House of Disorder

A work of fiction, by

Daniel F. L. Endicott

Copyright © 2026 Daniel Endicott
All rights reserved.
ISBN: 978-1-971406-03-9

Contents

1

"There was a man – with a sword. He was standing casually with his legs apart, the tip of the sword resting on the ground and both hands on the hilt – one on top the other. This was at the beach, the other day. Just past the outcrop of rock – just past the cave. Just on the end of no-man's land. I came around the corner, and there he was – just standing there."

"How much were you drinking?"

"That's the thing: He could almost be the guy from the bottle. He had boots that came up almost to his knees, and he had one of those shirts like musicians wear. You know – with the little frilly stuff."

"A poet shirt."

"I've never heard them called that."

"How 'bout – tuxedo shirt."

"Maybe. But the point was, he had on one of those, and his pants were like a pirate's: Kind of ballooning from the boots. Reddish-brown. And, on top of that – literally, in this case – he had a cloak. Bigger guy with a full beard – a little gray coming in – just standing there with a big, honkin' sword, dressed almost like a pirate, but also – he's got some kind of sorcerer's cloak over his head. Stone-faced and staring across the ocean."

"Did you get a name?"

"Ha,ha," precedes, "You're funny."

"Okay – facetious. But we've seen blue-faced girls with horns, dinosaurs, Roman soldiers… Why's a Viking sorcerer more off? And – not facetious – did you ask?"

"No. I didn't ask. I came around the corner and there's this big guy with a sword – a big ass sword. It came up to his chest. So – no: I didn't ask. I kept my eye on him while I passed and made sure he didn't follow. And, I didn't see a photographer. I looked around to make sure he wasn't part of an army – and I looked back a couple times. It was just him, and then the third time I looked back, he was gone."

"I'm…"

"One more thing. I forgot to mention – I did mention: The guy had a cloak – I told you that. But I don't think I said it had a hood over his head. It kind of shielded his face – I could mostly see his mouth and beard. But on top of the cloak, the guy was wearing a crown. Almost exactly the same color as the cloak – a mottled, greenish-brown. Pretty simple. All the same material and points every couple of inches. It was just a really weird look."

"I'd say that answers your question."

"How so?"

"It's a look. Probably a character from a show. If you search for Viking wizard you'll probably find him."

"Still… Something seemed off. And why just stand there?"

"Because," as it was obvious: "Long distance shot for perspective. Either you missed a guy camped out on the rocks or he was shooting from the cliffs. Maybe you even came across the guy – actually – playing the role. You'll probably see that shot in a promo."

"Yeah. I guess." A quick search and brief scroll through images, finds, "That's actually a thing. There's actually a Viking wizard thing. A Viking mage: Check it out." The device is held for the friend to see, "No sword, but that's pretty close to what he was wearing."

"There you have it. You met the king of the Viking wizards."

"Yeah. I guess – I guess: You're probably right. And maybe he was the actor, because he was playing threatening real well."

"He startled you. You interrupted his shoot. He's irritated, you're jumpy and imagination runs wild."

"Seems stupid but it's really been buggin' me. Like, all night I kept having dreams about the guy."

"Corbs…"

"Wha…?" A twisted smirk of disapproval brings, "Okay, bud. More like I end up on a spit and become their dinner. Like I said, it seems stupid now."

"Corbyn."

"Wyliart."

"You wanna go hunt the Viking king?"

"Viking-wizard-king, and no."

"Come on, Corbs. We'll pack some heat and we can poke around. Better, Corbyn, we can hike down to the campground and see if anyone's run into the Viking king. King-king. Wivi-king – something. They'd know at the store if there's a shoot."

"How did he become a Viking, anyway? I thought he was bringing us rum."

"That's why you should have asked. We don't know if he's a pirate or a Viking."

"At least we know he's a wizard."

"Yes. The wizard, pirate, Viking king. I think my slim-Jim's in the closet. If you wanna grab that, I'll get a couple guns."

"Two things, Wilson: Number one – I didn't agree. Number two, you can get my back."

"Suit yourself. Does that mean you agree? We've got to track down the wizard king?"

"Now I'm curious."

"You should've asked."

"I should have asked."

In the brief time a weapon was retrieved, second thoughts began to filter through but a cheerful return, and, "Let's go get this guy," shuttered them back into second.

However, as the door began to close, an arm shot out, and third thoughts brought, "You know – maybe I'll grab that slim-Jim."

Humored banter clatters on choices and decisions, but after protection was secured, attention turns to, "Walk, or drive?"

"Ten minute walk," and, "I don't know why I got paranoid again. This guy – I'm telling you: There's something off about him."

"Corvair: I think there's something off with you."

"Look, Wylie, I'm not the one that suggested protection."

One stopped, and then the other, because, "Carbon. You raise a good point. I don't know what made me suggest that."

"Big guy," Corbyn suggested; leaned in and whispered, but harsh: "Big sword."

"Oh wizard," announces the onset of the search as the cliffs are neared, but the walk otherwise finds silence as footsteps start to move with purpose.

The evening is pleasant and the cool, ocean breeze is only a nuance to the adventure. There are hours of daylight, still, and more than two until high-tide partitions the beach.

The cliff-breach to the beach is taken with the same enthusiasm as it was taken thirty years before, with feet striking sand and slipping down to elongate and degenerate the entrance as eons of feet have done before. It is a break to the beach and a break to the silence as reflection brings voice:

"I was thinkin' about – the guy. While you were saying it. You were goin' on. Talking about some dude in a robe, with a sword; with pirate pants. That's where that came from: You know – grab a gun. 'Cause I was imagining this guy out there swinging a sword. I was, like, sword or not – I got an answer for that."

"Profound."

"Profound – not. I was just imagining this guy you're describing. Thinking about why you thought he was a threat: Reality – it's just some guy and cosplay."

"Old guy. And, no – not just a costume. It was beaten to hell and the sword looked like it could cause some damage."

"Yeah: I got it, Corwin. But I'm imagining this massive, Viking warrior, swinging the sword in a monsoon. I'm seeing you duckin' the swings and running for your life. So, that's where it came from. I'm imagining us blasting this guy as he comes for us."

"Willard: Promise you will."

"Promise, Cobain. But it's just some dude doin' his thing. If we're lucky, it's more involved than that and we stumbled on a shooting."

"Meaning," is questioned, however, "Cobe: For a show. Get yer shit together."

"In case you missed it: We're out here 'cause it isn't."

Silence drops: Worlds of calliope ring what's said with memories of hopes, and dreams, and failure at all their ends.

Shoes battle past the slip of sand and driftwood to the sated beach where feet can move more easily, where they move directly for the south and the high-point of the cliffs that rise above. Where the rock molts from the earth, concrete, and sand, and licks out against the ocean.

There is heaviness on the ear from the salted air, and footsteps fall in metered coordination, though opposition to the waves that threaten. The crash against the shore is the crash against the words that were spoken and to history.

It brings worry: "Good Corbs?"

"All good," is answered, though it never is.

"You wanna tell me where you're at?"

"All good," is restated, but the cynicism drips heavily. A step – a kick into the sand – frustration: "Sucks, is all. Just sucks – you know: Don't know. You don't know, Wyl – you are the luckiest fucker in the world."

"Corbs…"

"Hey: It's good. I'm just saying you have a good thing – wish I did." Empty pause is followed: "Still." And that omnipresent conversation is blunted, with, "What happened to the lizard king? We're getting sour."

"C-bo. You-n-me can take down Kaiju. But I gotta have you there to do it: Let me in to where you are."

"Good," is repeated again, and it's emphasized, "All good. There's a list but – no stress. Nothin' I can do about it."

"Shit," is offered as a wave creeps up and soaks a foot.

It brings the joy of friendship that is absent most experience and life and a battle rages after an attempt to share – a quick shove towards an encroaching wave. But distraction falls apart with another, and alarm: "You said high tide is when?"

"Seven-thirty. You wanna bail?"

"Nah – that's plenty – but let's roll through no-man's land."

They cross the rocks that are already being sprayed by crashing water, and seen concern turns a device displaying, "Seven-thirty."

"Alright. Seven-thirty is acknowledged and concern is left behind as they drop to sand.

It's a stretch that's difficult to access when the tide comes in, bracketed by the ancient flow to the north, and a narrowed beach with scattered rock that makes passage during waters' peak extremely treacherous. The duo walking through have both escaped the trap more times than they could remember, but the one way leads to certain saturation and often injury, while the other is a climb that feels more perilous every time.

Wyllem wonders, "Would the magic, pirate king live in the cave?" It is asked to mock and tease but said good naturedly, and the cheerful repartee between them continues as they approach the opening.

It is the end point of an ancient lava tube of which ten yards remain accessible with the rest back-filled with sand and stone and sediment, packed in by time and violent storms that can transform the coast in an instant. It is also a place of shelter when weather becomes inclement, or a break against the wind; a space for gatherings around a fire in the evening – especially for older children:

"Looks like someone had some fun."

"Looks like we should've brought a bag."

"Looks like you should've looked a little harder."

"Well, look at that, Corduroy. Why couldn't they just pick their crap up in the first place?"

"Kids – you know."

"Don't I know."

"I really don't – you know."

"Corbs."

"All good. What the heck is that?"

Stabbed into the earth near where the sand meets the apex of the cave is a small dagger. The metal hilt is worn and pitted and it appears to have seen extensive use and years. In contrast, the blade is well-honed and glints the light as it's examined.

"Interesting," and it's offered, "That's a keeper. You think your Viking left it?"

"Who knows," however, "You think it's marking something?"

"Well… If you feel like digging – go ahead. Someone probably just forgot it."

It's agreed, but fingers dig in anyway. Fingers dig and start pulling more aggressively – and then stop, as they meet the edge of a wooden box: Head turns with wide eyes sparkling and mouth agape, and the look's returned as the other slides along the incline and begins clearing away a side.

They extract a small box. The wood is dark and covered in stains and damage but it is unremarkable, outside of the calligraphic words, "Property of Awrol."

The reaction of both is summarized in the single word Wyllem croons: "Ho-ly." He sets the box squarely in the other's hands and slips the small, brass latch free. The lid is lifted and they observe a tattered book that fills the box almost entirely.

"Let's get in the light," and both move closer to the entrance, still far enough in to evade most of the wind.

The book is worn and the corners have been eroded. The binding is cracked and the title is barely made out – black ink on dark blue cover: "Stratygyes & Pryncyples."

"Ho-ly," is offered once again, and the box is turned so the book can be viewed and opened.

It is filled with writing and diagrams, drawn on thick pages of an unfamiliar material – firm, but soft and fibrous. Many pages are torn, and edges are worn and damaged. However, the contents are exquisite: Drawings elegantly arranged and labeled, and the handwriting is perfectly even and straight. It is also, largely unintelligible – random letters seemingly replacing others and making it difficult to follow.

Yet, it is examined intently. Pages are turned, strange words are examined, and patterns emerge in the diagrams. It is quiet between unquiet friends as the find's examined, as each page is turned as if the next will offer clarification. At last, it is turned to the final page and that holds a single word. As with every word written in the tome, the writing is clean and elegant, but the one word written is written large, and it is, "Wyn."

"Think that's your dude's," is answered, "Yes," and the book is closed, the lid rolled back, and the clasp seals it back in safely. The box is returned to where it was found, and it is re-buried, knife set through the sand above it.

Corbyn sounds the name, "Awrol."

"You think? Could be more like Awrol."

"Owl?"

"Ah-rooo," is howled, but it isn't met with humor, it's met with, "Let's get out of here."

"You know, Cordoba, let's dig that back out and grab a few. I wanna try a reverse search and see what comes up."

"I don't think so – let's go."

"Cardavan – wait a minute: If he didn't want anyone to see it he wouldn't have left it there. He wouldn't have stabbed a knife into it. It was left behind like everything else in here. Almost like he wanted us to find it."

"Exactly. That – Wilted – is why we should leave it alone. They're probably incantations. Why knows what would happen."

"Wilting enthusiasm even further. I'm getting pictures."

"I'm getting out of here. If he materializes and cuts you in half – I warned you."

"I'll be ready," is promised, and with amusement, it's suggested, "You be the lookout. Tell me if you see our Viking wizard."

Wiliart is told, "Shit."

"Corbs?" A turn finds his friend at the entrance with a hand held to his head. "Corbs? What's up?"

"The fucking tide's in. How is the fucking tide in?"

A quick search, and the answer's returned: "'Cause high tide's five-fourteen. What the hell were you looking at?"

"I'm an idiot."

"Why? What'd you do?"

"Spelled it wrong - I'm a fucking idiot."

"Well. At least we're protected from the wandering warlock. Let's get a better look."

"We gonna climb, or get battered?"

"We're gonna get some pictures – Cornfused. I prefer the climb if you're up for it."

2

Knocking at the door is answered, "Open."

It does, and a face peers prior to the inquiry, "Got a minute?"

"'Til about four. Then I'm into fish guts."

The door closes and Wiliart shares, "Kids've started calling you hermit Corb. It's a bad mix of eulogies but they make a point."

"You have a point?"

"Listen – Carbonation: You've been off. That stresses me, and that stresses Corsh, and then the kids get stressed. How 'bout you agree to dinner with the fam and we can eliminate the stress."

"Wyl."

"Corbs."

"Wall: I'm already in your hair. I don't need to bother your family."

"This – is where we have the problem: Corbyn."

"Formal."

"Listen."

"Listen, yourself."

"Stop – for a minute: I wanna be serious."

"I have 'til four."

"Can I ask you something you don't want to answer?"

The answer is, "No."

"Last time you saw A-k."

"The answer was no."

"No, Corbs: You're checking out on everyone – and that's the point. I won't hassle you about anything – except that."

"Still no."

"Still your daughter."

"Still doesn't want anything to do with me. Still doesn't want to be forced to spend the weekends here, and still doesn't have any interest in anything about me. I text, reach out, and there's nothing. I'm not gonna force her to waste her time with me."

"Can ya promise you'll keep trying?"

"I'm guessing the wife said something."

"Man – come on. I'm just saying, make an effort with your daughter."

"Man – I'm just saying: Tell me your wife didn't say something."

"Corbyn," is stated with flat intensity: "My wife is right ninety-nine percent of the time. She says you need to keep making the effort with your daughter, and she also says you should join us: Eat with the family."

It's agreed, "I keep in touch. She has almost no interest in responding." And, disagreed, "But I don't need to bother your family. I shouldn't' be here. I'm grateful, Wyl, and make sure your family knows that."

The mission shreds as two old friends come together with understanding and a seat's taken at the small table that's the only furnishing in the small cabin besides the bed.

The cabin was built as a pool house for a pool that was lost to erosion, many years before. It turned into a novelty for multiple generations of children, and then a source of income for the prior owner: Renovated, source of heat added, and the remote location made it ideal for someone seeking serenity. The selling point had never been put to use by the current residents, and it again became a novelty for their daughters, when they were younger, and then storage for a body that had become increasingly withdrawn:

"Crossed paths with Ani," brings the conversation back around to where it started.

"Apparently on a bad day."

“I think she’s so used to piling on it’s just like, “how’s it goin’,” anymore.”

“I know, Collards. And you know I see it like you see it and so does Corsh. But your daughter’s there and she’s agreeing with what she’s saying. So, she says, light a fire, and maybe lure him out of the hut. They’re valid points, Cromeo. The kids were asking if you died.”

“Just on the inside – so far.” Fingers type, “How’s it going? Hope everything’s good,” and the device is turned to show the first point isn’t needed.

“I’ll trust you on that, but come up to the house, once in a while. Say – dinner.”

“I’m up to my waist in fish guts after four.”

“How about – join me for coffee in the mornings.”

“How about – I try to stay out of your way as much as possible.”

“No, man: See… That’s where we’re failing. There’s no, in the way. We said, make this your home – as long as you need it. And maybe we didn’t think that meant forever, but if it is – then it is. This is why Corshae told me to say something: You’re hermitting.”

“I – hermitting.”

“Yes. You’re becoming a hermit.”

“Sounds like an interesting sport.”

“Face time, Corby. The family wants to see your pretty face. And – maybe – that’s also what your daughter wants.”

The device is held to show there is no response: “That’s how it goes. I text or leave a message, and that’s the end. But fear not, Wylie, I will continue coming up with creative ways to say the same things, and ask the same questions I ask every day.”

“Rolling my eyes, Coralberry – just like AnnaKay: Ju-u-u-st like AnnaKay.”

"Coralberry… You ready to clock out – Wylful pest?"

"Just roll up the hill once in a while. That's all I'm saying. Well, that and the kid but I feel like you're on that. So just rolling."

"Sounds hard."

"It is – that's why I'm saying it: I get tired of having to climb back up after I come down here. There's gotta be some reciprocation."

"Make me a promise."

"Of course – I promise."

"Promise me this: If anyone's tired of me – let me know. I don't wanna bother you guys."

"Sure, Cortyard: We're tired of you not coming up to the house. You'd better rectify that."

"Are we off the clock?"

"Right after I say they were valid points: They were valid points."

"I'm rolling – my – eyes."

"Roll all you want but I had to hear it ten times longer."

"Got it. If you're done, I was thinking about a quick jog down the beach: Any interest?"

"I'm on the hook for lawn darts. You've still got time for a couple rounds."

"I'm gonna pass. I'm looking for some quiet before the market, not a chance of injury."

"Got 'em filed down real nice. Solid risk of serious injury. Tell me you'll take peace of mind over that."

"Maybe next time."

"Here we go."

"Off the clock, Wylburn."

"Fine. But I am definitely gonna spear you when we do."

"Not if I strike first."

"Not gonna happen. I'll see ya, but you're on the hook for hospital games."

"Alright," it's agreed: "I'll see ya."

A brief brush of air combs the cabin as the door is opened, but it is swallowed by silence as it closes. The figure leaving is briefly watched through the square of the entry's window but is quickly lost to bramble, brush, and elevation.

The thought towards movement and fresh, sea air collapses under the weight of the rumination it was meant to combat, stirred deeper with the complaints delivered. Stabbed deeper into the chest – already heavy – already weighed with regret and a mind's eye only seeing failure: At every turn, in every corner, and an albatross on those the least deserving – those that gave the most, and cared the most, and claimed occupation of their tiny cabin was not an imposition.

It is there that regrets become focused, as they are present and addressable, and the pull towards languor is conquered by the inability to ever express the appreciation, and gratitude, and especially the love as fully as it should be – if only briefly. If only a chance to see anyone and simply acknowledge their existence, because as was noted – increasingly that was absent.

Regret.

Sorrow, and self-pity.

They replace the anger and vitriol of prior years. They sapped the battle over custody and property, and they killed the relationship with the only child, though, that had been suffering since the beginning.

From the beginning.

When words were spoken that a child couldn't comprehend, only intended as a jagged shard against the psyche. Words honed over years to diminish and devalue, and eventually, they landed without a battle.

"Uncle Corbs," calls enthusiastically, with a chorus joining, "Unca-C."

The bike pulled up the steep incline that was earlier observed gives weight to complaint of onerous returns, but all thoughts scatter as the two jaunt over to offer greeting. They're embraced warmly, and told, "Your dad said you thought I was dead."

They laugh, but Lia shares, "I said, if you died, no one would know."

"'Til your body rots," her sister teases.

There is amusement, and there is joy. It is the reinforcing emphasis to the lashing words their father shared, because it's always so. They are the only people remotely close to family, anymore – that feel like family, anymore. But as with everything, there is guilt and regret lingering on the edges.

"Still ticking," ignores all of it.

"Too bad," Shey teases: "I was gonna move into the cabin." It is only meant as humor and residence has been held so long she doesn't understand the reason it falls otherwise, but she does understand there's something, and suggests, "We could trade. Then I wouldn't have to hear Lia snoring all night."

Immediately, Lia fires back, "You snore, cow."

"You'd hate it," Corbyn suggest: "Smells like fish guts."

With no hesitation, Lia says, "Just like Shey."

"Ladies," they are scolded, "Play nice."

Shey says, "That's nice for Lia."

"That's nice for Lia," is mocked in return, but they laugh together, and it's contagious.

"I've gotta gore some fish. Let your parents know I passed through so I don't get another lecture."

Says Shey, "Tell me about it," which finds the sympathy of her sister, who agrees, "The worst."

"I'll see you guys."

"See ya unc."

"Unca-C," is called enthusiastically, and brings burbling happiness that forces a smile.

The ride to town takes nearly forty-five, but considerably more on the return as it's considerably more uphill. The ride is taken along bike lanes that were never added – only defined – and it can be harrowing as vehicles race down the mountain well over the posted speed. As log trucks struggle to maintain their transport, or, downshift in near-proximity which it's presumed is intended to antagonize.

But it is also a ride that is an outlet even in the darkest times. Where burning legs and heavy breath drive off the thoughts that eat the soul when reflecting on experience. A solid ride that brings an elevated state of mind to the only place that stuck after many failures. One that brings the same on the return to the only other people that notice extended absence. Two hours of exertion that keeps mind and body healthy, to a degree – at least – they otherwise would not be.

The ride to town is more down than up but it still takes significant exertion, and the final stretch ascends a bridge that crosses the bay. Once across, there is a sharp dive down to the docks that is almost always taken far faster than is sensible, and far faster than any vehicles anywhere close to the posted limit.

But that's for safety: To keep drivers in control. To have vehicles arrive at a speed from which they can easily stop quickly. However, there's no cross traffic, nor pedestrians, and fools on bicycles are only dismissed as putting themselves in the way of harm. Or, sometimes they're greeted cheerfully:

"Hey – Corbs."

"Corbyn: How was the ride?"

"Good to see ya, Corbs."

The response is somewhat breathless but always enervated. It is another place that breathes life into the mind, if mandated by necessity: To survive, buy groceries – but mostly covering child support. But after years it has become another part of life that would be less full if it was absent.

"Afternoon," is offered to the person behind the counter. There are several in the store and two directly occupying attention – there is nevertheless, a cheerful, "Corbyn. How was the vacation?"

"Good. It was good. Mostly just stayed home. Did some reading. Did some hiking. But it was good to just have time. You need help up here?"

"All good. Sometimes that's the best, though – just taking time to yourself. Good to have you back, though."

It's claimed, "Couldn't keep me away if you tried."

Past the counter and through the swinging door finds the operation that the tiny storefront belies.

There are more greetings than could be individually responded to, and so a wave, and, "Hey, all," is the greeting that's returned. They're told, "It's good to be back. 'Cause – I'm broke."

Laughter follows. Fond conversation spills across the floor as a slow course across the floor pulls inquiries from those that come into proximity:

"Nothing much. Did some reading, did some hiking; caught up on some rest. Mostly stayed at home, but it was good to have a break."

"Corbyn," brings an end to the wider conversation: "Good to see you. You ready to move into action or you need a few."

The push for work resumption brings assumption, "Decent haul?"

"Not bad. Not bad at all. It's good to have you back." That conversation ends with the shouted, "Hey: Over here."

It is a handoff to a station, after a breakup of conversation: The foreman's gentle way of saying, back to work.

Everyone present got the message, but there are still words passed, if quieter and only in nearest proximity. That is abandoned as a fouled glove is pulled away, sweaty hand swept across the apron and then raised to greet and embrace at the point of destination:

"Welcome back, partner."

"Yeah: Good to see you, man."

"Ya had a good one?"

"It was good – yeah. It was good to have some down time, but I do start missing the routine – this place."

"The people," it's suggested: "Could do without the game."

"Yeah," agreed: "Mostly the people. Slide me a victim so I look like I'm doing something."

"Gotta keep up appearances."

"You know."

"Yes, sir." A knife's pulled out, but before it's examined or hit with stone, it's shared, "They're sharp. A little welcome back to let you know you're missed. Hope it's good."

"You're the best, Chel."

"You know: Down time."

"Yeah. Down time – I know. I appreciate you. How's the family?"

It's warned, "Incoming," by another.

The foreman's on a round and makes the observation, "Good to see you jump right in. Good to have you back, Corbyn."

It's claimed, "Couldn't keep me away if you tried."

3

Legs burn as they're pushed relentlessly. Muscles spasm and feel incompetent like rubber ligaments, that jab at angles to turn the wheels: Multiple rotations for a single turn of the wheel.

It's the final ascent back home. The last incline before the perch atop the cliffs where dismount will find legs unstable and threatening to give away. It is a push that's made irregularly, and an effort made on the last day of the third week back on the last day before the weekend. A push made that would find the next day difficult if it was spent processing at a table. It is a push made knowing the next day will likely be spent hermitting.

As the crest's neared, the lever's slid up three gears and the chain janks down with a jolting stiffness on the pedal, tired legs slogging against them to reel in the final stretch.

It is a property that was once the propriety of an artist of some repute in the region – notoriety briefly stretched into the falderal of southern California. That momentary serenade of interest brought the finances to create a cliff-side compound that was envisioned as a retreat and artistic crucible. The vision was doomed from early on as finances crumbled – as did the cliffs – and all that remains of the original installation is the home intended as a welcome center, and the hut that was once adjacent a pool. That hut is four strides from the edge of the cliff and one bad storm away from being swept away.

The home is swept past to avoid the accusation it's being avoided. A, "Yo-ho-ho," announces arrival and serves as notification for what is observed to be no one present. The bicycle is rambled past the drive and towards the steep descent to the little cabin. However, that progress is stopped by a call from behind that claims, "Corbyn."

"Oh." A quick scan confirms the car is absent as are the children that would typically have something to say. "Sorry," is volunteered against presumptions, which were, "I didn't realize anyone was here. Ya know – cars gone. No Unca-C's."

The obvious is, "I hung back," and Corshae offers, "Care to join? I've got most of a cold bottle of Riesling."

There's a minor laugh in a minor key that reflects back on a conversation, and it's the reason, "I hate to turn down the invitation." However, "I smell like fish guts and just pushed the ride harder than I probably ever had. So, I'll take a rain-check. I'm just gonna clean up and take an ice bath."

"Corbyn," interrupts the attempt at disengagement, and, "Maybe I need to apologize," brings, "For what?"

"For asking Wyl to talk to you."

A swirl swings back to the conversation that brought the laugh, and concern: "Why? Have I seemed off."

Corshae confirms, "A little."

"Corsh," is a plea to otherwise: "Like he said, they were valid points. I thought I'd been doing good."

"You know: I talk to Anika."

"Sure. Of course."

"But she told me some things, and I didn't even question it. But I've been thinking: How would you even be at a mall?"

For one, there is pure hilarity at the question. For the other, there's concern.

"Hoo-boy," Corbyn begins, and ponders, "Maybe I need that wine." A switch was flipped: "I flipped out. That's what she told you."

Confirmed, "Kind of – yeah."

"Look. I'm not gonna sugarcoat it."

It was a culmination. Ten years of frustration coalesced into a moment. Almost a month of texts and messages left that went ignored and unreturned. Two weeks of sharing plans. Rejection, and then – there they were.

It had been almost a year since the previous visitation. The conversation, and contact, and arrangements had always been problematic, but the past year had met near silence. The push to meet, to speak, to simply share a meal was mostly disregarded and met with silence.

It was always challenging. After the settlement was met, there was an immediate petition to the court to allow for distance. Like everything else that was asked for, that was granted. And while that always posed a challenge to meet the terms of the agreement, it was agreed that sacrifice was acceptable to take care of their child. It was agreed that the distance would be mostly closed by parent, and that visits might be daytime and exclusive of other obligations.

That had initially seemed viable, and early years saw their daughter spending nights at the hotel with her father. But over time, the solidity of that arrangement was eroded to the point that conversation, connection, and visitation was almost non-existent. In the month prior to making the trip, there had been no response to texts nor messages.

But an idea spawned: Make the trip with the excuse to see the game. Buy the tickets and tell them – in town: Let's get together. An excuse to be there. An excuse to see their daughter, and leverage with proximity. However, no one ever responded.

And then – they were there.

"You were there."

It's admitted, "I was. Probably everything she told you's true: I pretty much lost it."

They were there. In a store where the price of anything was out of reach. They were there, laughing, and spending, and, "I just lost it."

"I don't take sides. I promise. But I could hear AnnaKay agreeing. That's why I asked him to say something."

"I know," is not followed by what's known: Shortcomings, failures; temper. I know's not followed by anything that's acknowledged, only, "I bought two tickets. It's not like I thought she'd join me, but I bought two – just in case she might."

"Corbyn: I know you're trying. The girls are just at that age."

"It's almost a year since I've seen her," is blurted out: "Almost a year: I have parental rights, still. I'm supposed to see her on the weekends. This has been a joke from the… From the beginning, and here I go again. You don't need to hear it."

"I get it."

"I just want to see her," sadly reflects that the feeling isn't mutual: "I get she can make decisions now. I'm not asking for her entire weekend. But maybe, ya know – get together for lunch. Have dinner. That's all I'm looking for."

"I'm sorry. I know it's tough." And the offer's made again: "Sure you don't need a drink?"

"Nah – I stink. I'm sure whatever she told you's dead on. I definitely could've handled it better."

"Can I just ask – why – you went after the store."

There's more laughter. Because, "One purse in that store costs what I make in a week. I'm never gonna say I shouldn't pay what I pay to take care of my kid, but we all know they can afford whatever they want. I'm moochin' off my best friend and his family because I can't afford shit. It was just everything coming together – and I lost it. I'll leave it like Wyl always does with you: Ani's usually right."

"Yeah, well – she isn't always."

"No?" Considering, it's wondered, "When's she been wrong? Outside of getting married to me, anyway."

"I gotta say to you what I say to her – I don't wanna be put in that position: I like both of you. And I agree with you – and, Wyl – she janks you by not getting married, but I also see her perspective. So, let me stay in the middle. How 'bout you come up and have a glass of wine and we can strategize."

There is appreciative laughter, however, "I smell like fish guts. I'll have to take a rain-check."

"Rain-check yourself 'til you're cleaned up," is suggested, as is, "Come back up and you and Wyl can mix some cocktails. We'll break out games and make a night of it."

"I," looks for excuses not to, though the most presentable have already been used. The rest are waffled by the claim, "You know, my two think the world of you. If you need proof you have anything to offer, look to them. They love their Unca-C."

"Ooh," is offered because it's the band-aid to the stab wounds in the conversation: "That is a cheep shot. I might think about it."

"I'm telling them you agreed."

And, "Fine," is agreed: "A sucker punch if I ever saw one."

"Still need to see you around more often."
"Don't want to be in the way."
"You never are."
"I have been for almost a decade."
"Corbs," Corshae says: "I'd be fine if you slept on the kitchen counter: We do what we got to – right? Just work on you and the kid and come back tonight. We got a deal?"
"Fine. But to make my point, I texted her when Wyl came to lecture me and I still got no response. There's not much to work on if she's got no interest."
"She's fifteen."
"And she hates me."
It's claimed, "Goes with the territory," however: "Not yours," meets protest: "It's different," and that's agreed, "Yeah: You got great kids. They also got great parents. I'm gonna clean up, ice, and nap, and then I'll come back to disrupt your family."
"Corbyn?"
"What?"
"You are family."
There's a scoff, and, "Yeah," and opinion: "I'm a pain in the ass." But there's also a nod to the effort made to the black sheep that wanders amongst them: "You know I appreciate you saying something. Ya know – pushing me – everything. You guys are all I've got."
She says, "We're not," but that's answered, "Yeah," and bitterly.
"We'll see you later?"
"I'll see you later."
It's a handoff to the thoughts that battle: Time together with the family are the best times had. But there's a hollow knocking that reflects against the family that was. To a failure to hold family together,

and failure to maintain any connection with a child whatsoever.

Waves of regret wash in regret and feelings of incapacity to have coopted the space, and place, and lives of another family. To accept kindness and generosity, and find it impossible to escape the rut of existence ever since.

There's a wholeness with them – with lifelong friends, and with their children. In times together with them there is a sense of inclusion and belonging – a sense of value and that it's worthy to continue. However, it's an echo back to those feelings with a family – from a marriage and a child that are gone. From a time and place where it felt like they forged together, forward, but that was abruptly, and brutally brought to an end.

A knocking at the window brings eyes to open to blurry light, and, "It's open," is said because it always is.

The door scrapes open and brings admonishment: "Corshae says you promised."

"Yeah: Yeah-yeah. I'll be there. What time is it?"

"Eight-thirty."

"Ooh…" Tired bones are brought upright, and it's claimed, "I meant to. Just fell asleep – I'll come up for a few."

"Minutes? Or, drinks."

"Yes, and yes, Wylful reclamation. My body's angry I pushed so hard. That's all. I was coming up."

"After you."

"Alright – alright: I'm going."

"It's curtains for Corbyn if you don't."

"I already said, Wyl: I-art going to."

"I don't know. I don't think that one worked like you wanted it to."

"Do they ever?"

"You've got a point, Carbonation. But the delivery was a little flat."

"Nice. Also, I just woke up. My brain's not even at full dysfunctional operation."

"Seems like it is."

"You're on a roll."

"Like buttah."

"Ba-boom: Wyndham is cookin'."

"Corbyn," greets them as they enter the home, as a glass is delivered in a rain of, "Unca-C."

"Thank you, and I just fell asleep. How are you two?"

"Trouble," their mother answers.

Lia asks, "Do you wanna throw lawn darts?"

"In the dark?"

Shey fills in, "Better chance of blood."

4

"Unca-C," breaks through the misty-morning fog.

Feet pound beside the surf – shoes dancing against the water's edge – as cool wind blows off of the ocean, useless against the heavy sweat that's dripping.

"We're gonna stop you, unc," is claimed, but it isn't true, and neither is, "I'm gonna beat you."

"Not," is said, "A chance," as Lia's passed, said with the exhalation of heavy breaths. But arms are raised in victory and the sound of laughter is left behind as the sprint along the coastline continues.

It's the final and favorite part of a morning run. The end stretch after running along asphalt and the undulating foothills. It's the slip down the sandy slope and over slipping footsteps of windblown sand onto the water-matted sand where the final push concludes. It is the last leg to a 20k, and every last ounce of energy remaining is expended.

There was a time the exertion pressed was believed to hold a purpose. That was a time before failure and where expectation and belief still staked the future. There was a time where speed, and energy, and the push of the body was believed to hold value and it was expected the effort would, likewise, find value. It was expected there would be reward returned for the effort made. And then there wasn't.

Instead, there was disaster – to expectations, the future, and family.

A gun fired.

Bodies kicked against their marks.

Legs sprinted.

Feet pressed.

Tempo increased and groups coalesced as the track was run. And then, on the third circuit of the track a desperate lunge was pressed in a futile effort to stay relevant:

Bodies collided – bodies fell – and effort to avoid the pile resulted in a mis-step and collapse as a tendon exploded. The years hoping to return to relevance found none and everything else falling apart, including – marriage. Including parenthood.

Including everything.

Feet press against the sand with rapid desperation. They move at a pace that would still be worthy of consideration – but at a pace of someone with twenty fewer years that was looking towards improvement: They look at a past that sees the times plateauing, and probably getting longer. Feet dig, but times are no longer getting better, only – sometimes – closer.

Feet pound away from the cheerful calls that follow, dancing against the limit of encroaching waves – occasionally losing and washing in the ice cold waters. Legs strive even more at the teasing claim of getting old – one of the girls says something about being shirtless in the winter, but the brunt of it is lost to distance, wind, and the crashing surf.

The final sprint pushes faster, yet, to the finish line of shallow stream that cuts a ribbon across the beach. It's own, terminal finish becomes lost against the ocean's wash and the sand it pushes back against the flowing water.

Feet high-step through the water and the splashes of cold water against the flesh feel good after the exertion. But as pace staggers to a close, the time is checked, and what had felt like the best run in forever finds it took most of an hour.

The stream is told, "Well, fuck," and the words called to taunt the passing runner lose their humor.

There are days that runs are struggle, and days that legs feel like they could continue to the southern border. Most days that legs feel good, times fall into the middle fifties; the push to move back into the forties looks increasingly like a fading window, and the latest one, that seemed like one of the better ones of late, instead is one of the slowest runs in months.

Cool down begins with kicks against the water as the stream's crossed-back, again. A slow slog in the fog led by the heartbeat flashing in the distance. The sight turns thoughts towards recovery and the heartrate's checked and finds it's already settling.

"Getting old," is said with spite, because it doesn't feel it, but run-times speak to an erosion from the peak of fitness. Pushing into lower fives takes a concentrated effort that undermines the tonic that running finds.

There is a quiet, laughing scoff as the swirling mist unveils enough that a distant figure can be seen still sitting on the massive rock.

They were recognized the moment they were seen through the heavy fog, despite they were unrecognizable: They way they moved and interacted. Ghostly figures of familiarity to raise the spirit and bring joy with the barbs flung in passing.

"You lose your family?"

"Dash: I thought you were running to California."

"Well, as you pointed out – I'm getting old. I'd probably break down if I tried to make it."

"I'd break down if I thought about putting on running shoes."

"The fam head back?"

"The fam is back, wild-Wyl: Packing up for school."

"You just couldn't wait to see me, or did ya pull a hamstring?"

"Just takin' a minute. I love it when the fog's this thick."

"Yeah… It's pretty cool. Do you get that thing where you can see your heart beat?"

"Ah – what?"

"When you look into the fog. Like, through distance: You can see your heart beating in the fog."

"I don't think – that's normal."

"I'm sure it's an eye thing. Like, your eyes are trying to focus and there's just a washout – probably subtle pressure changes cause it."

"Seriously, Corbs: I don't think that's normal."

"Seriously, Wylting warrior – it's not uncommon. Lots of guys have it."

"More seriously, cardiac-kid: Maybe you should talk to your doctor. I really don't think that's normal."

"A – chill. B – like I have a doctor."

"Maybe you should get one."

"Listen, Wyner: Take a poll – lots of people get it. It's not abnormal. It just came to mind when you said you were staring at the fog: Yeah – it's awesome. Sometimes I like it better than clear skies and sunshine."

"Now I'm very worried, Carbonara. First hearts beating in the fog, and now – sunshine? I've never heard of it."

"I'm pretty sure it only exists in Egypt."

"Ah. That would make sense. You wanna join me for a coffee, or – whatever you people consume after running."

"A thing called water, typically."

"Interesting. I thought that was just an ingredient for coffee."

"Probably a little better for you on its own."

"Says fog-heart."

"I'll have to pass on the coffee. I've gotta clean up and get to work."

"Not to be rude, but don't you disembowel fish?"

"Not exclusively."

"My point being, Cartwright, You're gonna smell like fish guts anyway. You might as well spend fifteen shootin' the breeze with me 'cause it isn't gonna matter."

"I appreciate your insight, but I prefer to work my way into the scent of dead sea life. I'll catch you tomorrow."

"Catch me for dinner, tonight, and we'll talk about it."

"Eh… I told Chel I'd hit Belli's with him and then I was gonna hit the gym. If you wanna make me a doggy-bag I can make it lunch, tomorrow."

"No promises."

"I'll keep my expectations low. I'll catch ya later."

"Yeah, Corbs: I'll see ya later."

Tired legs complain as loose sand is met, and more as the large, semi-intentional steps are taken through the cliff-face.

Exit from the beach arrives behind rental cabins and adjacent a parking lot for those with camping equipment. Yards to the left there is a wall of marionberry, strawberry, and weeds that has grown several feet tall, except for a path that's been maintained and winds through it to a small clearing of grass with a fire-pit.

When there are renters, and especially those with children, there are often raucous celebrations around the fire that are unfiltered by the tiny cabin-home that is just strides away, the other side of another wall of vines.

The weather is cool, and with the delayed return, the shower is just a rinse. Run-day routine follows, which is the same as every other day but excludes sitting and staring out the windows: Two glasses of water downed, then, one apple and two protein bars are zipped into the bag. The little home's departed for the second time of the morning with extra time to spare in consideration of legs that had been imagined moving at incredible pace.

The cool weather is cooler still on the ride and especially downhill, as humid cold works around the protection of the jacket. By the time the mid-point's met cool air brings relief as the body aches protestation against further exertion.

It is an uneventful ride with little traffic, and the exit ramp is taken with the usual lack of care – too fast, and on the edge of out of control. The abrupt stop is met by mostly silent greetings from the few that are present – mostly grunts, or nods, and one says, "Hey."

It's more of the same once in the plant – polite, "Mornin," is given and returned, a, "Hey," a, "How's it goin'?"

At the station, arrival is announced with, "I think you sleep here."

"Mornin' Corbyn," is offered with a smile.

"Ready to battle?"

Chel answers, "They don't have a chance."

"No," it's agreed, "No they don't. It's a battle lost already."

"For them," Chel says. "We're just startin'."

It begins another day of processing the haul: An average pull with nothing unusual. Four hours of scaling, filleting, cracking, and slicing into steaks. Product for the tiny storefront, but moreso, to be moved to restaurants and wholesalers. After four, there's a thirty minute break where conversation can range from absent to exuberant.

There is little as the two bars and apple are consumed, and two more glasses of water are downed. The second part of the day will end when everything's been processed; even on the best days it's rarely another four.

"Empty," announces the conclusion is at hand.

Chel notes, "Not even four. You wanna grab a drink at Billy's?"

"I would," Corbyn begins, and then declines: "But I was hoping to get a little time in at the gym – and I promised I'd get back for dinner with the fam. Maybe tomorrow, though."

"Maybe," Chel agrees: "See how deep we get into the clock."

There is immediate complaint from muscles as the ramp is climbed, as quads and calves push back against another round of effort. But that only lasts for the ascent – from there, a coast over to the gym and a workout for the upper body. Before departure, a brief run loosens up the muscles in preparation for the ride back home.

Afternoons and evenings are more harrowing than the morning rides. There is much more traffic, and it's on the outside lane where the road ahead sometimes appears to disappear into the heavens. In places, the walls are not as tall as the bike seat and are all that protect from a, likely, fatal fall. It is also more uphill than down and already tired legs are grateful for the one advantage to that side of the road: Scenic lookouts where they can rest.

They are magnificent views of the ocean and rock formations. Of cliffs and sharply descending mountainsides. Like foggy mornings, they are the reason it's difficult to move – a suggestion made many times in counterargument.

There is, of course, more opportunity in the city. It would remove the issue of distance. And when the child was younger, those arguments held weight, but there had been overwhelming bitterness. Bitterness over everything:

The disintegration of the family. Dismissal of every argument and claim through the proceedings. The lies that were put on public record. Being ordered to pay an amount that would leave nothing to survive on. And after losing everything and every argument, the one bright spot that remained were the weekends: The arrival of AnnaKay. One weekend in, an order was delivered that declared that arrangement was going to change.

A cool breeze blows the hair as it blows the waves below, and it's reflected on whether it would have been better to follow. If any mote of a relationship could have been salvaged.

"Excuse me, sir." A young couple approaches, and asks, "Can you take our picture? With the sun in the back?" And the woman gloats, "We're on our honeymoon."

"Sure," is offered over an emotion punch that came from nowhere. That came from reflecting on relationships, their failures, and then being presented with another that wasn't: "Perfect. You guys look great. Congratulations. You couldn't have picked a better place."

The man questions, "Are you from around here?"

He's told, "Yeah. Lived here my whole life. I can't leave it."

A thought that isn't held the first time. It's what brought the strain and challenges. It kept the distance and made arrangements complicated. Insistence – obstinance – at least a part of the reason why the relationship had deteriorated to the point it was almost gone.

Thoughts swirling like they hadn't since a plan gone wrong on the last trip to the city fuel burned out legs the final stretch of the return. There is a thought to roll past the driveway and slip quietly down the slope without detection, however, reflecting back finds memories of devastation where a best friend offered kindness and support. When he'd offered, "Stay in the cabana. However long you need."

It turned out to be forever.

Knuckles rap against the wooden frame and a face peers through an adjacent window. One that seems to fill with joy on observation, and declares, "It's Unca-C."

"Well. If it isn't Cancorsaurus. Come on in – I didn't have a chance to fill a bag with dog food, yet."

However, Corshae offers, "I could heat a plate up for you if you want to stay a while."

"You know," Corbyn begins, and everyone – even Corbyn hears it in his head – is expecting an excuse. Instead, they're given, "That would be great. Chel had to cancel so I didn't get a chance to eat."

Shey jumps up to announce, "I'll get a chair," and dashes off.

"Have a seat, Cornucopia. You look gassed."

"Passed gassed," it's admitted, and the offer is accepted.

"Here ya go, Unca-C," but the arrival finds disappointment he's already seated. That's quickly righted as the chair is slipped beside, and Shey delares, "Here – I – go, Unca-C. Can I get you a glass of wine."

"No," is offered with amusement, but Corshae offers, "Something stronger," and she's told, "You could twist my arm."

"The usual for ya, Carbonator?"

"That'd be great, Wildebeast." There's laughter, and it follows, "You guys are too good to me. Some day I'll find a way to pay you back."

"Lawn darts," Lia suggests.

"In the dark," says Shey, and her sister makes the claim, "We sharpened them last night."

Their mother says, "Now girls: Not 'til after he eats."

"And drinks the good stuff," their father complains: "You better pay me back for that."

Corbyn looks at a friend that deserves one as good as he has been and it is on the edge of emotion and breaking down that he is told, "You know I'm not gonna do that – Wilfred."

5

Sunrise is a cast of shadows at the seashore. They start at mountains, gain more at foothills, and the shore-side cliffs add a final curtain to the sandy expanse before the surf.

It is not uncommon to find the mornings cloaked with fog and that often drapes more blinding curtains of its own. Runs often find figures abruptly in the path and there have been several collisions over the years. Especially on the last leg, where the mind's become fully immersed in thoughts and endorphins. Only once was anyone seriously injured.

It is a morning that feels warmer than it is – because of exertion, because of the fog, and because the wind is quieter than it often is. Drapes of mist gently drift over the sand and ocean. Sheets of cloud sweep through one another forming a kaleidoscopic haze.

It is the first time in years that a run broke the five-minute mark, and that revelation as time was checked has brought a sense of calm to a psyche that never has it. It brings a sense of fulfillment and satisfaction that is carried by acceptance that it will probably never happen again.

It was a run that found something not felt in years. Another gear where legs just moved like liquid. Where there was no sense of effort, nor pushing – akin to the last leg of the ride from the highway down the offramp: On the edge of control and careening at the border of capacity. Legs pulled instead of pushed and led the way.

Sheets of fog scroll across the beach and in the misty distance there's a mar that registers as the aberrant rock that abuts out of the sand. There is a spike in spirit as it momentarily appears there is someone near it: A figure, or an abscess in the fog – undetermined.

Memories bring to mind the conversations there: With Wyl, with Corsh, and with their children. There is a flash to a memory of AnnaKay – stood upon it and proudly strutting. But the vision in the clouded distance brings dissonance to those memories, as it doesn't evoke the sensibility that's found of those that are known: Movement, shape, and mannerisms. The memories slip away into the dissipating clouds of time as the present returns thoughts to legs, and time, and wonder if it is a barrier that will ever be crossed again.

The foggy landscape is a shroud against the bright mood and clarity of mind brought from the run and from the numbers that were found. There is a feeling of calm and resoluteness that is unfamiliar, as if every step falls on solid ground, as if there is an answer for every question, and no problem can't be overcome. There is peacefulness and calmness of the mind that is unfamiliar, but it is not rejected. It is accepted, absorbed, and reveled in.

The figure down the beach is likewise standing resolutely, between the rock and waves that have begun to slowly ebb. It is the second time the person crosses thoughts, and as proximity grows closer, they become a focus, after failing to meet the trademarks of those familiar – except: They are familiar.

The figure is large and appears to be wearing a cloak – seen blowing in the wind. As that registers, the rest of the familiar costume is imagined and the identity of the person becomes certain: The mythical viking, pirate, magi king.

An image is clicked as identity clicks, and it's sent with the message, "Guess who's back?"

Wyl questions back, "The fog?"

Another shot's taken, and it's shared, "The Viking."

Wyl replies, "I see nothing. Are you hallucinating?"

"Give me a sec," is answered back, with the intention of a close-up – Viking permitting.

The person is as remembered: Boots, robe; the crown. The only difference is that they were not stumbled on, and the sword is stashed along his side. But he is otherwise as found before – stoic, and staring out, over the ocean.

As he's neared, his size, abruptly stumbled on – alarming – is again noted: He is well over six feet, and broad. Consequently, and remembering the sword, he is approached cautiously. Distance is kept, as, "Excuse me," opens the introduction.

There is no response.

He continues standing perfectly still with eyes fixated over the ocean.

More firmly, he's offered, "Hey." With nothing, still, he's questioned, "Excuse me: Can I ask you what you're doing?"

There is the slightest turn. The man turns his head ever so slightly but it does not appear his eyes have shifted to see who is interrupting. Position is taken more directly, so they can view each other head on – caution still pulling back slightly to one side:

"Hey," begins the effort, once again: "Last time I saw you, I just walked by. A friend of mine said I should have asked you what's going on. So, what's the deal?"

The explanation finally earns the question, "Is your inquiry – directed – towards myself?"

The man's voice is calm, and smooth, questioning as if surprised that anyone might wonder about a magical viking, pirate king standing on the beach.

A quick glance finds few others within eyesight, and no one near, as noted, "No one else is here. Is this a cosplay thing? A reenactment?"

Bewildered, the man inquires, "You can see me?"

The question brings feet another step away, and, "Yeah," notes the obvious: "We can all see you."

He protests, "No: When I am still, I – am – invisible."

"Ah – okay," and another step's taken. It's suggested, "Everyone sees you. Maybe they just walk past because it's kind of alarming to – ya know: See you. Dressed like that. With a sword. So, they just walk past and hope you don't follow."

He questions, "What difference does that make?"

"I – I'm sorry: I don't follow."

The man turns to squarely face and questions, "Do you distinguish between invisibility and disregard? Do you feel there is a degree of separation?"

"Ah," brings clarity – a feeling of hilarity – and much of the concern begins to drain: "I get you. I feel invisible a lot, myself. But yeah, to answer: There's a difference. If you were invisible, I couldn't have told people about you. I tried to ignore you 'cause I came over the rocks and – there you are. But you weren't invisible. I saw you – just like I see you now."

"You have," the man questions – smooth voice grown stern: "Previously imposed upon my occupation?"

"Whoa," is thrown up as a warning as concern returns: "Hey, man: I'm not imposing on anything. I was walking down the beach and you were standing there. Apparently, you weren't the only one that was invisible."

"Mercenary," the man growls, and his hand reaches for the hilt, as he demands, "What liege to you proffer to?"

"First of all." Concerns become the more familiar anger, and it's shared, "I might be half your size, but I'm in great shape, and – worst case scenario – I can definitely outrun you. So, chill with the theatrics."

"A challenge," he says. His eyes grow wide and light glints off them beneath the hood, giving the man a sinister appearance. Before protest can be had, he shouts, "Accepted," and pulls the sword free, raising it above his head.

In anger, "What the hell is wrong with you," is shouted back. Steps are taken back, but the man is challenged, "Are you mental?"

Corbyn is told, "Draw your weapon."

The man is told, "You're freakin' whack. I don't have a weapon, ya nut job. Put the frickin' sword away."

The sword swings down and stabs into the sand, and eyeballs roll into the cranium – head shakes – the blade is raised and held forward for examination: "It's plastic. I believed you to be a member of the consortium."

"Well – it looks real as hell."

Proudly, he answers, "Thank you."

"So, it's a game you play? That's the deal? You wander around the beach picking plastic sword fights?"

The man says, "I do not appreciate the litany of derogatory terms you have used to assault my conquest. As someone that assails hills and sand with extensive frequency, I should think you would comprehend."

"Assails," Corbyn questions. "By assails, you mean – run? Is that what you mean?"

He says, "Only one of us concludes our venture with a victory."

It hits deep, and, "Yeah," finds there is sudden resentment, because, "You have seen me. So, let me ask you again: What's the deal?"

"What's the deal," is repeated: "You run and keel, chasing shadows from the past you will never reach. What's the deal," is asked again: "You run to a future that you will never reach because you cannot return to where you've never been."

"Okay – then." The man is offered a curt wave, and Corbyn turns. However, anger is never far from the surface, and he turns to shout expletives, but it never happens. Two middle fingers never fully raise, because as he turns, the man is seen walking into the ocean. Instead of anger and vile words, "Hey," is shouted, and, "What are you doing," is questioned.

It momentarily stops progression, but only long enough for the man to say, "Develop a new line of inquiry. Yours has become as tired as I have become waiting for the enemy."

"Are you," Corbyn wonders: "Are you trying to rhyme? Can you actually be a poet-talking, magical, Viking, wizard king?"

"Enough," is bellowed, and it feels as if the word fills all the air surrounding. He demands, "End your insulting drivel. You do not carry the weight to pass judgment on another. Return to your hovel and discard all memories of this encounter."

"Okay, look – hey: Fair enough. But it's kind of alarming you seem to have some insights about me. That's kind of weird. But you're also right: I've got no shade to cast at anyone. I just wanted to stop you from going in the ocean. It isn't safe here."

"It isn't safe," the man questions incredulously: "It isn't safe? Your neurological pathways have become corrupted. Your interpretive skills are completely lacking and dangerously designed with ignorance. Do not presume to understand what is safe for me."

"Can we cut it? Big man? Can you drop the act for a minute? 'Cause I've lived here my entire life and I've – seen – people pulled into the water. Once it's got you – there's no coming back."

He begins to reply, but stops and looks thoughtful.

He decides, "You are not irredeemable. And your concerns towards insights are justified, however, you are a passing voice that is frequent. A presence often encountered as I seek my enemy."

"Well," says Corbyn, "I'm not your enemy. And, I don't wanna see you swept into the ocean and drowned. Then, your enemy wins – right? So, I'm gonna recommend not going in the ocean, here. There are some protected beaches down the road, if you're into that."

"I am aware. I have never considered you an enemy."

"Okay. Then, just listen to what I'm telling you: Sand pits and rip tides are my nightmares. They're a bigger enemy that whoever you're looking for."

"No," he says, and turns, to resume his march into the ocean.

In panic, Corbyn calls, "You've got no enemies here. Maybe the guy's a no-show."

Progress is stopped again. The man turns, again, and looks back with the look of a disappointed parent. His face is tinged with sadness, that he shares, "El-Assissi-Syrianni-Afrahm is never far."

"You're Awrol – right? I found your book in the cave a while back. Maybe you can explain what any of that means, or, who – whoever that guy is. Just, promise you won't go in the ocean."

"It is – Awrol. You should not have touched my property."

"Well," Corbyn suggests, "Maybe you shouldn't leave it in a cave."

Awrol suggests, "It was protected."

"By the knife? 'Cause that didn't do a lot. Ya know – pulled it out, and dug it out – the book. Box – whatever. Or, is that part of the game?"

He says, "This is not a game," and begins walking back, again.

Corbyn offers, "Thank you. You've had me all sorts of off, today, but the last thing I wanna see is you wash out into the ocean."

As he nears, Awrol extends a hand, and it is taken. The moment it has been, he pulls the two together into embrace, and there are several heavy slaps against the back before release.

He says, "You have demonstrated many admiral qualities. However, you are deeply mistrusting. You run from a past you never had – towards a future you will never reach. You are splintered. You are shattered. I do not know if you will ever be whole."

"You are a freakishly big man that knows way too much about me. So – I'm gonna trust you'll stay out of the water and do what ya said: Forget this ever happened."

"I am afraid," Awrol claims, "You have committed fealty."

"I have committed nothing."

"You raised a challenge – and submitted. You will do my bidding."

"I'm not doing anything for anyone," Corbyn counters. "I'm trying to keep you from killing yourself – and that's it. I'll see ya, man. I'm no part of this weird shit."

"Unca-C," the mans says, and he smiles. It is a smile over a sour stomach. It is a smile that knows what follows. It is a smile that gives the opening, "I will walk into the sea, but there will be no harm. I walk into the waters – they will not receive me. I will walk into my submersible, transportation vehicle. From there, I listen to the voices on the beach."

"No." It's said with utter disbelief. It's said as it is simultaneously realized the fog has mostly lifted. It's said as reality strikes back, and says, "There's no way."

Awrol turns and begins walking, and this time, there is nothing said to stop him. He is watched as he continues into the water. He is watched as he continues through the water as waves crash around him – waist deep, to his shoulders; over his head. At that moment, panic sets in again, however, just as it had, a crowned, and cloaked head re-surfaces and Awrol slowly reemerges.

He walks fully back, and points out, "Not a drop of water upon me."

"There is no way."

The man should be dripping. His clothing should be saturated. He should have been swept away and drowning. But as noted, he is completely dry.

"I'm gonna regret this, aren't I?"

"No." Awrol says, "You will not."

It's supposed, "I'm either dead or hallucinating."

"You are neither."

"Well," says Corbyn: "I expect both of us know where this is going."

"These are the terms," it's explained: "You have challenged and submitted. You are therefore indentured until you choose to challenge and defeat me. That will only take place after the current conquest and is also – highly unlikely. Your other choice is to continue running."

"I've gotta work," Corbyn counters: "I've gotta take care of my kid – I've got friends."

The man that's claimed to be Awrol replies, "C'mon, dude: Like all of us don't have a life. You wanna see what it's about – those are the terms. I'll give you an out after the campaign, but you've gotta stick through to the end of it."

"If I don't?"

"Nothing," Awrol says: "Nothing at all."

It is a sentence already lived. It's experience for the prior decade: "Except the family. I don't deserve them. I can't repay what they've given me."

Says Awrol, "Who can? Who does? We are undeserving. We give to others because they are."

"Show me," says Corbyn: "We walk into our grave, we walk into our grave. I'll follow you and do what you need me to do. Just – don't ever touch me again."

"Fair play," is agreed, and "Follow."

They walk forward towards the ocean. Awrol leads the way and is waist deep as waves crash against the shore. He is unaffected and continues, but the water is cold and saturates the scant clothing quickly. They continue on until heads are just above the surface and regrets, and second thoughts begin predominating. They begin considering alternatives and the foolishness of trusting a complete stranger. Yet, feet continue marching on.

They walk onward until the last ebbing wash no longer clears their head, and the inevitable feels present – yet, it isn't:

They walk forward into a blast of warm air and they are found to be standing in a structure.

"There's just no way," speaks to the improbability. They stand in close quarters, in a structure with walls of wooden plank. The ceiling and floor – both are metal grates. There is a sealed wooden portal on the wall they face, but a look behind finds darkness – as if an infinite expanse of complete emptiness. "There is just no way," speaks to the inability to comprehend any part of it.

Awrol moves to the door and begins winding back the dog. There is no invitation, only the observation, "It's fortunate we're early in the campaign: There are plenty of provisions. However," Corbyn's warned, "We will need to gather more."

It's information that's not processed. Little is processed, other than awe: At the small space through the portal. Of a vessel – not large, but with space for navigation, with berths, and a small kitchen at the fore. It is not large – two people could not pass between the berths and navigation – but it is a remarkable wooden vessel decorated with brass detail: Pipes running overhead. A rail on open walls. Brass trimmed panels and wheel at navigation. It feels old and it is astounding. That is verbalized by Corbyn, who says, "There's no way."

6

Sunlight stretches fingers through the treetops on the mountains. Light pierces into the still darkened sky to the west as the sun reaches from the horizon. It is a cool and misty morning, the sort of morning held as ideal for early morning runs, and there's laughter as that crosses through the mind:

Appreciative, but also with awareness of the obsessive nature it had become.

That amusement is still carried as knuckles rap along the door frame, and as a surprised, "Unca-C," serves greeting.

Shey's asked, "Where's the enthusiasm," and her sister shares the obvious:

"Goin' to school."

"Lame," Shey offers.

Her sister agrees, "Lame."

"Lame," is agreed, however, "Do better than me or you'll end up like Unca-C: That's extremely lame."

"Livin' the life," Lia claims.

Shey says, "Could be in school," and their father ends the conversation:

"You pull something?"

"Interest," Corbyn answers. "Thought I'd see if you can spare a cup of coffee."

"You got it, Cococabana. But seriously – you injured?"

"All good – all good: Thought I'd come up and have that coffee you're always promising."

That conversation is interrupted by the surprise observation, of, "Corbyn."

"Corsh," is answered: "Hope it's alright. Coffee and all, and – what have you. Trying to encourage the girls."

"No." She says, "No: It's great to have you… Have you – join us? I mean…"

"I mean – weird: Right? Tell me to split if it's a pain in the ass, but I thought I'd come up and grab a coffee. And – tell your girls to bust ass in school."

"Lame," Lia says.

Her sister says, "Unca – Unca g-leaque. We thought you were in the league."

They're told, "I'd take g-league. They're getting' paid to play: Beats swimmin' in fish guts."

"Gross," and, "Take the guts," are the responses offered.

They're told, "I take the guts – y'all can do better."

"Take care of him," Wyl's told, and she says, "Out the door girls. Let's get moving."

"See ya, unc," and, "Later, unc," see the pair ushered from the home. Their father waves hands in question, and that's answered, "Have a coffee, ya say. If you've gotta move – I can come back another day."

"Capybara – look: It's just – we had a routine. We say, join us, and then – you make excuses. Showing up and asking for coffee… That's just extremely rude."

"I was hoping I'd see more of the girls, but I got distracted by the morning: It's absolutely beautiful out there. Sunlight reaching over the hills and through the trees. A little mist to soften everything. This is why I didn't wanna leave. It's why I'm stuck here. Seeing my favorite people in the world completes it."

"Corbs. What the fuck? I'm giving you shit, and you come with this?"

"You got time for coffee?"

"Yeah, Unca-C. Drop a pod in. Everything cool?"

"Cool," it's agreed: "Everything is very cool. Except," it's said, "Your kids gotta go to school. They would've fed the energy."

"And – what's that?"

"Things are good."

"Good?"

"Things are good. I meant to get up earlier so I could have a few with the family, but I couldn't get my ass to move. And then – I walk out and it's just incredible. I had to take a few."

"Coffee," is delivered, to, "Corterly."

"I appreciate you."

And that's given, "Don't appreciate you. What's goin' on?"

"You know: Nothing new, Wilber. Just – kind of reflecting. Where I am – what I do with what's left."

"To clarify: We're good – right?"

"Oh yeah. Everything's good. You guys? Gallery's good?"

"Yes, Cormorant, the gallery's good. Family's good. Not that you're not always, but you've seemed – maybe – a little more off than usual. Reflecting makes me worry."

"Chill – Wyl: Nothin' like that. I was just talk – that's right: Remember I said I saw that guy again?"

"Our Viking, wizard, pirate king."

"Yeah – he's not that. He's actually a really interesting guy. Really, really weird, but I don't know if we have time for that. But he asked what I was running from – or for. I had just broken fives…"

"No: You broke fives?"

"I did."

"Corgi: You're makin' this up."

"I'm not, Wilted. Four-fifties – but I'll take it."

"Specifically, Cornwall."

"Specifically, four-fifty-threes. Point eight."

"Damn."

"Yeah."

"Holy hell, dude. I mean, Corpuscle – that's outstanding."

"Yeah. It was a moment. Real good run. Legs were liquid, lungs wide open: Best run in longer than I can remember. I stopped the watch and I felt this incredible elation. I was, like – I did it. But then, right after that, I was like, that's never happening again. That's why Awrol's question really hit me. 'Cause, what am I running for?"

"Awrol: The big guy – with the sword."

"Plastic, if you're wondering. But yeah – big guy with the sword."

"And, you talked to him?"

"Several times, now. He is a very strange person, but the whole uniform is what he wears when he's on a conquest."

Coffee sprays, and, "Warn me," follows: "Corona. When you're gonna say something insane."

"You've got no idea, Wilmington. These campaigns go into a level and detail that is absolutely – insane. To give you an idea of how insane it is: The guy patrols the coastline in a submarine."

"Corbyn," his friend scolds: "You're screwin' with me."

"Hundred percent not. The thing looks ancient – beat to heck, ya know? All wood, and it's got brass pipes running across the ceiling. Brass handles and hatches. It's an incredible machine – not huge. It's got four bunks but I think four people on that thing would be claustrophobic."

"You've," is questioned skeptically, "Been on it?"

"A few times. And the most incredible part about it is, you just walk into the ocean. You're cold – soaking wet – and then you walk into a chamber at the back of it and you're hit by this blast of hot air. It blasts the water off, and, same thing going out: It forms, like, a bubble around you so – literally – you walk out of the ocean completely dry. Absolutely incredible."

"Corbs," his friend suggests: "You are making this up."

"Willow – I'm not. There's a bunch of people that are part of this consortium, and they have these conquests where they spy on each other until – well: They battle. But there's a lot more to it than that."

"Corbyn. I am really, seriously asking you to tell me you're screwin' with me. Otherwise, I might suggest you get your head checked."

"It's a lot to get your head around – I get that. We've just touched the tip of the iceberg, but I'm thinking of joining them."

"What?"

"I challenged him, and I lost, so I can do a test run on the current campaign, but I've gotta swear my loyalty to him. Do what he says – that kind of thing."

"Okay. I'm backing up. Do you have a picture of this guy?"

"I meant to get one but it was overwhelming. Like I said, we were talking. And then, he convinced me to walk into the ocean."

"So, you're gonna follow this guy around on an ancient, wooden submarine so you can have a plastic swordfight with someone else. That's what you're telling me."

"Pretty much."

"Corby: That's fucking nuts. What you are telling me is fucking nuts. Tell me you're making this up."

"No – I get it. It's fuckin' nuts. Completely get it. And maybe it was just the timing hit perfectly. I broke fives, and then I see this guy again."

"Okay. Pirate wizards, aside – tell me what's going on."

"Awrol."

"Whatever. What's with the running and thinking, Corbonkers."

"Like I said. I broke fives, and – what am I doing it for? It's the first time in forever and it might end up being the last time. Like he asked, what am I running for."

"Exercise? 'Cause ya always have – 'cause you've been obsessed with times since we were children? At our age, breaking fives is outstanding."

"But that's the point, Woodrow: That's a benchmark from the past. I haven't been competitive for twenty years."

"So, you're just giving up running to play swords? To float around the ocean in a deathtrap?"

There's laughter, but, "No. Not giving up. Just letting my body run where it feels good. That's not gonna be getting faster, and I'm alright with that. And I was going there before I ever talked to him. I saw my time and it was like I was looking through a window."

"As long as your going from charcoal, to paint, to clay and not actually walking into the ocean."

"We do," it's shared: "I figured I could swim out if there was nothing there. But there was – definitely – something there."

"Alright." There's movement from the chair to gain a second cup and wonder back to another thing that was mentioned: "That's what you reflected on? And, going forward?"

More laughter, because, "Tip of the iceberg, Wafflestreuse."

"Call in."

"I can't."

"Then run me through and I'll drive you in. Otherwise it's b to a p."

"Don't follow."

"Corpse. Instead of Corbs. Sounded better in my head. Tell me what made you join the submariner corps."

There's laughter again, and, "Wylobee," is said with great affection. It's shared, "More of the same – looking back. That run was just the end of it: I broke fives, and I never will again."

"You might."

"Ten years from now, I will not be breaking fives. That's my point: I still push myself like I'm training, but there's no reason. I'm still pushing like I'm gonna make a comeback."

"So, move on, Corburrito. Run for fun and move on to other things. Or, ya know, pretend to swordfight. Whatever grips ya – ya know?"

"It was also what happened with Anika."

"Oh boy…"

"I spent the last ten years busting my ass to have a relationship – and I'm the asshole I get mad they won't return my calls. I was – definitely – an asshole. But it was, like, the final straw. Seeing them shopping at that fuckin' store – I absolutely popped a screw loose."

"That bad?"

"If it sounded bad – it was worse. But at this point, she's gonna have to make some effort if she wants any kind of relationship. I've tried – I have tried, Werner."

"Corbs: Ya can't stop."

"I'm not. But I've got about two more years of child support, and then I can actually think about what I want to do. If it's fish guts, it's fish guts, but I'm not tied to anything, anymore."

"You've got a standing offer."

"Gimme a break, Wiggles. My skillset's fitness and massacring sea life. Not a great match for a gallery, but – actually – pretty on-point for plastic sword fights."

"Last chance, Chubs: Tell me you're makin' that up."

"It's for real. Maybe I could open up some kind of cult-like fitness program. Like, a nature-lovers defender corps. Charge exorbitant fees to have people break their bodies. Complete the program, you get a certificate you can proudly display."

"The cynicism smells like fish guts."

"That's the smell of the hemp-paper certificates."

"The cynicism smells like burning morals."

"Yeah. Either way, Wilshire, I can finally stop mooching off you."

"Corbs?"

"Shut up. I'm leaving if you start a lecture."

"There's no mooching."

"Yes. There is."

"In all seriousness, Corbyn: We love you. If you need proof – just ask my kids: They adore you. We just wish we'd get to see you more. You check out a lot."

"Here we go."

"You live in my backyard, and no one's seen you for days."

"Scouting," it's suggested. "And that's my point. Thanks, Wylamette."

"Okay. You interrupted us for coffee. I'll leave it. But what about some kind of fitness program? I think if you market it right – ya know, tie it in to art therapy at the gallery – I think that's not a bad idea."

"Again, Wylizard – don't wanna drag ya down. Everything I touch ends up breaking."

"Okay. So, let's go back thirty years ago."

"No. Please – no."

"You were the guy."

"Hey Wyl: Let's not. Ten years later and I was definitely not."

"I'm not gonna say you couldn't have done some things differently, but a lot of that was crap luck. Just – random chance."

"Being a shitty husband and father."

"You were busting your ass trying to get back to competition, and she crushed you."

"She saw all the dollars that sparkled in her pretty, little eyes start disappearing."

"And that's your fault that's what she cared about? There was a freak accident. It was random. So, yeah – you put in a lot of training, but that was the source of the dollars – if you wanna make that claim."

"Obsessive, violent; fits of rage. There's a mall camera that supports that opinion."

"When a dam breaks, there's usually a reason. I remember the kid everyone wanted to hang with, that still came over to an awkward, shy kid that just wanted to make weird drawings."

"'Cause they're frickin' amazing."

"And you told me that. It meant everything, 'cause all of us expected we'd be mooching off of you."

"Ha: Finally admit it. Busted in the act."

"My point is, most of what happens to us is random. You got taken out by other runners, and just when you're getting back to competition level, ya got taken out by Anika. You should've pushed back harder."

"For what? She had the money to come after me. They were killing me."

"After," it's suggested, but that's answered, "Nah. I was already struggling to keep in touch with her. Let her mom say, you're dad doesn't wanna take care of you? I've got two years and I can finally stop moochin'. You gonna pick me up or make me walk it back?"

"You're gonna walk, 'cause you're a pain in my ass. I got to say, Corbyn's my best friend, and that was something I really, really needed. Having your support for what I do helped me continue."

"Corshae disagrees. Besides, Wyliecoat, I wanted that dragon."

"Yeah," and they laugh back into their memories: "What book was that on?"

"No clue. Still got my dragon."

"And, I still got my best friend – Crosshairs. Life socked ya: Least I could do was help you up."

"Kept me on life-support."

"Don't expect mouth-to-mouth."

"I'd rather die, Wyllips."

"My point's made, Clyde?"

"Loud and clear: You should've been mooching off me."

"You're hopeless."

"That's what Ani says."

"Corbs."

"You driving? 'Cause I've gotta practice my knife-work."

"You – ready?"

It's asked with doubt, because the usual sack is missing. That's explained, "They've started doing sushi at the counter. Just like everything – I'm obsessed."

It's agreed, "You do have that problem."

7

"Corbyn," is offered mutely as a greeting as the bike slows in proximity.

The ramp down was taken with brakes applied, to take in the view on arrival: Not particularly breathtaking – row of buildings against the docks, and three ships moored – but a decade of existence had never taken a moment to take in detail. There is nothing particularly interesting and most that came across it would probably describe it as run down and dirty. But it's a place that holds appreciation, because of familiarity – because of the people: Passing ships that offer vacant greeting before moving on to obligations.

"Morning," is offered back – and a pause: "You just getting back, or heading out?"

"'Bout an hour back," is answered.

"Anything good?"

"For the time of year – it's alright. They bought most of it but it's not gonna keep ya late."

"Alright," Corbyn claims: "Always appreciate you."

The man says, "Yeah. Alright. Have a good one."

Inside, the little store holds several, though most seem to be connected – a family, or families that came together. Most likely, tourists.

The woman behind the counter's offered, "Mornin'. Everything good up here?"

"Corbyn – actually," she says: "Can you spot me? I need to take a break."

"Not a problem. Just let 'em know I'm here."

"Yeah. Thank you, Corbyn. I'll do that."

She leaves quickly, and the counter empty.

Corbyn asks, "Anyone need anything? Any questions?"

A gentleman inquires, "What would I need to feed fifteen people?"

"Lots." There's a whole case of fish, "But if you're lookin' to keep it simple, you could bake a salmon. Low effort and most people like it."

The man asks, "Can you tell me how to do that?"

Corbyn says, "They think of everything," and pulls a card off the counter: "They even sell the seasoning."

"Some potatoes," the man suggests: "A salad." There is enthusiasm as he envisions the feast, and he says, "Yes. That's what I'll go with." A simple solution – a prospect that seemed overwhelming, and he walks away happy, unburdened, and very pleased to return back to where he came from with success. He says, "I really appreciate you," as the transaction concludes, leaving six behind that are certainly together.

There's a hostility, or irritation between them. There are three adults and three children and anything anyone suggests is shot down with a litany of reasons, by several.

Corbyn offers, "I feel like you're not looking for a meal." And, it's guessed, "Road trip?"

An older man complains, "They're taking us on the ocean."

A near woman adds, "They've got nothing for the kids, so they sent us here."

"Oh," says Corbyn. He shares, "I never liked going out until recently. Give it a chance. You might really like it."

The woman says, "You got something kids might like? Something – not junk food?"

"A couple things," Corbyn suggests: "It might not sound like something you'd like, but the jerky's really good. Let me get you a couple samples."

The third adult that had not previously spoken, says, "Don't bother."

He is ignored, and while those samples are distributed, it's further suggested, "The smoked fish is another good one – another one you don't have to keep refrigerated. It's a little messier, but it's really good. My favorite's the peppered, but a lot of people like the teriyaki. You can't go wrong with the original, either."

As it's suggested, samples are offered, and a little girl says, "Mama: I want this."

"Grab some crackers to go with it. We've also got some Tillamook cheese sticks that are always good."

The woman says, "We were hoping for some fruit," and she's told, "This isn't that. The smoked is pretty healthy, and the jerky's not terrible – it's got salt. But nothing's terrible for you. But we've got no fruit."

She asks the older man, "What do you think?"

"The smoked," he says. "Pepper and the regular."

They're sent away with both, with jerky, with cheesesticks, the crackers, and a six-pack of water, walking out as relief returns:

"Thanks, Corbyn. I was hoping I could grab one of you coming in."

The usual greeting are met beyond the swinging door: Acknowledgment – commiseration. The foreman says, and cynically, "Thanks for joining us."

He's told, "I was spotting up front. Didn't she tell you?"

That's answered, "This is where you're paid to put your time in. You wanna play around up front then come in early."

"Really." It is a challenge, and the old nemesis of anger charges: "She needs a five minute break and no one's gonna help her? Are you really serious?"

"Yes," he says, "Corbyn: Is that a problem?"

Anger liquifies and circulates, but it's understood the answer's, "No." He further adds, "Got the message. Loud and clear. Heading to the station."

The rest that's said is left ignored, and the greeting, "Corbyn," is answered, "Chel."

His partner asks, "We havin' a bad day?"

"Hadn't been. Thought we all agreed to help out where it's needed. Guess I missed the meeting."

"Time of year," Chel suggests: "They're gettin' pinched. Everybody gets pissed about everything."

"Yeah," is agreed, but there's amusement, because, "I got no room to criticize. I'm worse than anyone." There's protest, but by the time, "We doin' alright," is asked there's recognition that seasonal tension's effecting everyone, and the man's told, "Yeah," and, "Just hope another load comes in."

The foreman moves on, with, "You and me both."

Conversation continues. Mostly with Chel, but with others in proximity. It's garish, and casual. Trite, and brutally truthful. Mocking a cut is followed by a cut to the soul as a diagnosis is shared. As concern about a child flitters loose in the middle of a filet. There is laughter and caustic commentary that circulates throughout the room until it's interrupted by another observation, or complaint, or random thought.

It continues until, "Empty," is called, and it isn't even noon.

It brings to mind an earlier conversation, and Corbyn recalls, "They said it was light, today."

Chel says, "Shit. I need to get paid."

It's agreed, "You and me both."

"Scrapin' boogers off boats," Chel objects, but it's one place there's dollars, off-season. He says, "Shit," again, and, "Fuckin' seems like it's worse – every year. Shit gets shorter every year."

"Hey, man – sorry: Ya know? If I could spot ya, you know I would."

"Yeah," Chel says: "The broke brothers. Scrapin' our knuckles for the kids. You wanna send it off with a drink at Billy's?"

"Belli's," Corbyn returns, and that's answered, "Billy's." Corbyn says, "It's Arte Bellis."

"Motherfucker: It's Arty Billy's. That's the name of the fuckin' bar."

"It's," is started, but Chel talks over: "Billy's. Why do you got to always do that? Billy-bella – who gives a fuck? You always gotta correct everything."

"What the fuck Chel," is fired back. "When do I correct anything?"

"Steaks too thick. Missin' the bones. Cuttin' too deep. All day long I gotta listen to that shit. We all get it: You're Mr. perfect: It's fuckin' Billy's."

"Chel," says Corbyn: "We shit on each other all day long. It's fuckin' around. Do you think I give a shit if you miss a bone, or cut too thick, or whatever the fuck it is you're talking about? You've told me I don't know how to sharpen a knife since I started here."

Chel says, "'Cause you don't. Wanna grab a beer at Billy's?"

"Yeah – you asshole. Arty Billy's."

He asks, "Really?"

"Yeah," Corbyn confirms: "Dyin' to try this new place – Arty Billy's."

"Here we go…"

It was a bar called Gracie's until a half-dozen or so before. It was meant to be high-end Italian but high-end Italian only comes through in the summer, so they leaned into survival mode with a street food menu that was more affordable. Most locals still consider it a bar, just with better food.

The bar is crowded, like it always is. Like anywhere with decent drinks and delicious food: Arancini, sciatt, and scartrosso de pesse amongst the favorites. The bar is crowded, so seats are taken at a table. It is a crowd that does not match the atmosphere. In the summer, that will improve, but it will never meet the proprietor's original expectations.

The menu's scanned – eyes flit from drinks to food – and as pangs of hunger drive growing salivation, Corbyn shares, "I can't remember the last time I had a beer."

Chel says, "I'll have a hangman."

The woman at the table asks, "What can I get you, hon?"

There are many choices, but the description of, "The Scotch ale," holds the eyes. There also a question of, "Are we sharing food, or just getting whatever?"

Chel instructs, "Separate bills," which brings the man across from him to order several of the small plates – relatively inexpensive but three adds up to more than's usually spent on groceries in a week.

It's a luxury that would never have been considered, a month before. Not before breaking fives. Not before joining a campaign. But an erosion of everything held sacred has reached a melting point, and the small account funded in the hope of every leaving a good friend's shed is recognized as pointless: It will never be enough with the little added to ever reach that goal.

With an endpoint to financial strain in sight, it's no longer clung to with hope of moving forward. It's a few thousand that offer the opportunity to enjoy life, occasionally, until that endpoint arrives.

"Nice place for something called Billy's."

"Sure, Corb," and he leans in closer: "Let me guess – you've never been here."

"Yeah. I was here before they made it – Billy's."

Chel says, "Good to see you're learning to let things go."

There's laughter as the beer arrives, because, "Just starting. I do have a hard time letting anything go, but I'm trying."

"I'll let you know."

"Okay – let me know," and then it's asked, "How's the family?"

Chel answers, "Good."

"Kids are good?"

"Yeah, Corbyn. Kids are good. How's your family?"

"Everybody's good."

"I mean," Chel clarifies, "Anika. How's the ex and your girl?"

"Also good," Corbyn answers: "Last time I saw them I reminded them why they're glad I don't live any closer. I haven't talked to them since, so – good. Did Gyles figure out what he wants to do?"

"Corbyn…"

"Hey – just a question. You've mentioned it a few times."

He says, excitedly, "While shootin' shit and slicing fish. I just came here to have a drink. Talk about the game, or anything else."

"I didn't know that was crossing some boundary."

"Corbyn," he says: "I've been married twenty-eight years. My kids are grown. They'll figure it out. All I got is goin' to work and comin' back. Sometimes, I like to stop here and have a drink."

"Got it. Most of my information about the game comes from you. I'll just say, it looks like they could do okay, this year."

"I got you – not really a fan."

"It's a complicated relationship."

Says Chel, "What isn't with you?" There's laughter, and for once, it's shared. And with drinks and food pulling the edge of disappointment, he further asks, "I'll bite: Why's it complicated?"

"A-K was a huge fan when she was a kid. And the last time I went up there, I bought tickets for us to go to the game. Then I blew up, and everyone left angry."

"She didn't want to go?"

"I don't think I asked. I'd been trying to get in touch any one of them in forever. I went up, hoping to try in person, and then I saw them shopping at the mall. I lost it, Chel. I blew up. I said a lot of things that are true, but it wasn't the place or the right way to say it. The kid ran off in tears and I got removed by security. It was a real good look."

There's a moment of silence, a sip of beer, and a few bites taken as the information's sorted, and what Chel finds, is, "That's kind of sad, man. In actuality." He looks across the table at a person considered pompous, considered a tremendous egoist, and he sees a broken human. For the first time in the ten years that he's known him, he has insight into the person he guts fish with:

"You know, man – let me be honest: My wife and I don't get along like we used to. My kids are still at home and the best they can do is get away from here. But that's like jumping out of a plane without a parachute. So, I come here to drink because I don't know how to fix any of it. I didn't mean to be a dick, but that's talkin' about family."

"Shit sucks."

"Shit sucks – that's right."

Corbyn suggests, "We should go to a game."

It's questioned, "You want to go to a game."

"Yeah. Make a weekend of it. I'll spring for the tickets, but we'd have to split everything else. Ya know – child support takes ninety-percent of it."

It supposed as humor, and Chel chuckles, "Yeah?"

"Yeah," is answered, and Chel follows, "Really?"

"Really. I slosh around in sea life sludge to make the payments. Almost all of it goes to the kid."

There's silence, again, as thoughts conflict, and it's thought its best to leave it at, "Sounds tough."

However, the source of resentment is bared, as it's shared, "She drives a G-Wagon, Chel. They live in a million dollar mansion – probably millions. I'm doing everything I can to make the payments, and it's nickels to them. It means nothing to the kid – they have everything. That's why I lost it. I'm struggling to come up and see my kid in person, and then I turn around and they're shopping in this fucking designer purse store. I flipped my lid – looked like a fucking idiot."

"Shit, Corbyn. You always make things sound alright."

"You opened it up."

"Yeah, well, I'm gonna go home and take my wife out. I'm gonna go home and give my kids a pep talk. I'm even gonna tell the dog he's not so bad. I think you just put my whole life in perspective."

"I'm jealous of you, Chel. I know you're joking, but I've got all that without a family – that's the worst thing. He took my wife, and he stole my kid. I swim in fish guts to take care of my kid, and it means nothing. I'm no one to her – I'm an embarrassment to her. I don't even get to see her."

"I ain't just joking: You're makin' me feel like shit. I'm gonna go home and put my arms around my wife and tell her how much I love her – that is not a joke. We just get into routine, you know? Maybe we just need a hobby."

"Even – watch a movie together."

Chel says, "That's not it: We will never agree on a movie. You got any hobbies? I mean, not the gym or ridin' your little bicycle."

"Well," says Corbyn, "Gym and bike keep me in shape for the hobby."

"I don't wanna know."

"You don't," is laughed out loud: "You don't."

"I'll tell you what, Corbyn. How 'bout you work on those tickets and let me know what weekend we're gonna make that happen. I'm gonna go home and work on my relationship – s."

"One more?"

It's agreed, "Yeah – I'll have another." But he laughs. There's a smile as he says, "Only 'cause i wanna see you ride outta here after a couple of those."

8

It feels like legs just began to warm up as the run draws to a close. It feels like an inadequate start to the day. It feels like another stretch of beach should be taken, but it isn't. Feet splash through the shallow river, and there's a mental strain to avoid it – but it isn't. Practice, conditioning, and obsession bring eyes to the watch and there's laughter on observing time well under fives.

It's understandably ridiculous. It was expected. If it was more, it would bring concern.

A stroll's taken further down the beach, eyes on the soft, cotton fog that wafts across the sandy shoreline – a woman bursts from a cloud. She's pressing hard and obviously well into her run as she approaches – digging hard: Pushing her body. She's given a nod of admiration as she closes, and she offers the same, though, it's not deserved.

There's another laugh into the clouds of morning. Another laugh at the absurdity. Another laugh at decisions, and another laugh at a body that's only getting slower as it ages. It's laughter at the obsession of it held until recently. As if there could be a return to the strength of twenty years before – twenty years, or more.

Looking at time and the places that it's gone brings the mind to darker places, but there's also a beam of sunshine that's leading to the future. There's a rip in the fog that finds a way forward into new adventures: New possibilities. New interests. New obligations. Most of those revolve around sword fighting, and that thought brings more laughter, again – a laugh that draws a concerned look from a woman that's returning.

She's told, "You're killin' it. Keep digging."

She nods, and there's a brief smile. A smile that's known. The sort of smile that comes from self-consciousness. One that breaks the mind away from the intoxicants spilled from a good run. The sort just beginning to drip as feet dipped in the river.

"That's a good feeling," is said only to the surrounding emptiness as a turn is made to head back home. An acknowledgement that not every day will be ending before legs and lungs have been pushed to their maximum capacity.

The walk back is pleasant, as the temperature is relatively comfortable, and the fog has begun to lift. There are no heartbeats in the mist – even with efforts to see it – no muscles cramping; no recovery.

Waves are licking at the large rock embedded in the sand, as it's neared. It's impossible to know if they're moving in, or falling farther from the shore, as they alternate between coming near and being washed back out. The brief observation only finds that none of them surround, and it's mounted, and climbed to the highest end.

It is where the world is perfect. On the beach. On the coast. Standing on the farthest end of the country overlooking the ocean. It is the peace and serenity of Awrol as he was found the first time. It is where the darkest thoughts, and anger, and frustration have been washed away, through the years. It is where ideas are born. Where thoughts have found conviction. It is where decisions are made and find confidence. It is the end of the world, and the beginning of everything. It is violence, and it's calm. It is the beginning, it is the end; it is renewal.

"Looks like the fog's lifting," breaks the quiet and is a reminder of other decisions that are slipping away as everything is considered.

The passing stranger's told, "A little early, today. But it's a little warmer."

"Have a great day."

"Yeah," Corbyn says: "Yeah – have a great one, yourself."

He leaps from the rock, and makes for the cliff-face.

Legs do not complain like they usually would. There is strain to take the crumbling steps, but not the ache felt after the runs of the past decade. Simply a push, and move, and gain – to the grassy opening behind the cabins.

There is one man that is sitting at the picnic table and he makes no motion to acknowledge the interruption. He is a stranger from the cabins, or from a camper. He is staring into the distance, over the ocean, and it is a mirror to the man once considered threatening. Someone with whom little has been shared, and little has been shared. But there is recognition, in the moment, that he is someone that comes from somewhere and shares the gaze into the distance. Feeling invisible in that space is familiar, and hollow, and a common experience for many.

The stranger is left to silence because there are no words that find a voice. The bramble patch is navigated to the cabin, but it's bypassed and the stretch up to the home is taken.

Rap against the frame is greeted by, "Unca-C."

She's given, "Morning, Lia. How are you?"

She says, "Goin' to school. Can you call me in?"

There's laughter, but she's told, "No," and asked, "Alright I come in?"

She holds the door open, but says, "Not if you won't call me in."

"Corduroy," greets the entry, and a device is lifted to view the time: "Skip the run again?"

"Nope," he's told, "Four-four-nine."

"Are you kidding me," erupts in question, as does, "Are you serious?"

"Corbyn," is said, as Corshae enters the room. She says, "Good to see you. Can I get you anything?"

She's followed by her daughter, who immediately suggests, "Have I got the thing for you." She strides across the room and pulls a box out of a cupboard, and tells him, "This is your thing. It's got no sugar, no salt; no flavor. You're gonna love it."

"Corbs was telling me," Wyl shares: "He hit four-four-nines. That's competition level."

There are words of congratulation. There are words that claim they're impressed. Until Corbyn shares, "It was a five: Five miles. I figure I'll cheat time with shorter miles while I can."

"Unca-C," says Lia, and it's admonishment.

But her sister adds, "I'm gonna cheat on my history exam, today."

Coffee's offered and a seat's taken at the table as Lia's offering's delivered. "It's not bad," is accused, "Only you would say that." There's laughter, because, "It's true."

Lia sits and asks, "Did you hear dad's gonna be famous."

Says Corbin, "Yeah? They puttin' a Wylrus in the Louvre?"

"More like the loo," Shey says.

Corbyn asks, "What's up?"

It's claimed, "Not a big deal."

Refuted, "It is – a big deal," by Corshae, and she shares, "He got a commission to create a mural for a Portland station. It's a very big deal."

"Potentially," is refuted by his spouse: "It's a formality. Just to make sure his idea meets their expectations. I'd show you but he's packed it up. But it will exceed their expectations."

"That's great, big Wyl. That was the trumply thing?"

"Trompe-l'oeil, but yeah."

"Dad's famous," Shey proudly gloats.

"The most famous," agrees her sister.

Corbyn agrees, "Well deserved. That's really cool, man. I didn't realize that was a done thing."

"It's not," is refuted by his wife: "It's set in stone: He's under commission – today's just the final approval. It's just a formality – and a free lunch."

"No one deserves it more, my friend. Make sure you get the bag up front."

Corshae says, "That's the formality."

"Oh – man." Another bite's stuffed in the mouth, and it's marveled, "That's outstanding. That's so – exciting – man. I'm so happy for you. That is really, really cool."

"It's not a big deal, Corbel."

"Corsh," is asked, and answers, "It's a very big deal."

"Shey." She prods her sister and points over, "He's eating the whole thing."

"Ooh. Why you doin' that, Unca-C?"

"Your sister called it. I wouldn't say, love, but it's right in my zone. You guys taking up residence; long days on the road? Both?"

Wyl answers, "I don't know. I think long commutes while I sketch it out, but probably some overnights when I start really working. Playing it by ear – seeing what happens."

Corshae suggests, "Convince him it's too much driving. I think, one way per day at a minimum."

"I bet you get completely wrapped up in it, Wylkie. You'll be gone weeks at a time."

He suggests, "Then, I'd have to hire a babysitter, Corblits. Someone's gotta look after you."

Coffee's denied it's target because laughter follows, because, "Ya got me. I thought – the kids. But – bip: Ya got me. Good one, Wylshire, but if you need the time, I can keep an eye on the place."

"Sure. You'd like that, Crosby: Wild parties – trash the place. There'd be nothing standing after a week."

"Ooh." Lia suggests, "Then, can we stay home?"

"No," her father answers, and further, "You'd probably bring the stabby crowd. I can't even imagine what they'd do in a civilized setting."

"Oh," says Corbyn: "Nowhere we go is civilized. Only chaos and mayhem."

"I'm in," Sheys says, and her sister says, "Me too."

Their enthusiasm is interrupted by their mother. She asks, "What – exactly?" Corsh questions, "What is it exactly that you do? Wyl's tried explaining it, but it sounds totally bizarre."

There's laughter, because, "It is."

She asks, "You sword fight? You dress up and pretend to be knights, or something?"

Wyl gets up to get another cup of coffee, and shares, "I tried," but he knows his wife is not digging for an answer – not satisfied by the incomplete, disorganized description that he gave her. He suggests, "How 'bout a two-minute summary. I told her sword fights, submarine, and spying. I also remain confused, Corbinaer."

"Two minute summary," Corbyn reflects: "It's actually really complicated."

"Dang," Shey says – to her mother, "Guess you've gotta call me out."

She's more serious than she should be, and says, "No." Attention turned to Corbyn, she admits, "I'm actually a bit concerned by it. He's said you walk in the ocean. There's a submarine – you spy on people on the shore. I don't know that any of that sounds alright. And then, there's sword fighting."

"Has this been a discussion?"

"Yes," Wyl answers, "Corbination. I've tried to normalize what you're into but it only sounds worse every time I say anything about it. If you'd like to put our minds at ease – go ahead."

"All of you," Corbyn questions.

"Not me," says Lia, and so'd her sister: "Not me, too."

"Guys," Corbyn pleads, "It's not a bad thing. It's just a bunch of us that participate – ya know: It's, like, an elaborate game."

"With sword fighting," Corshae points out.

"Plastic swords," Corbyn explains. "And these guys put a ton of effort into making them – their uniforms. So, there's really minimal contact, unless."

"Unless," Corshae questions.

"I mean – we practice by fencing. So – you can – make a fencing challenge. There's more contact during that. But usually they just track each other down and use the moves we practice to catch the other person off guard: Fake stab – that's a point. No one's getting hurt."

"Can I ask," Corshae does: "Do you even know anything about this guy?"

"Timothy Brandt – used car salesman out of Newport. In uniform he's Awrol, and either way he's a really great guy. Really nice – really, super smart. If you ever need a car – that's your guy."

"Maybe you," Wyl suggests, "Should get a car, Cornberry."

"I don't think he has anything crap enough I could afford. But when Shey's old enough to drive, he'll set you up."

"Concerned," Wyl says, though he clearly isn't – mostly: "Have I been replaced?"

He's told, "Never. But Tim's taught me so much, already. And, I love fencing – if I'd known I'd have been doing this instead of running. I would love to have you guys join us fencing."

"Stabbing," Shey asks – she says, "I'm in."

"Ooh," Lia imagines, "I can't wait to stab you."

"Girls," their mother says, and a hand is raised, and they go silent: "Tell me what you do."

"Corshae," is begged. She's told, "It's mostly planning. Mostly practicing. Some spying, but mostly working on moves."

In case it wasn't clear, Wyl clarifies for his wife, "To make fake stabbings."

"Yaay," is said quietly by Lia, as is, "Woo," by her sister.

Wyl adds, "Woo-woo," but there is clearly something more behind the concern and suspicion falls the more is Anika.

"This is what I'm built for," Corbyn explains. "This is what I've been training for my entire life. The running, the gym – I'm in ideal condition to join the consortium."

There's a discernible roll of the eyes that's abbreviated, still – unmistakable.

Wyl tries, "So, you aren't part of it yet?"

"I'm in liege to Awrol."

"Liege," Corshae questions.

"He's in charge. He tells me what to do. My loyalty is to him."

Asks Lia, for everyone, "Forever?"

"Right now, I'm just learning, so I'm just gonna do what he says anyway. But I can challenge him to be on my own if I felt like it. He also said he'll let me go after this campaign, but I don't wanna do this on my own, so I'll probably just stay in liege."

Corshae says, "This sounds like some kind of cult."

"It's not a cult," Corbyn laughs: "This is what I've been trying to get back to for twenty years. There's a physical aspect that feels so good, and it's competition. I get to compete again. This is what I've missed. And it's such an interesting group of people. I know it seems weird, but it's just a bunch of really creative people that created a game. It's just a kick. I really wish you guys would at least try fencing."

"And, there's a submarine," Corshae points out: "That some guy built. That he sails around and spies from."

"Well," Corbyn admits, "That is true. But it's an amazing machine. And it's not deep diving – it just sits right beneath the surface. And Tim's no nutjob: He built this thing to handle a lot. He's got life jackets – it's loaded with technology. Ya know, trimmed out in antique brass, but it's not just drifting in the ocean. One day, I'll give you a tour."

Immediately, Shey asks, "When we goin', Unca-C?"

Wyl breaks in right after, because he knows what's coming. He suggests, "Why don't you tell us what the consortium is – the campaigns: What are those?"

"Aren't the girls gonna be late for school?"

Their mother says, "I'll call them in."

"What," is the expression of shock, and joy follows: "You're the best, Unca-C: Keep talkin'."

"Corbs," Wyl coaxes, "Can you give a brief run down?"

"Consortium," is explained, "Is everybody that's involved. The campaigns are led by whoever either wins a challenge, or the campaign. We're hoping to challenge the guy that set up ours up because it's kind of stupid, and it's obviously rigged."

"Do tell," suggests Wyl.

"The current one? We're supposed find a thunderegg that looks like an existing nebula. We've got a few that are – sort of – like one, but obviously, this guy's got one or that wouldn't be the campaign. So, we're gonna have to challenge him but he's been laying low."

"Do you just attack them," Shey wonders: "You just jump 'em while they're walking down the street, and – stab?"

"Only when they're in uniform," Corbyn explains: "You have to be available for challenge at least five hours a week, but trying to find a person when they're in uniform is the biggest challenge. We've gotten a tag on him a couple times but so far – no luck."

Wyl asks, "You know who it is?"

"El-Assissi-Syrianni-Afrahm."

"Ala what," Lia asks.

"El-Assissi-Syrianni-Afrahm," Corbyn repeats. "I won't even go into how much information we have on this guy, but we can't pin him down in uniform."

"So, it's just," Corshae supposes, "Some weird, elaborate game. You play dressup and pretend to sword fight. I don't get it."

"It's really involved. I mean, I get you don't get it. The amount of effort these guys put into it is insane. But it's been so much fun. I absolutely love being a part of it. It's weird, it's insane, but it's also incredible. The more I learn, the more I wanna be a part of it."

"So, Cornerstone, if you guys jump this guy and win, what's your campaign?"

"No idea."

"Let me guess: You didn't ask."

"I've kinda been in shock – from the moment I walked on the sub. He's been explaining how everything works since then: There's a lot."

Corshae wonders, "But you can't run the campaign because you're this guy's liege."

"Well, he's my liege. I swear fealty and liege homage."

To Wyl, Corsh asks, "Do you understand any of this?"

"I – honestly – can't even remember what you asked him. But I think, I feel, like it's – okay? Would you agree with that?"

She points out, "A submarine, Wyl. And why did you challenge him in the first place?"

"Oh." There's laughter as it's recalled, "That was a misunderstanding. He was thinking about starting another campaign and he thought I was a member of the consortium. I didn't mean to challenge him. But I was trying to have a conversation and it got weird. I don't remember exactly what I said, but suddenly – sword's out and he's coming after me."

"Starting – a campaign," Corshae questions, "You can just randomly start a new campaign."

"Like I said – it's complicated. You can challenge anyone in the consortium at any time. You don't have to – but you can. If you win, then you can run a campaign with them. You can have as many as you want, but even one's a lot. He was getting tired of trying to track down El-Assissi, so he thought – why not. He figured I'd be an easy take down."

"Took ya down a rabbit hole, Cornbread."

"Yes." It's agreed, "He did do that."

9

"Damn, it's cold." This is an observation made in advance of several hours of sitting in it. This is an observation made that recognizes they came poorly equipped. Chel is realizing, "Man – I gotta get somethin' to put on." He is realizing they will be sitting in an outdoor stadium for several hours and it's already unpleasant, and furthermore. "God dammit, Corbyn: It's gonna fuckin' rain."

"It does look like it." Feel like it – smell like it. It's an observation made after a miserable night sleeping with another person in the same room. A night of violent dreams and brutal flashbacks exacerbated by the sound of heavy snoring. It is something not experienced for a dozen years and as the cold digs in and the threat of rain looms, it's an experience that is not envisioned as ever being welcomed, again.

"Wife said," Chel complains, "He's got no one. Say's, he's reachin' out. Tryin' to make connections. I'm like, no, but she don't listen." A gust of wind brings irritation and a moment of awareness that the complaint is being made to the person in question. He tries, "I said, Corbyn don't need no one. He does his thing – do whatever you want to, right? She tells me I should do this. Probably wants me the fuck away for the weekend."

"I just thought it would be fun to go to a game. We were talking, ya know? We've been slaughtering sea life together, forever. I thought it would be fun to hang."

"I ain't sayin' nothin', Corbyn. I'm just sayin', I go to work, I come home, and maybe that's what I like – I know: You heard me complainin'. But maybe you get to where you are 'cause that's where you wanna be."

They walk on with the wind increasingly gusting and it feels as if the temperature is falling further from the already unpleasant cold they'd walked into. The misty air is growing heavier, and footsteps follow. Footsteps fall heavy and exhausted by travel, company, and uncertainty. There is an onus that was almost forgotten. A baggage not carried for years because it had been alleviated after moving into the cabin. There was awareness, and interest, and thoughts towards those that offered it, but there was no expectation that decisions would take others into consideration.

It is nominal in the present circumstances, but notable in that it's present. It brings thoughts back to reflect on whether there was a lack of it, decades prior. If focus on resuscitating a career had superseded the well-being of another. If it had disregarded their needs, and opinions, and desires. If a child had been disregarded and ignored, and left to be cared for by their mother.

It brings a heavy sigh, which brings Chel to air thoughts also falling into a similar category: "I'm not sayin' somethin', Corb. It's just, it's cold as hell. We were in the forties – I'd be alright with that. I was goin' back and forth, but I was thinkin' – I wouldn't mind catchin' a game. I just didn't expect it to be so cold."

"Cold sucks," Corbyn agrees.

"Look: Maybe we can hit a bar and watch the game. I'll pay you back for mine, but I don't feel like sittin' in this shit for three-four hours. You good with that?"

They'd left after work, which was fortuitously early – seasonally early, because the winter was never good. But it had still been a late arrival. It had still been six hours on the road after five spent processing. It had been nearly six hours on the road steeped in the scent of fish guts, and they'd arrived exhausted and starving.

They'd checked in, and crashed down to the hotel restaurant where one did not enjoy microwaved ravioli, and Chel struggled through a tough and rubbery steak. The restaurant had a four-star cumulative, average review, but it was undeserving.

The lousy meal was followed by watery drinks, and a miserable night of attempted sleeping. Morning's promise was quickly dampened by sour waffles, thin, bitter coffee, and fruit that was on the edge of expiration. They'd still left the building with inspiration that the day would be rewarding, but that was dampened not long after – after being chilled, and finding the temperature would not be rising. Finding the heavy air would likely grow heavier, and by the time they were in the stadium, it was expected it would be raining.

Chel's told, "I'm going to the game."

"C'mon, Corb: This sucks. I'm not spendin' half the day in this crap – and it's supposed to rain. I'll pay ya back for both the tickets. We can find a place to watch – I'll buy the first round."

"I'm gonna go to the game," Corbyn says, and explains, "This is the second time I came up here to catch one, and I'm not gonna miss it again. You can do whatever you want, but I'm gonna catch the game."

"Damn, Corb. I cannot see myself sittin' through this."

"Yeah," is said. There's a look up through the fog into more gray of heavy clouds. There is shared objection to the unpleasantness of the weather and understanding that will only grow worse with time and degeneration. That the prospect for the day is less than positive and their time in the stands will grow increasingly unpleasant. There's no retreat from position, but there is acknowledgment of the other's, and with appreciation it brings thoughts towards a solution. That is one that jogs the memory, and thoughts, and prior visits to the city: "I know exactly where we need to go to lunch."

Chel questions, "How does that cover anything we talked about?"

"Because," Corbyn explains, "It's at the mall." He explains, "There's an amazing place and they've got amazing food, but their empanadas are insanely good. You have got to try them. And after we eat – we gear up: Another layer. Rain gear – we can make this work."

"I gotta be honest: Even the worst I thought about this whole idea, I never thought it'd be as bad as it has been. To be honest with you, I just wanna go back home."

"Man. I could not agree with you more – everything about this trip's sucked."

"You ready to head back home?"

Corbyn says, "I'm going to the game. We can eat, warm up, and if you don't want to, we'll meet up after. But it's the second time I bought tickets: I'm gonna go – even if it sucks."

"Man, Corbyn." Chel looks into the mist that's close to rain already. The cold wind paints it across bared skin with an unpleasantness that draws anger. However, there's a crack in the hostility, formed by the same things that his wife observed, from the time spent together while they've worked, that he'd suggest it in the first place, and by a conversation held at Arte Belli's. There's an opening, however Corbyn's told, "Don't get your hopes up. There might still be an opening, but it's small as hell, and it's lettin' in a cold-ass wind. I'll have lunch and then I'll let you know."

"The mall's that building over there. They've got one of outdoor stores; that's probably our best target for staying warm."

Chel complains, "Where it's twice as much as anywhere else."

"Yeah," Corbyn agrees, but an image flashes from the past: "A-K used to like playing on the bridge – ya know: They've got a little stream running through it. She'd try to pet the ducks…"

He's asked, "You gonna start rainin', too?"

There's a soft laugh, and, "Nah," because, "I don't know where that came from. I haven't been there in a long time."

"Yeah," Chel continues to complain: "And here we go. This is how you get me – I mean: How my wife did."

"I didn't mean to."

"Let's just focus on gettin' somethin' to eat, and maybe get a drink – try to make the most outta what's left of this thing."

"After that crap sleep, last night, I'd probably pass out in my seat."

"Yeah," Chel agrees, "It sucked."

"It did. This whole trip's sucked, but I'm still going to the game."

Chel says, "I know," and it's with acceptance that won't change.

They arrive at the mall, and it's teeming. The building was once a warehouse that once became a department store and then remained abandoned for over a decade. It was considered for removal, but it's also a landmark: A recognizable feature of the city built with enough character that the thought to loss turned to ideas for redevelopment. That became, "The Mall." Six stories of shops, restaurants, and entertainment. Restaurants being a collection of offerings with walk-up service. The one walked up on was the one touted as outstanding – food once offered from a food truck that had since become used only for catering.

Corbyn promises, "At least this won't disappoint you."

He's told, "My expectations are extremely low."

For the first time since their adventure began – beginning with a drive filled with strained and awkward conversation – for the first time, there is genuine humor shared between them. It is a rise to spirits buoyed by the aromas as they approach the kitchen.

A variety of empanadas are ordered to be shared, as well as sides for personal consumption – street corn, a salad, and a water.

Chel observes, and says, "I feel like you need something to fill your stomach:" Speaking solely for himself.

There's a pause, as he tries to interpret the items on the menu, but he's shaking his head. The man behind the counter suggests, "Try the Mofombo. Shrimp is the best."

Chel asks, "What's he tellin' me, Corbyn?"

He's answered, "That's also good. If you hate it, we'll find something else."

It is not hated. It is, "Strange," but another bite follows. An empanada follows, and the conversation begins to find the legs from around the cleaning station.

It's within the lighter mood that Chel is asked, "Any chance you changed your mind?"

"Alright, Corbyn." He says, "Alright. We can see what they have. But I'm still fifty-fifty."

"That needle's movin'."

Chel suggests, "Don't get too excited."

They're walking towards the outdoor's store, when a woman says to Chel, "I think these would look great on you."

He questions, "Yeah," and as he does, she slides sunglasses on. She points to a mirror and he mugs, and asks, "How much?"

She says, "Seven-fifty."

He laughs and starts taking the glasses off, and entertains, "If there's a point after the seven then we can talk. Otherwise, you got the wrong guy."

She says, "Have a nice day."

There's laughter, and Chel says, "You have a nice day, too," and just after he does, there is a, "Hey," spoken in near proximity.

One turns with a skeptical eye, but a father hears a voice that won't ever be forgotten and has to mute what would otherwise be a cry:

"A-K. It's great to see you – how are you? It's great to see you: Annakay – how are you?"

She says, "Good."

"I," he says, and stumbles. At a loss for words and observing that she's miserable. He says, "This is a friend of mine – Chel." And he turns to look at the man to proudly introduce, "My daughter – AnnaKay."

Chel takes a moment to look her over and says, "No shit."

"Are you," Corbyn tries – trying to find anything to begin a conversation. His eyes scan and find the two suspected to be responsible for the interaction watching from across the court – clutched together like incompetent cohorts trying to pull a fast one. Corbyn checks down his thoughts and tries to sound cheerful, as he questions, "You guys out shopping or just passing through?"

He's told, "Mom said I should say hi."

It's no lie, that, "I'm glad you did. It's great to see you. You look – I mean: You're very… Ya know – it's been awhile: It's great to see you, A-K. Things are good?"

She answers, "Yeah."

Her father says, "Good. I'm glad – glad things are good." But it's clear she has no interest in being there. It's obvious she wants to be anywhere but in conversation with a father she hardly knows.

It had once been different. In the early years there was immense enthusiasm when they got together, but that had waned and eventually disappeared altogether. To the point there was almost no communication whatsoever.

From the awkward pause, Corbyn suggests, "I should introduce you to my ex," to Chel.

That brings a, "No," from AnnaKay. She says, "They just told me to come over here – they thought you saw us."

Corbyn says, and sincerely, "It's always great to see you, Annakay." And then, "Come on – let's say hello."

He leads the way against protest that isn't voiced but demonstrated through hostile body language. That's expressed through forced huffs of breath rasped from the chest.

The pair looks warily on as they approach but a gesture of decency is offered with an extended hand. It's suspiciously taken and given a nod, as Corbyn says, "It's good to see you guys," and it doesn't even sound insincere.

Plinio, says simply, "Corbyn," and Corbyn follows, "It's nice to see you," to Anika. He says, "A-K tells me you're making a day of it. Getting a little shopping in." In a nod to the other in their presence, he says, "That beats what we're looking at."

The pair are made aware another is included in the conversation, because he says, "I haven't committed to anything."

Plinio tries to find grounding, by claiming, "It seemed like we – like AnnaKay – should," and his thoughts dead end at a loss for words.

"Yeah," says Corbyn: "Good to see you guys – always good to see you, A-K. I don't wanna keep you guys from your plans, but I do need to apologize for last time I saw you here."

Plinio attempts to move away from the conversation, by saying, "It isn't," but he stumbles off his thoughts, again.

"It was out of line," Corbyn says. He starts, "I," but then, it's understood, "No excuses: I've got no excuse. I lost my shit and it wasn't… I got – nothing: Just an apology. To you guys. To AnnaKay – to you: I'm sorry, A-K. Not the time, not the place, and none of you deserved it. I lose my shit – Anika: You know it. None of you – A- K: You especially. None of you deserved it. I'm sorry I'm an idiot."

Anika breaks her silence to say, "It was humiliating. You're lucky I didn't file with the court."

It's expected that she tried, but she's simply told, "I wouldn't blame you. Chel," Corbyn says, and the dissonance progresses positively, to, "You ready to split?"

He says, "Yeah. Sure."

And Corbyn turns back, to claim, “It was great to see you guys. Great to see you, A-K. Drop a line, or text – anytime: If you want.” There’s a pause, and quiet, and the only thing that is absolutely true, is, “It’s always good to see you, AnnaKay.” She continues looking miserable. The two she’s with look back as if expecting something to follow. As if something was done and they think they’re caught. They say nothing, and neither does their child, so Corbyn ends it. He says, “I’ll let you get back to what you were doing,” and turns.

An elbow’s jabbed against Chel’s ribs, and the cue is taken to follow away.

They haven’t walked far, when Chel says, “I just learned everything I need to know about you.”

He’s asked, “What does that mean,” and is answered, “You’re full of shit.”

The façade of calm from the moment before shatters, and, “What the hell does that mean,” is filled with anger.

“That,” says Chel: “That’s real. That bullshit back there was only bullshit. All these years I’m thinkin’ your bullshit’s real.” He says, “I see you, now.”

“Whatever. You wanna split – whatever: I don’t give a shit. We can go.”

Chel says, “Hey man: I’m just sayin’, I never understood who Corbyn was until I saw you talkin’ to them back there.”

“I’m an asshole? I thought everyone knew that. Let’s check out and get out of here.”

“Corb,” Chel says: “You are feelin’ fucked, right now. Let’s do what we gotta do to shake it. Then, we’ll hit the game.”

"I don't care," is an admission that the observation's accurate: A brief moment, few words, and everything that sucks the life from living was encapsulated. "I don't care," is a claim that washes against more than a game. It's the window that shattered and let another person through: "I fucked up. Last time I saw them – here. I needed to apologize. That's all – I fucked up."

"Chill," is a suggestion that is understood to be unlikely. But Chel says, "I see a lot goin' on there."

"I – just," Corbyn says, "Maybe. Say something? They might react? For A-K, ya know? I hoped she'd say something. I guess – I don't know… I don't know… Let's just go home."

"Take a breather." They are standing and staring at the entrance of a store they'd intended to enter. It was the reason that they walked to the mall through miserable weather – hoping to find a shield against it. Chel shares, "I've been listenin' to this pompous ass talk about run times, about his bicycle, about the shit he does while he's livin' outta some garden shed – some family and kids – and I'm thinkin', what a self-righteous, entitled fuck. Apparently you're just as fucked as the rest of us. Well: Fuck it. Let's see what they got to make this less miserable."

"Chel," says Corbyn: "We can go. It's fine. This whole trip sucked."

"Second time you bought tickets," Chel reminds him. "Shit ton of dollars to throw away: We're here – get some gear. Let's do it." There is an attempt at protest, but Chel says, "Win or lose, you need an outlet for that shit, 'cause it's killin' you."

10

The sound continues, after waking. It transforms from the gunfire splitting rocks in a crevice of a canyon in the subconscious, to a sound that is more familiar: Knuckles raps against the door frame.

There's still ill-ease as the transformation happens. There's still uncertainty and tension as the knocking at the door continues. It is still pitch-black. The mind is still cloudy. Igniting a device finds it's shortly after three. The knocking continues.

Whoever is on the other side is not told, it's open, as per usual – though, it is. There is an effort to assess who's interrupting the night's sleep: Body turns and pulls to a seated position, but the world is hazy and whatever is beyond the door remains cloaked by the night. Feet meet the floor in a turn to silence, as the knocker no longer presses.

Through the rectangle of glass that is approached, the little light that travels from the home and any from the moon and stars that is able to pierce through a growing haze, outlines an amorphous form the other side. A large figure that is draped in fabric with a distinct ring pressing in atop the head that is known to be a crown. There is tremendous relief on recognizing who is present, and a thought back to a search for him, nearly a year back, where weapons had been procured as protection – thoughts falling to it might have been advisable to have one.

The door is opened, and, "Awrol," is acknowledged through a yawn.

He whispers the reason for his presence, "Located," and it is a warning that every word, every motion is being monitored.

Eyes stretch, and a nod is offered back to confirm. Arms motion away as an invitation, and the prior nod is given reciprocation.

Corbyn turns back in and moves quickly to ready for departure: The advice to always be prepared, ignored, but it makes little difference as the space is small, and anything that could have been prepared is accessed easily: Socks, shoes, and several layers to protect against the cold.

It is only a few, and they are stumbling across the landscape in the cover of darkness. Walking through the bramble, across the lawn, and then down the broken staircase to the sand.

It is known they will be walking into the ocean. It remains a leap of faith that a machine will be waiting for them and the cold water that saturates will be sucked away and dried in merely seconds.

They walk across the sand and towards the ocean, and as they meet it, footsteps do not hesitate. They walk in against the undulating waves until they are submerged. Breath is held as the cold water digs against the skin, as the red warnings flash against the brain, and only trust, and faith in the other leading allow feet to struggle forward.

They emerge into the familiar blast of air, and it's instantly warming. Water is stripped away and the bitter chill of December water is peeled away. As that transformation is embraced, the dog's already being turned and Awrol is moving towards controls. The hatch is pushed closed and wound tight, before it's questioned, "You have him?"

"Something strange," is explained.

"What's going on?"

"Observations have found," Awrol begins, but he turns, and says, "Something is off. Completely straight – I need us to communicate clearly. Right now, I need us to be you and me – Tim and Corbyn. Because I can't figure out what's going on."

Corbyn asks, "What is?"

"I have a ping," and that's unusual, because, "We've been chasing him for months. He's elusive – he's invisible – now: Here he is."

"A setup," is suggested.

"A setup," is mulled dismissively, because, "Why?"

"Force the challenge," is suggested, but Awrol replies, "That serves no purpose."

"He fails, and we are victorious – it is a disastrous miscalculation. If he is successful – nothing changes. Engagement does not offer him any value."

"You still have him?"

He's told, "Florence. It appears they're in an establishment that should be closed."

"Complacency," Corbyn suggests. "Or… Maybe he got tagged from another challenge. Maybe he's taken on more than he can handle."

That's given, "No."

There is quiet as the vessel gets underway. They begin moving from shore into the open ocean, heading south towards the position marked on the screen.

What excitement there was drips away, as the mighty vessel is many things, but it isn't fast. Of remarkable note is the unyielding focus of its captain, faultlessly wary of other vessels, of physical threats, depth, and of course, their target.

"Maybe," Corbyn suggests, "He crashed there for the night?"

It is not an unreasonable conclusion. The ping's remained stationary since first observed. All the more reason to think, "It's a setup. He is up to something."

The night winds on and the journey crosses an hour. Throughout, the captain remains focused, and the target does not move. The passenger, on the other hand, makes the best of it and lies down on one of the bunks.

The nap seems brief, when, "Unca-C," is called. The captain's answered, "We there?"

"Close. Our quarry has moved. I believe our subterfuge has been compromised."

Corbyn wonders, "What does that mean?"

"They signal us to let us know they are on to us. They are aware of the sub-surface transportation. A flex to demonstrate we no longer move with secrecy. A show that despite our efforts to move without detection – they remain impervious."

"Now what?"

"A matter of time – only a matter of time. It was a good run and provided copious data. We will still land as we planned to land, and if the demon known as El-Assissi-Syrianni-Afrahm is daft enough to show his face – then I will challenge him."

Attention is drawn at the declaration. Corbyn walks over but there appears to be little change of position – it isn't questioned. What is, "What will I do?"

"At three points scored, I will give the order, strike. You will run over, grab the bottom of his cloak and pull it over his head. Today, this will be our exclusive strategy. If he scores three, loudly narrate what you see."

"I don't have to worry about anyone attacking?"

"Unca. C: I will call you C. Find a name for yourself. If successful, this is your first challenge. Watch, listen, and learn how they are undertaken. If someone does challenge you, decline. You are not required to engage with them."

"But I can?"

"No," Awrol says: "You will do what I say. If we work together in the future and you gain your independence – then – you can make that decision. Today, your focus is on learning."

"Decline – got it. Did he move any more?"

"He is waiting," Awrol decides. It is observed that the vessel is heading towards the shore, however, it appears, "We're going in a river?" That's answered, "Yes."

"We're going up the river?"

"The town is on the river," is explained with a salting of irritation: "Push the scope and survey what we're approaching."

They move through a narrow waterway. There is little to the west – sandy shore with assorted growth – and scattered buildings on the shore opposite: All residential.

"What am I looking for?"

He's told, "Anything," but there's nothing. It isn't mentioned.

The move through the river is excruciatingly slow and there is nothing observed that's worth reporting. They finally turn such they are almost heading east when, "Bridge," is noted: "There's a bridge."

"Got it," indicates the news is irrelevant, however, "Now: Eyes on the north shore. This is it, C. Tell me what I'm looking at."

The scope turns north, and it's reported, "Ah… There's a thing. You see that thing in the water?"

"Forget the thing. There's dock, or wall that's jutting into the water. Do you see that?"

"Ah," is reported a second time: "It looks like there's some kind of floating dock, and that runs past a pier – like, up higher. Is that' what you mean?"

"The floating deck – the one closest: That's on the water."

"Ah – yeah. Floating dock sticking towards us on the water."

"Along the pier," Awrol demands, "That's floating dock?"

The scope's turned, and it appears, "It looks like a ramp. It goes from the floating dock to the shore."

"We will breach the surface. Step on the dock and follow the ramp. Announce, 'Awrol arrives,' and I will follow immediately after."

He's told, "Got it."

There is near silence as the captain carefully navigates the shallow water. There is a slight jolt, as the bottom of the ship comes into contact with the riverbed. With serious intensity, the vessel is carefully turned and guided, moving with precision into position.

"Screw it:" They lurch back and the vessel is thrust against the shore. Awrol revises, "I'll lead the way. Follow me."

He moves quickly, and Corbyn follows into the mucky edge of the riverbed. They dodge around a small shed and ascend the steep embankment to a sea of asphalt. There is a short fence that is smoothly spun across, and then simply leapt by the man's compatriot. There is nothing and no one obvious, but Awrol strides to the center of the lot, to declare, "El-Assissi-Syrianni-Afrahm: Show your wicked face."

With no response, the sword is drawn, and he begins walking towards the pier.

It is a platform that holds two buildings – two restaurants. Between them is a stretch of open pier, and it is towards that Awrol is heading. With the sword raised high above his head, it is demanded, "Show your pathetic face. Your cowardly intrafage will no longer disgrace this conquest. You will be vanquished and dismissed from your ill-gotten place. Come free of the shadows. Step forward and face your defeat with honor."

Seconds pass, and it's enough time to wonder if they chased ghosts. It's enough time to consider if they hadn't, the objective wasn't battle – and concern turns towards the submarine. But then:

Heavy footsteps plod across wooden planks. A pre-planned march and show of force step through the doorway of the western building.

It is an impressive show. It is more than a dozen, and the one assumed to be El-Assissi-Syrianni-Afrahm wears a costume befitting a knight – a king: Possibly a medieval assassin. He is not as tall as Awrol, but he is the human equivalent of a bank vault. He is clearly rock-solid, despite the clothing, and he stomps forward with a confidence that demonstrates the upper hand.

It is noted that Awrol fights a smile. That he sees someone that has been absent for some time and he's glad to see him. He fights a smile, and it's observed that the other does, also. They approach one another as friends coming together after a long absence. It is clear the words are empty and there is comity between them.

El-Assissi says, "You: This is a grievous error. You will be submitted, and the contract you have petitioned will be ended. Prepare to fall, yet again."

He pulls his sword free, and the others step away. Immediately, Awrol charges. He swings, but the challenge is met – swords come together but there is minimal contact.

Swords spin – combatants spin: Cloaks splay and twist with the motion. It is a remarkable dance to watch: Feet step and bound, and twist and lunge, all while the swords spin, and thrust, and probe. It is fencing with a mind toward minimal contact of the weapons. It is a swordfight that is all strategy and skill with the express intent to not cause injury, and not to damage weapons.

Unfortunately, "Point," is called by El-Assisi. He met a swing and instantly plunged under, falling to the boards and taking – it could certainly be considered a cheap shot. He dropped and stabbed the point of his blade at the back of Awrol's knee.

Shoulders slump, and there's clear disgust at what happened – though it isn't evident for what: Clown move, or that he wasn't ready.

They resume. They continue the dance, and there are multiple additional attempts to create openings, but Awrol is clearly familiar with the tactics and brushes them aside. Unfortunately, another, "Point," is called, as a swift-faux-deflection is followed by a spin, and – Awrol's ready: He brings the sword down but it was likely with the memory of a prior interaction, and it comes up empty. A second jab is stung, and it's two to nothing.

There is a brief pause to the battle, as Awrol takes a step back. He offers a nod and with evident appreciation says, "Nice."

El-Assissi answers, "Thank you," smiles briefly, and lunges forward.

He is easily repelled, as are all the attempts to score again. The two work around the perimeter of the open pier, taking care to avoid the edges and the crane near one end. They move quickly with spins and lunges, circling one another with increasing energy. Increasingly, as if they are very much enjoying themselves.

Corbyn takes position just beyond the crane, in a corner where he won't be in the way and also where no one can slip behind him. He watches those gathered but like the others, he is mesmerized by the battle.

Awrol deftly turns away a plunge, twisting the blades together, and he then quickly pulls, bringing his weapon around his back and directly into El-Assissi."

"Again," is stated with frustration – that it worked – before the delighted Awrol, says, "Point."

They resume and it is a frenzy. They are clearly both skilled but El-Assissi increasingly has an edge, and he manages a flurry of blows that result in, "Point." Immediately after, he orders, "Waffles."

Corbyn calls, "Left – rear."

Awrol tags the attacker and the woman falls to the deck and begins to dramatically die. Laughter begins to form, but there is a blindside strike that nearly sends Corbyn off the pier.

He gathers his feet and begins to turn to assail whoever hit him, but eyes have scarcely turned when two fists punch heavily into his chest and send him over.

The word, "Hey," is shouted by El-Assissi and it lingers in the back of thoughts as everything else goes silent – like a greasy film that won't wash away.

The world slows as the lower deck's observed, as it's sailed across and thoughts are focused on avoiding contact – specifically, the thought to avoid contact with the head. But it's cleared, and there is a sense of satisfaction that the landing will end with wet and not with death.

The silence ends. Shouts erupt from the pre-dawn night just as the sound of the body's impact breaking water falls. They are quickly drowned by the abrupt submersion. Everything goes dark and the icy water aches a chest that begs for air, and to gasp at the sudden, frigid submersion.

The breath is stalled, but there is panic as there is no sense of up or down. In the seconds ticking past the mind races to recall orientation: Eyes spread open looking for any glint of light.

The cold begins to bring an ache, and arms desperately dig into the water – feet kick with a prayer they push the right direction.

There is a punch against the temple and in the mind's eye, the dock stretches just above. But the puncher found the target and grabs onto hair. There is a fierce pull and in the second before lungs were filled with water, Corbyn is pulled above the surface.

The gasp finally has its chance, but it is halting as hands grapple to cling onto whatever pulled. The hand pulls again – pulls him higher from the water – but only to drop him down against another body, and a thick arm wraps below the chin and begins to pull.

"I've got you," is a shivered promise from Awrol. He pulls hard for the far end of the dock, the little submarine slumping on the shore behind it, but the current is too fast, bodies are too cold and weakening, and they sail past, feet from an outstretched hand.

As they clear the dock, it is observed that the others are running along the shore. El-Assissi splashes in the water to yell encouragement – to reach closer for his friend, but he's pulled back as the water reaches his waist.

Bodies are completely numb, but Awrol continues. He slowly brings them closer to the shoreline until others are finally able to form a line and reel them in.

Corbyn is incapable of moving. He is pulled onto the muck and lies frozen, outside the violent wretching of his body. Awrol crawls onto shore on his hands and knees, and efforts to bring him upright end with failure.

Voices color in a night that only feels worse as it continues:

"Can you hear me?"

"We have to get them inside."

"Corbin:" El-Assissi crouches down, feeling for a pulse, feeling the cold – himself saturated with ice cold water. He questions, "Can you hear me?" There is just enough blood flowing that Corbyn can manage a shaky nod, and he follows, "Let's get you up."

Hot hands pull, and Corbyn is brought around to a seat. The mind's slow calculus finally turns to the one that saved him, to find him looking back with a worried face.

Behind, and coming from a distance there is a woman racing from up-river. She carries bundles that she tosses down as she arrives, and two attempt to get Corbyn to his feet. They shake the blanket open and wrap it across his shoulders and begin dragging him up the embankment.

Voices continue shouting:

"Get some cars."

"We need to get them inside."

"We need heat – let's get 'em up here."

"What around here's open?"

They manage to drag the pair from the river, and they stumble with their guides – muscles weakened, extremities in pain. As they make the street, two vehicles approach at a high rate of speed. The first turns sharply just before it reaches them and stops with passenger side towards them. The driver leaps out and races around to open the door:

"The seats are warm. But it's gonna take too long to heat them up. Let's try the coffee shop."

It is still early when they arrive, and there is resistance to early entry, but the block of a man that is El-Assissi steps to the door and firmly states, "This is an emergency – two in the river."

The door is opened, with, "Oh shit." Awrol and Corbyn are quickly ushered towards a table at the back. They are seated and wait in quiet misery as the others scramble to find ways to warm their feet and hands. The proprietor offers, "I'll turn the heat up. You called for help?"

El-Assissi says, "We just pulled them out – no: We haven't. But call the sheriff and tell them we need medical attention. Tell them this wasn't an accident." He walks over to an old compatriot that is just beginning to feel his toes throb. He walks over to the man that has not taken eyes off him since he sat, and he verifies, "You know I would never put anyone in danger. You know – I had no part in that. You know I would never ask someone to do that."

"You stretch boundaries," Awrol accuses. "You stretch the rules. And this – is the end result."

"I know you're angry," El-Assissi says: "I know you're cold, so I won't argue. However, you have a submarine."

Awrol answers, "This was attempted murder," and it's agreed, "One-hundred percent:"

"We obviously suspend everything until we understand what's going on. We will get the authorities involved, and I will – I would like you to help me – investigate. The man is relatively new, but there was nothing about him that raised concern. I'll show you everything I have on him."

Awrol calls, "Corbyn." He sees eyes lead a head that slowly turns, and he begs, "Can you tell me how you are?"

He's told, "Feeling – a lot – better. I still – I still – feel cold. My hands are aching. But I think nothing's broken. You? Thank you, Tim: Thank you. You saved me. You're alright?"

"I am angry," he says. "This is not what we do."

El-Assissi agrees, "It's not." He moves to Corbyn and puts a hand against his shoulder. He says, "I do not have words that are adequate to offer you an apology. I am so terribly sorry. This is not who we are."

"The rule is – no harm. To our creations, but especially to people."

El-Assissi nods his agreement, and says, "This is our escape. We flaunt our creations, we push ourselves – and, limits – and we do it for the joy. No one is ever meant to be harmed. I am so sorry, Corbyn. I am distraught but grateful that Timmy found you."

A woman asks, "How's he doin'?"

He answers, "I think – I'm alright." And, wonders, "Do we know? Who was that?."

El-Assissi answers, "Argreave Topel. Do you know the name?"

There is a moment of reflection before Corbyn answers, "No." The name is not remotely familiar. He asks, "What happens?"

With great indignity, El-Assissi insists, "He will be arrested."

The door opens, and a man in uniform shakes off the cold before addressing the many present: "Mornin' folks. How we doin'?" He enters with the presumption he'll face conflicting stories; he is surprised to enter to many people dressed in peculiar uniforms. Several are unnatural colors. He asks, "What – is this?"

A woman explains, "We role-play. We're all fencers – sword fighters. We get together and challenge each other. But tonight, a guy tried to kill one of our members."

Awrol pulls dripping feet from a bucket to stand. His imposing presence brings a raised eyebrow, and then wider eyes as he shares, "We have a name. We know where he lives. This man – needs – to be held accountable." And he waves a hand towards Corbyn, to emphasize, "I nearly lost my friend, tonight."

The man is somewhat overwhelmed by what he's faced with – role players, sword fighting; some sort of organization. He falls back to presumptions, and asks, "Anybody want to give an alternative perspective?"

"No," reverberates the room and stamps the prospect from existence: Awrol says, "We saw what happened. That person tried to kill my friend. We are all witnesses, and all of it was recorded. There is no question of his intent."

El-Assissi agrees, "There is no dissent and no question. His intent was to cause injury or death. Our friend risked his life to save another. More than one was placed in grievous danger. There are no alternative perspectives."

"Okay." The sheriff says, "You got that video?"

A woman walks forward with a device held towards him, and says, "I got it right here, hon."

11

The last leg of the run begins at the rock embedded in the seashore, where a pace already pressed pushes to absolute capacity. Feet pound the water matted sand and muscles burn more with every step. The end point is quickly gained, and at the little river, direction turns to chase the river's flow cutting through the cliff face. The sand matted by the ocean is quickly lost, and so is pace as soft sand absorbs footsteps.

Hands reach to the back to stretch the aching back and to open lungs for the heavy breaths as a brief walk is made onto the shoreside river stones. A turn back finds a familiar face approaching, and she's given a nod of approval just like every other time they've passed. Except, she doesn't continue.

She stops across the river, and asks, "Are you alright?"

Skin crawls with paranoia. Fear and nightmares feed thoughts that question, "Is there somebody behind me?"

She looks confused, and says, "No," and wonders, "Why would you ask me that?"

Eyes turn back because the sense of someone approaching is omnipresent, but no one's there. No one close and no one threatening. She's answered, "Long story. But why did you stop?"

"Because," she says, "You didn't go through the water."

"Yeah. I didn't. I decided I don't like water. That's why you stopped?"

She explains, "You didn't go through the water, and then you didn't check your time. I thought you might've been injured."

There's laughter, in that, "I'm that predictable?"

She says, recognizing in him what he sees in her, "It's what we do."

A quick glance finds, "Fifty-one, ten." A shrug, and, "Not bad," is suggested, but times aren't being chased, anymore: Running is the only place where there's a sense of control.

"What are you running?"

"Ten-milers," he answers.

She laughs, and mocks, "Not bad?"

Corbyn recognizes, "I guess I broke fives. I did that a few – a couple months ago, I guess." He raises a hand as a means of introduction: "I'm Corbyn, by the way. I never say anything 'cause – you know: Don't wanna bother you."

She laughs, through, "I appreciate that." She moves through the river and the sound of splashing water washes the bright morning with black and sends a chill down Corbyn's spine. He is paralyzed as she shares what she believes to be an amusing anecdote: "I used to try to avoid the river as much as possible. You know – aim for the little islands between the water. But then I'd see you go full throttle through it and it looked like a blast, so I started doing that, too. That's the only reason it seemed weird you didn't. But then I saw you didn't check your time. And that seemed really off." She says, "Corbyn," as he stares into the icy blackness of midnight water. "Corbyn," she questions, "Are you alright?"

The water ebbs it's tendrils from the mind, and he apologizes. "I'm not," he says with honesty.

She questions, "Should I call someone?"

He looks up and meets her eyes, and shares, "Some guy tried to kill me."

She says, "Oh my gosh." She qualifies, "I don't know what to say," but asks, "What happened?"

"It's – it's a long story."

"My gosh – I'm sorry." She extends a hand, to share, "I'm Jesty. Did that happen, here?"

"No," he says: "South of here. I can't figure out if he's just a psychopath, or if I did something to piss him off." He shrugs, but it's mostly against, "I can't remember ever seeing him before."

Jesty asks, "Did they catch him?"

The answer is, "No," and why runs are ten miles, again, and pushed like they never have been, prior. Because, "We know who it is. They've got his name and address, but he's laying low. Somewhere." There's a laugh, because, "Now you know why I asked if someone was behind me."

"Oh my gosh," she says, again. She says, "That's crazy: What happened?"

"Long story," Corbyn says, but there's concern, and so he shares, "I'm part of a fencing club – ya know: Swords, and masks, and white uniforms. But we also get together sometimes – for fun. Some of the guys make elaborate uniforms, and we get together and spar. I'll keep it brief, but at a certain point, other people on a team can get involved – but it's harmless. Ya throw a rubber chicken, or, if I got the call I was supposed to pull the guy's cape over his head. Just harmless, prank-type things. Well, the other team got the call, and that's when this guy dumped me in the river. Middle of the night," and her eyes light up, and with equal parts disappointment and humiliation, it's observed, "Oh. You heard."

She asks, "Down in Florence?"

"Florence," he confirms. "I can't figure out why. I don't even think my ex hates me enough to kill me."

She suggests, "Maybe he's a sore loser. Maybe he held a grudge from another – whatever they are: Meetings."

"That's the thing: I just got started. This is the first time I was ever part of one. I keep trying to think of anything where I might've pissed off someone, but I can't think of anything. Not recently, anyway."

She asks, "You don't think it was an accident," and she's answered, "No," and sharply:

"It wasn't an accident. You can watch the video, and you ca..."

"There's a video?"

"Yeah," Corbyn says: "They record the meets. I'm sure it's out there."

She asks, "You have the video? They said they weren't sure it was an accident."

The conversation has become irritating, and Corbyn says, "Yes. I have the video: It was not an accident."

Sheepishly, she asks, "Can I see it?"

"Yeah," he says. "I guess," he agrees. It's a video that's been viewed ten-thousand times. Every frame is familiar: "These are the combatants. I'm over here behind the crane. Right here – you see the guy score a point. That's when someone else can get involved, and you see this woman start charging. As soon as she pretends to die, this guy – right here: That's the guy. He charges directly at me. Right here – he drives his shoulder into me, and I almost went down, right there: There's another dock down on the water, just over the edge. I was thinking, I don't wanna fall and break something. But then – right here: I manage to regain my footing, but just as I start to stand, he punches me in the chest. Let me play it back in real-time."

They watch as the scene plays out again, as a point is scored, a woman charges, and then falls to the boards to prostrate in death. In real time, the ensuing attack is quick, and violent.

"That's not an accident," Corbyn insists, and Jesty shakes her head: She agrees, "No. That's not an accident."

"That's why I don't go through the water," Corbyn shares. "The sound of splashing gives me a panic attack."

"Sheesh," she says: "I'm so sorry that happened to you. Can you do me a favor?"

"I," says Corbyn: "I don't know. What do you need?"

She asks, "Can you let me know when they catch him?"

"Sure – I guess. You want me to flag you down? Or, maybe fly a flag upside down?"

She laughs and shares, "I'm only fives, right now but I'm trying to work up to a marathon." She pulls a pen and small notepad from her fanny pack, and rips a page free. A number's sketched and she hands it over, with the offer, "Any interest in training together?"

He says, "Maybe. Maybe once this blows over."

She smiles, and says, "Nice to meet you, Corbyn. Make sure you call."

He answers, "Sure," with scrambled thoughts more scrambled from the conversation. Initial thoughts decay and settle for the only reason for the contact was concern. And so, he tells her, "I'll let you know."

She smiles and offers him the nod they've always shared, and he does the same, completely uncertain of her intentions. She strides to the hardened sand and resumes her run along the beach.

Corbyn follows the same direction. He walks slowly back, knowing time is slipping quickly and he should be moving faster. But the world's become a scramble of experience, and it isn't just unpleasant. It's just unsettling.

For the prior several days that was due entirely to the late-night, river plunge. It kept sleep from settling – it kept thoughts electric. The mind had been unable to find calm. That had been fought with increasing physical exertion, but the salve had only been temporary.

Corbyn laughs at himself.

When the number was handed to him, his first thought was there was interest – and that was awkward and uncomfortable: The woman was closer to his daughter's age than his. There had also been no thoughts towards relationships in over a decade – recognized as an indictment of himself. Of his failings as a spouse, and as a father. However, the longer thoughts simmer, the more likely it seems she simply views him as an experienced runner and wants exactly what she claimed: To train. To work towards running a full marathon.

By the time the decaying breach into the cliff is climbed, there is audible laughter at his own self, that he had considered she had interest. It is also a release, and relief that he hadn't spoken what crossed his mind. It is the first time in days that the brain begins to decompress.

The bramble is cleared, and Corbyn moves with a lighter step than he has in years. He approaches the cabin with all the weight accumulated over years lifted from his shoulders. The heaviness in his chest, the bolus in his guts, and the cloud that darkens his mind are as absent as they have ever been. He has laughed aloud numerous times as he reflected on thoughts, and conversation, and experience. And then, he sees motion through the window of the cabin.

He drops immediately to the ground.

He crawls across the lawn with the mind re-activated into deep paranoia. He slides to the window and very slowly rises. He briefly peers, and then falls away, expecting a gun to be pointed and firing. But he falls, and looks to the sky, and asks, "What the hell?"

Feet are taken, and he walks to the door and enters, and wonders, "AnnaKay? What are you doing here?"

She says, simply, "Hey."

He asks again, "What are you doing here? What's going on?"

She says, "I just came to see you."

He asks her, "How?"

She says, "I drove."

Corbyn takes a moment to recalculate. He breathes in deeply, and guesses, "You got your license?"

She says – yeah.

"You got your license. You drove here. Does your mother know?"

Her eyes roll. Arms cross. She says, "I spent the night with aunty Didi. I decided to come see you."

The mind calculates: Four hours – two from there. It is still early, and even the short trip from a former in-law means departure was pre-dawn.

Corbyn resets his brain to comprehend there is more going on than a random visit: Likely conflict. Likely something that made a visit to an aunt an acceptable destination – mid-week.

That isn't mentioned. All of the scenarios are brushed away, and the reset offers, "I'm glad you did: It's great to see you, A-K." He says, "It's good to see you," and there are waves of heaviness that crash into the soul carrying the disappointment, and frustration, and sense of failure that seeing his only child had been so infrequent.

A moment of quiet, and awkwardness will not be allowed a stake – Corbyn says, "You got your license. That's great: Congratulations. That's got to be great – to have that freedom: To move around." He says, "Good for you, A-K. I'm glad you came down."

She looks back like she will soon throw up. She is miserable, and Corbyn is aware enough to know he is incapable of digging her from where she's buried. He says:

"Everyone always asks: How are you? Are you okay? Those questions, ya know? But it's hard to really answer them. Ya know – honestly. I accidentally did, today, and we had a good conversation. But I can't begin to tell you how we ended. I have no idea what the expectations are. And it's just like that: I have no idea where you are. I'm not gonna pretend like I can solve your problems or fix whatever you're dealing with. I can't even fix my own. So, let me know what you need from me, and I'll try to do that."

"I just came down to see you," she says, and he says back, "I'm really glad you did."

There is a moment where eyes meet. A moment where a child looks to a long-lost parent and wonders why they're absent – wonders why they've been abandoned. It is a moment where a parent sees the hurt and recognizes that their child does not understand the forces that have shaped their life – they are only seeking confirmation that they are relevant – they are important: That a person that is supposed to – cares about them.

In that frame of reference, there is extreme regret to share, "I'm supposed to be at work in a couple hours." It's offered, with hope it's an acceptable solution, "You can hang up at the house. If you want. If you're sticking around."

She says, "I'm not."

"Okay," Corbyn offers, and he doesn't address the reasons why she's present, but she does:

"I just wanted to see if you'd come to my concert."

"Okay," he says, "I definitely want to be there. When's this happening?"

She answers, "Saturday."

"Ooh." He cringes. They are thoughts out loud, that Corbyn says, "This Saturday? I had plans."

It is thoughtless and plans are immaterial and can be changed, but it is read for what's expected, and AnnaKay rises and heads for the door. With deep resentment – with disparagement – she says, "Mom said you wouldn't."

"A-K," he protests: "I'll see what I can do. I just – you know… You heard what happened?"

She pauses at the door, curious enough to wonder, "What?"

"It doesn't matter," because she clearly hasn't, and all that does is that she came to see him. So, he tries to explain, "I just told a guy I'd help him this weekend. I only hesitated because I literally owe this guy my life. But I'll," he tries, but she isn't interested.

She says, "It's fine. I didn't think you would. I just," she says, and there's an attempt to intervene: "Listen."

But she says, "No." And whatever is weighing upon her shows as her face is flushed, and she is on the verge of tears. She grabs the handle of the door, and accusations spill: "I knew you wouldn't. Mom told me you don't care. I just thought – maybe she was wrong."

"A-K," he says, emphatically, "I care. So much – you're all I care about."

"Then why don't you ever call," she asks. She is angry as she says, "You could even text me – anything. But you don't even try to see me."

Firmly, "That is," Corbyn says, "Not true. I call you. I text you multiple times a week."

But she's not listening. She lifts her device, and claims, "Nothing." She demands, with tears now breaching, "Don't lie to me. Don't tell me things that I know aren't true. You never do anything for me. You don't even talk to me."

"Hey," Corbyn tries – an attempt at gentle intervention, but it still falls on unwilling ears: "The only reason I get up and go to work every day is so I can take care of you. I have tried," but she says:

"No. You don't. You never paid anything. You never call, you never text – you never do anything. It was stupid to come down here."

"I certainly," Corbyn says, "Pay child support. Almost everything I bring in goes towards child support – and I am not complaining. I've never said I don't want to take care of you. I have," he begins to claim again, but she stops him.

She says, "Mom says you don't." And she asks, "So, who's lying? You – or mom."

Corbyn admits, "I don't have an answer. I don't know what your mom says."

Annakay suggests, "Prove it. Show me you pay her."

Corbyn is looking at a child in distress. He is mired in a battle of which he has no understanding, but he knows he's caught within a minefield. He sees there is conflict and knows lighting fires will help no one. He attempts to be neutral:

"Your mom gives you everything, AnnKay. I do what I can, but your mom – and Plinio – they make sure you can have whatever you want. I'm not gonna argue that they haven't."

"So, you can't. You can't show me," she says, and he tries, "I don't know how that would be helpful."

It was an attempt to stay in neutral, to not refute the claims made by her mother – to not ignite a powder keg. It is an attempt that fails, and she pummels him, with, "Figures," and slams the door.

She storms away, and Corbyn is left paralyzed again, back in the frigid waters and just as helpless. She disappears up the hillside, off through the bramble, and the world is only dark – splashing water reverberates across the mind.

"A-K," he says weakly, and it is a plea that clears the mind and recognizes potential danger.

Heavy feet are pulled away from their cemented place, and he moves to follow. His tired legs stagger up the hill, towards the home, and he rambles in, and pleads, "Is A-K here?"

Wyl, answers, "What," in a manner that shows that he's confounded, and it's everything he needs to know: She's not there.

With more urgency, Corbyn jogs down the driveway, towards the highway, past the cabins and to the campground. He arrives just in time to find a vehicle turning from the lot. He arrives just in time to watch it head north, and for the driver to look through the window with teary eyes that stab with hatred.

He immediately calls, and it goes to voicemail: “AnnaKay: I need you to listen to this. I was sorting out my thoughts, but I want to be there. Tell me when, and where, and I’ll make it happen. Please call me, or text if don’t wanna talk. But please let me know you’re alright.”

Another call follows – made to her mother. Like daughter, the call is immediately sent to voicemail. Corbyn shares, “Hi Anika – it’s Corbyn. I don’t know if you’re aware, but AnnaKay drove down here. You won’t be surprised, but in our two minutes of conversation I managed to piss her off. So, please reach out and make sure she’s alright – she was heading north. So – hopefully – she’s on the way. Please call me back and let me know.”

He follows up with a text to AnnaKay: “I know things have been complicated, but I do care very, very much about you. Please let me know you’re okay.”

12

The morning begins with sprints: From the rock to the river, and then recovery – walking back, again. This is done to remain local, on the chance a submarine arrives with a magical Viking. The sort that is impervious to frigid water and can rescue those foolish enough to enter.

Corbyn takes a knee.

It is the position taken before every sprint: Take a knee, set, and wait for the gunshot. Of course, there are no gunshots. There are only sea gulls and waves crashing at the shore. He sets, and with a gull's mocking laugh, he launches for the river.

It is unknown how many times the stretch has been run. They were counted until seven or eight, at which point it was no longer clear if it was seven or eight. Trying to remember while continuing further muddled numbers and eventually, thoughts began to wander. It had been almost an hour – not continuous: But, mostly.

With another walk back to the rock it is leapt upon, and Corbyn stands on top of it to survey the landscape.

It is warmer than it's been. Not warm, but not cold. The perfect temperature for running – for long distance running, but that was not happening on the current day. Instead, sprints were taken, because it was a day of training. A day to better understand the rules of the consortium and how to participate during a challenge. It has been repeatedly stressed that committing murder is strictly forbidden.

The beach is only softly brushed with mist, and that is most obvious in the distance. But the blue sky is mostly clear, the sun has almost cleared the mountains, and the wind is almost absent. If it wasn't for the gulls constantly interrupting the rhythmic rushing of the waves with obscene laughter, it could be considered the ideal start to a day.

The gulls cry their laughter, and it's annoying; it's appreciated: The sound of the shore.

There is a point in late summer, where this sort of morning occurs more than occasionally. Where days are not expected to bring rain and it is not uncommon to forgo a shirt. Those days are months away, but the current one still finds Corbyn standing on a rock without one.

Because he almost never wears a shirt when he goes running.

This is a habit that goes back to childhood. In any weather, athletic pursuits found him shirtless. This is reflected on, because of continued conversations with Awrol: Conversations about becoming a full member of the consortium, and as such, considering what sort of uniform might be adopted. The suggestion of only shorts was strongly frowned upon.

Corbyn stands on a rock and considers shirts, consortiums, and the exquisite landscape. There are thoughts of tsunamis and how to escape, and they turn to thoughts of being thrown into a river. Thoughts of drowning turn eyes back to a child driving away in a new Mercedes.

Staring through the window with hatred. Looking at her father with the belief that everything she's been told was validated.

The phone rings and goes straight to voicemail: "Anika: It's Corbyn. I assume if there was a problem you would have told me. Please: Give me a call and let me know she's okay."

The phone rings and goes straight to voicemail: "Hey, AnnaKay, this is your dad. I still have a chance to make it if the concert's this afternoon. Text, or call, and I promise I'll do everything I can to get there. Love you."

There is a lingering, thinking something else should be said, but the call is ended.

Corbyn stands on a rock under a cheerfully illuminated sky amongst a landscape that is subtly softened by mist, and watches as waves slip ever closer. He watches as they crash like a body hitting water, and threaten as if they are coming for him.

The device is lifted on the chance that anyone might have called and he somehow missed it, or anyone thought to send a text, but there's nothing.

There is retreat: Legs lope from the stone and fall to sand, striding across the still firm breadth that has been plowed by water. It gives way to the softer sand that rarely sees it, that reveals that legs have seen exertion, and it's felt as the climb is made upshore towards the cliffs, and the break that has been cut for access.

There are many children of varying ages running around the lawn behind the cabins. There are shrieks of joy as whatever they're engaged in evokes a response in response to something – amusingly reflected on as similar to the challenges of the consortium.

They are left behind for the empty cabin, left emptier with the memory of a child's visit. Of a disastrous conversation that had nowhere to go from its beginning: Doomed to failure without an understanding of what had driven motivation. But there was clearly something. There was clearly something weighing on the child that had pushed her to an aunt – and then her father. Her distant father that randomly appeared from nowhere and erupted in fits of rage.

It had happened twice – an indelible impression.

It is shortly before noon when a tall, broad figure is observed navigating the bramble. He emerges with cloak adorned, but he's otherwise out of uniform. He walks directly to the cabin and enters without knocking, taking the other seat at the table after closing the door.

Awrol questions, "Do you know Tarja Santini."

The head shakes as the name's considered, but the answer is, "No"

He says, "I'm going to read you some names. Let me know if any of these are familiar." It's agreed, and he begins, "Jayadeva Tse." There is a pause, and he then suggests, "Dyan Lemaire."

"No," Corbyn says, "I don't know them. Who are they?"

"Individuals with whom there was a potential encounter that are adjacent Agreave Topel. Let me continue: Manpreet Gebara. Tecumseh Bartesova. How about, Iqaluk Hafner."

"I don't know that name," Corbyn answers, and he's questioned, "Really? That's the one I would have bet on: He used to have a home at the shore."

"Iqaluk," is questioned, and Corbyn digests the name, but his head's still shaking: "I don't remember hearing that name. Any idea what he looks like?"

There's a quick search, and a device is thrust forward, with the explanation, "This."

It is an older man. His appearance could be interpreted as hostile, or – it could be pleasant. With no context, the man's a blank slate: "I don't remember ever seeing that guy."

"A couple more," Awrol says: "Asma Mala, and Treasure Dreyer."

"I dig the name, but no. What's their connection?"

"Those two are board members for the company that employs Argreave. Are you familiar with the AO9S corporation?"

"I've never heard of it. What's he do with them?"

"He was listed as their chief security officer," Awrol shares: "He's no longer listed."

Corbyn pulls himself straighter, and questions, "You think they're burying this guy?"

"I'm telling you to be alert. He presented Ryan – El-Assissi – with false information. He claimed it was his impression that's what we did. Because he openly admitted it and didn't hide from the fact, they continued to allow his participation. Now, Argreave has disappeared."

"Sheesh," Corbyn says. He wonders, "What the hell did I ever do to them? And why are you getting information and I get nothing? I call every day, and they always say, 'We'll keep you updated.'"

He explains, "We have connections. The consortium, it is – large. However, you should be aware that the sheriff views what happened within the context of what was happening."

"What does that mean?"

"Corbyn," Awrol points out: "We were having a sword fight. On a pier. In the middle of the night. They consider it to have been an extension of that: Sword fighting gone wrong, or a grudge."

"Well, I've watched that video more times than's healthy, and I can tell you it wasn't an accident. The guy knew what he was doing. He did what he intended."

"Corbyn…"

"He comes at me, nearly knocks me off my feet, and then punches me in the chest. I look at this and it looks like he's pissed at me. He clearly meant to cause injuries. Or worse."

"Take a breath, and hold it," Awrol instructs: "The video is why the case remains active. I'm telling you – they don't consider him to be an ongoing threat. I want you to be aware of who's around you, because we know that wasn't part of a challenge. We believe his interest in the consortium – was because of you."

"I don't get it. The only person I ever get into it with is Chel – but that's just joking. And if he did ever decide to kill me, I'm pretty sure he'd do it himself. Maybe this guy thought I was someone else that worked with you."

"Corbyn," Awrol shares: "I have experience, and I have technological superiority over most, but I am a minor player in the consortium. I have never, previously, coordinated with anyone."

"Then," Corbyn suggests: "Maybe I'm not really the target. Maybe someone's coming at the consortium."

He's assured, "That is also under consideration."

"I think, until we know what's going on, ya know: I don't mind the fencing – practicing with the swords – the submarine. Gathering information. But I'm not going to any meets until we figure it out."

Alwrol chuckles, to share, "They requested that you don't."

"Well, you can tell them – request granted. So, what's the company that guy worked for do?"

"It appears to be your average billionaire's, milquetoast shell corporation."

"With a security guy…"

He's answered, "Yes."

"So, you're telling me – eyes open/gun close."

He's answered, "Yes."

"I feel like I'm not winning this if he's comin' at me, so if you wanna ditch I get it."

"We have all raised our awareness. I have drones monitoring and weapons are always ready. I think it important that you regain a sense of control over the situation."

"Okay," Corbyn says, and he shares the reason for the offer: "If it's alright with you, can we keep it local? My kid's got a concert."

He says, "Of course," and asks, "What time?"

"Don't know," Corbyn says. "I'm hoping she'll call me back and let me know."

Mistakenly believing there's an iota of communication and echoing the request, Awrol wonders, "The concert's local?"

"Seattle," Corbyn says. "Somewhere around there. I was hoping she'd tell me when and where and I could steal Wyl's car. At this point, it's probably too late for that, anyway."

There's a moment of silence, as he's considered. There's a moment of silence where the request, and the ensuing lack of information beg to question, "Can I ask how you heard about this concert that is somewhere and at some time? I feel these are important details."

"Yeah," says Corbyn, and there's a heavy sigh, because despite obvious failings in the moment, any response from anyone seems reasonable. It's shared, "She came down here – she got her license. Ya know, brand new Mercedes – of course. But she was here and asked me to come to her concert. It's today, and I mentioned we had plans, and she got pissed, and left."

"Corbyn."

"Yeah," he says: "I should've just said I'll be there, but I'm workin' things out in my mind. I'm like, this is the guy that pulled me out of a river: I wanna be cool with him."

"Corbyn," is repeated. Timothy says, "This is a diversion. A very expensive and involved diversion, but that's all it is. Never – Corbyn – prioritize this over your family. If your daughter says, come to my concert – call me: Say you won't be there. This is why we meet in the middle of the night: We have other priorities."

"It's not like I didn't try to tell her that. I said, give me the time and place, but she was already done with me. I've called; texted, but like usual – nothing."

The games and pretenses are dropped as the man across the table is examined. He sits blankly with a slight edge. With a hostility that is just beneath the surface. The thought crosses Awrol's mind that it isn't a stretch that he could bring someone to the point they'd want him murdered.

But there's another aspect present. A person wounded and helpless with no ability to change their circumstances. Someone that lets slip pieces of their life, whether work, friendships, or a daughter who they've had little contact with for many years. Someone who pushes their body to extreme limits as a way to push back against problems for which they have no solution.

Timothy says, "You have a very broken relationship with your daughter."

He's told, "What gave it away?"

"I don't want to impose," says Timothy: "But I think your daughter needs you to do something about that."

“What,” is questioned. It’s pointed out, “She doesn’t want anything to do with me. I call, I text, and there’s nothing.”

“She drove down here. You said Seattle – that is not insignificant.”

“And left two minutes later,” Corbyn says. “You got suggestions – hit me.”

“Unfortunately,” Tim shares, “I have no experience as a parent, and I simply spoil my niece and nephews.”

“I can’t spoil anyone,” Corbyn complains: “Pretty much everything I make goes to the kid, and that’s just a drop in the bucket to her. You know,” he says, and the always ready angers rears its head, as he recalls, “She even claimed I don’t pay her child support. I’m sure the ex doesn’t miss a chance to point out how much more they give her.”

“What did you say,” Timothy questions.

“What did I say? To, I don’t pay child support? I said nothing, really. She was already pissed at me and I could tell something was going on with her mother. So, I avoided getting in the middle of that.”

“My brother told me once, you need to speak bluntly to children. Even though yours is older, I think you should speak truth to her.”

“And get into the middle of a fight she’s having with her mom. I’ve done that. I’m trying to salvage any chance to know her again.”

“I don’t have anything, as I said, to offer in that regard. I feed children junk food and let them stay up all night. It’s been mentioned on several occasions, that is not an approach most parents find amenable. If anything, perhaps a new approach is needed.”

“Yeah,” says Corbyn, and bitterly: “My ex says she doesn’t answer ‘cause I’m hostile and passive aggressive. Ya know, hostile I get, but I'm not passive about anything. That's what drew me to the consortium: I get to stab you."

"A draw for everyone of us," Awrol agrees. "I find you reactive – not necessarily hostile."

A device is held forward, to share, "These are the messages I send." The most recent asks for the time and location of a concert. As more are scrolled, they are found to mostly ask about well-being, to life experience, and many say, I love you. There is nothing passive-aggressive nor hostile. The device is dropped to the table in a hostile act of disparagement, joined by, "Got nothing to react to."

Tim questions, "You're sure that's her number?"

"Still her little voice when I get her voicemail: If I didn't mention it, it gets sent straight to voicemail when I call her – just like her mother."

"Who," Awrol questions, "Is her mother? And the person she's with?"

"Anika? She's with this guy, Plinio: Plinio Gauff."

"You don't care for him?"

"See," Corbyn muses: "Hostile. You picked it up."

"Yes. Is it earned, or just the relationship?"

There's laughter, because, "I guess you took your brother's advice: No. It's earned. He paid for the attorneys. I've always thought he was behind a lot of what was said – and I earned some of that. But not what they accused me of. That was bullshit."

"I find you confusing," Awrol shares: "You are reasonably intelligent, you are fit and push your body to extreme ends, and you seem to learn quickly. But you are also living in a pool house for a pool no longer in existence. You continue running towards the past but it has long been gone, and that has long been obvious. You look to the future but you have done nothing to find a way towards it. You continue to paddle when it has long been obvious that is getting you nowhere."

"Is there a question in there?"

"You need to do something to challenge the dynamic with your daughter. You have fought the same battle for ten years and gotten nowhere."

"A – alright: Hey," Corbyn argues, otherwise: "Ten years ago, I got to see my daughter. Wyl let me move in here so I could be close to her – 'cause I was as busted then as I am now. But then they moved. It's not the same battle – the battle changed. It just took me a couple years to realize what was happening."

There is silence. Timothy stares with arms crossed against his chest, and Corbyn says, "Just say what you gotta say, man. I get it – I screwed up everything."

The man sighs deeply, and suggests, "I have an idea."

Corbyn says, "Hit me."

"I have made you earn your way into the consortium."

"I'm in?"

He's told, "No." However, "There are other ways to become a member."

"How do you want me to do it?"

"Nothing changes," he says, "For you." He reminds, "I have told you I am a long-time participant. You have seen that others work in groups – I don't. I prefer to work alone. It is also evident that having assistance is advantageous, and of a complaint we raised of tactics used by another, it was suggested it could have been prevented if another was in the fold."

"Ah," says Corbyn: "So, that's where I came in."

"Of course not. This happened years ago. But to mollify our frustration my wife was given a pass to bring someone in without having to participate in the usual initiation."

"So," it's asked, "I am getting that – or, I'm not?"

"No," he says: "I will never work with someone that does not pass the rites of initiation. These are usually given for a spouse, but I insisted on earning my entrance. I am suggesting we give this to your daughter."

"Tim – Awrol, I mean. I mean – I can't. I couldn't accept that."

"Correct. You can't: Your daughter will."

"Tim, man – come on. I owe you my life already. I can't take that."

"I was losing my challenge."

Corbyn notes, "Yeah? And you think my kid's gonna help with that?"

"I think you will," he says, and asks, "What did you get your daughter for her birthday?"

"Random questions," Corbyn jokes, "For one-hundred."

"She turned sixteen, recently, and got her license. Did you get her anything?"

"You know," Corbyn rues, "What can I get her? A gift card? She's got everything: She'd never use it. So, I sent a card with a not hostile, and non-passive-aggressive message and a stupid thing I picked up at one of the art joints along the highway. She probably took one look and tossed it."

Awrol declares, "She will be delivered a belated-birthday gift: Certificate of membership and a sword. I think, Unca-C, that will initiate a conversation."

"Come on: I can't do that. I can't take one of your swords, or the membership. You don't need to get mixed up in my mess."

He argues, "I do." He says, extremely seriously, "If we are to work together."

"I'll pay you back," Corbyn promises: "Somehow." And he asks, "Between us: Corbyn and Timothy – how fuckin' seriously am I supposed to actually take this thing? I mean, all the rules, and the way you guys play it: It's goofy as hell. On the other hand, you go all out."

"Corbyn," he says – and he is Tim: "This is a diversion. Family takes priority. Health takes priority. Survival takes priority. I also expect you to follow the rules and procedures without question. I expect you to hold challenges, conquests, and the organization with absolute respect and to assist those who are members as you are able – however that might be necessary. The answer is – extremely seriously. As if your life depends upon it. I expect it to be on your mind every minute you are awake, and while you are sleeping. It is a commitment that must be taken with utmost sanctity. It will be your duty to honor, improve, and protect the consortium. Failure," and he is Awrol, "Will lead to your destruction."

"So," Corbyn suggests, "Don't fuck around – don't fuck with it."

Awrol confirms, "Fuck noteth with the consortium."

Corbyn is on his feet, and says, "Stay close is cool?"

"We have covered this. Your daughter calls, I will drive you there in under three hours."

It's suspected, "Connections?"

He's cautioned, "You are not a member – but those go deep. As El-Assissi-Syrianni-Afrahm pointed out, I have a submarine."

"I got you," he's told. "I'm digging this – I gotta tell you: My brain's blowing up. But I – don't – want to do this alone."

Awrol scowls, "I am your liege. You will demonstrate you have improved your broad sword work."

They depart the small cabin with the joyous decree, "I am definitely in the mood for stabbing."

Awrol cries, "To the land of no one."

A man in a mostly olive, but mottled, worn, and dirty robe leads another that is dressed unseasonably in athletic pants and just a tea shirt. They emerge from bramble to families that eye them with concern. They imagine the long bag slung over the big man's shoulder might hold a long gun. If they were aware what it really held, they might be more concerned.

They continue on. Down the cliff-face break, and then northward. There are few that come upon them as they engage in sword play, and those that do move quickly and avert their eyes. As hours pass, the chance to act on a child's call grows troublesome, as the path to escape grows perilous.

But there is no call, and the swordplay continues. It becomes moves they practice and develops into strategy. They engage in full battle mode until a swing, a clash, a twist, and Corbyn claims a, "Point."

"Lucky," Awrol suggests.

"Nah," he says, "I was born for this. I've spent my whole life gettin' ready."

He's told, "You need to ready a name. Make it meaningful."

He's asked, "Awrol's meaningful?"

"An ancient god," Timothy explains: "Unable to have children."

The sword drops, and Corbyn spits, "Shit. Fuck, man. What the fuck?"

Awrol tells him, "Fuck, man: Engage."

13

The home comes fully into view as the hill is taken. Every negative thought and every derogatory word in every language tangle in the mind to push the thought of stopping by to greet the family before work into the category of ill-advised. As those crash the brain into a desultory state, retreat is taken, with ambition turned to circumnavigation and a casual ride.

That attempt is halted with, “Corruption.” Wyl’s cheerful smile peers out of the doorway, and he asks, “You stopping in?”

“Yeah,” Corbyn lies – matching the cheer. He claims, “I was debating grabbing another protein bar.”

“Lame. We’ve got an outstanding feast this morning. Courtesy – mostly – of yours truly. Drop the wheels and grab a seat.”

“Why, Whistle,” Corbyn asks, “No one else will eat it?”

“Tart – but it’s not: Tortilla and roasted potatoes. Some of that other stuff you eat. Frew? Frew-it I think you call it.”

“I’ll take a look, but I’m not gonna eat something you put together.” However, the aromas, as Wyl is followed bring pangs of hunger: On the table, there is a dish filled with roasted potatoes, and beside, an egg casserole. With a waft of freshly brewed coffee the stomach commits, and the only question is, “Alright I grab a cup?”

“Wouldn’t want to waste it, Corbonculitis.”

A cup is poured, and a too-hot sip is suckled trough the lips with mostly air. A wry comment is brewing, but that gets interrupted:

“Good morning, Corbyn.” Corshae cheerfully greets, and then turns back to call up the stairs, “Girls: Hurry up. Your uncle's here." There is a sound from above of plodding feet, or, with insults offered one another, grappling. Their mother says, "Take a seat. I'm glad you joined us."

He does, and teases, "Wylchestershire claims he made this. Tell me that's not true."

His wife confirms, "All Wyl. I woke up to the smell of those potatoes. Dig in."

"After you," is offered, but Corshae presses the spoon into his hand. The offer's taken, and he wonders, "What's the occasion?"

"I missed my family," Wyl says. With a smile, he claims, "But I don't think they've missed me."

"Always," Corshae answers, immediately, and right after, Corbyn questions, "Were ya gone?"

"Ha-ha. I'm sure you were busy spying from your submarine, or, playing with your swords."

"Three kills – no scrapes. I'm unassailable."

"Ha," begins an off remark that is immediately executed, and finds eyes looking back that are wide – his wife also aware of the near slip. He says, "Haven't you gotten tired of that?"

Eye turn to the woman at his side, then back again – aware that something happened, but he just says, "No."

"Unca-C," brightens the morning, grown brighter with another, "Unc."

"Morning, ladies. It sounded like you were having a battle."

"Ugh," Lia emotes: "She's always getting in my way."

"You walked into me like a blind buffalo."

"You were standing there like a dead buffalo."

"Ladies," their father scolds, "Have a seat. Have some eats. Keep working on your delivery."

Corbyn notes, "Sounded like a hurd of buffaloes."

"'Cause Lia's got buffalo feet."

It sends both of them into a fit of laughter, and it's contagious. But there is sour as it invokes the last interaction with his own, and Corbyn watches the family interact with bittersweet appreciation.

"All good?" Wyl watches from across the table.

"Yeah," Corbyn says, but there's a sigh that follows.

Corshae tries, "These potatoes are so good."

Shey agrees: "Nice job, dad."

His other child says, "Burnt some."

He says, "That's what I was going for: A little char." He looks over, waiting for a slicing comment, but their guest is staring into the bowl of tubers. "Hey," he's called: "Potato: Straighten up and set a good example."

Corbyn scoffs, because, "I'm a bad example."

Tentatively, Corshae questions, "Should we ask?"

"You know," Corbyn says, and he slumps further. The fork drops against the plate as the reflection is as dark as icy waters.

He's prodded – Corshae asks, "Did something happen?"

Lia asks, with far too much enthusiasm, "Did you really stab someone," and he sister piles on: "Did you get the guy that dumped you in the river?"

"Hey." Their father lectures, "Let's focus on the positive."

Lia says, "I think it would be positive if Unca-C stabbed the guy," and she's high-fived by her sister.

Their mother says, "Girls," but Corbyn pushes back:

"No: They're fine. I love you guys. Especially you two – I love how well you guys get along."

Because it's in stark distinction to his own: No communication – no room for humor. No chance to clear misunderstandings.

"What happened, Unca-C?"

It brings a smile, because the question is from an angel – a whole family of saints and angels. He says, "You know: The usual."

"Corbyn." Corshae lectures: "If this is about your daughter, you need to get over whatever you're thinking and support her."

He says, "I do – I try," and Wyl inquires, "Have you talked to her?"

"I know weird, right?"

Corshae demands, "What happened," eliminating the absurdity invoked by the question.

Corbyn says, "Wish I knew." She moves to scold, again, but he says, "Look: I'd just come back from a run – a really solid run – and I'm, ya know: I'm feelin' pretty good. But then I get back to the cabin, and there's someone in there. I had… I had a massive panic attack. I dropped down instantly. I just knew that guy was gonna be in there waiting for me. But I crawled over to the window, and it's AnnaKay."

"Oh God," Corshae imagines: "What happened."

"Well, I tried to pull myself together. And, ya know – try to be positive. But everything I said just pissed her off."

Corshae asks, "Can you tell me what you said?"

"I think," Corbyn reflects, "It started when she invited me to her concert. I started to say I had plans…"

"Corbyn," Corshae demands – she is angry: "What is more important than your daughter?"

"Listen," Wyl suggests, "Let's move forward," But his wife snaps at him, "No. He needs to make sure A-K knows he loves her. You need," she says to Corbyn, "To focus on her. Not Anika; not your problems. You need to make sure she knows you care about her. You tell her that and listen. Let her lead the conversation."

A device is retrieved, as he asks, "How?" As a finger scrolls the hundreds, probably thousands of messages that have been sent without response. "I text, I message, and I get nothing back."

"Corbyn," Corshae says, "You have to keep reaching out. She came all the way down here to invite you to her concert, and you crushed her. What could possibly be more important than your daughter?"

"Nothing," he snaps. "Some guy tried to kill me – did we forget that? I had plans with the guy that saved my life. So the first thing that went through my mind, is, I've gotta break off plans with this guy that I owe everything. I've gotta have room to navigate things, because I am not perfect. I said I had plans, and that's all she heard."

There is silence, because one person is so disgusted, one is treading dangerously, however, the children find it hilarious:

Shey speaks for both, when she says, "Uh, oh."

"I told her I would find a way to get there. But she was ticked. Everything I said made it worse – child support. She kept asking about it. She wanted me to prove I was paying child support. I can't even imagine what kind of conversation that came from."

"I think," Wyl suggests, "We need to just be positive. Focus on what Corsh says – let her know you care about her. Start that, and, like she says, let A-K lead the conversation."

However, his wife suspects, "What did you say about her mother?"

"Nothing. I said nothing – I defended her. I told A-K her mother gives her everything and, ya know – appreciate that. I even called Anika to let her know she's down here, just so, ya know, someone she might respond to knows where she is. Of course, I've heard nothing. She could be missing for a week and I wouldn't know."

There hadn't been any mention of anything more than what had been, so Corsh accepts, "Just keep trying."

Corbyn says, "Hey: I try. All I've got's her number, so if you've got something else, I'll take it." And then, he laughs. Because, "Me and Tim even tried getting a response – but I guess not."

The heavy air that had lifted crashes down, again with the news. Eyes roll at seeing the information doesn't sit well, but the heaviness is everywhere so it goes unaddressed. The exquisite meal, the delicious food is eaten only to end the conversation. Without appreciation. In silence. Because no one wants to address what was said and why it affected the mood.

Except the girls.

Energy's just waiting to burst free: They see the tension, a hint of anger: Mince of frustration. It bursts:

"Okay:" Lia takes the reigns, and says, "I'll ask: What'd you do, Unca-C?:"

Corbyn smiles at her – at her sister: At the others at the table. He shares, "We sent her a certificate of membership to the consortium." There are groans. A hand smacks a forehead with disbelief. And then, Corbyn adds, "And a sword."

The children are falling out of their chairs, but Corshae is done. She rises abruptly and walks across the kitchen. Her husband can only offer the disappointed, "Corbs."

He says, "Delicious. You really outdid yourself, Wylmer." To the woman glaring from across the room, he says, "I'm gonna do what you said. I'll annoy the heck out of her, but it's all flowers and sunshine. I'll focus only on the kid. Maybe I'll even write a letter: I'll let you proofread it."

She stresses, "It's really important to get that message to her. She needs to know you care and you're there to listen. Please make sure she knows that."

"I'll do everything I can – promise." He says, to the two still tittering at the table, "I want you guys to give your parents a hard time. Don't do what they tell you. Stay up late and drink their liquor."

"Corburn," his friend says, "You know how to win 'em over."

"Whatever you say, "Unca-C:" Shey skips over to give a quick hug before running away. Her sister follows, with, "Bye, Unca-C." She looks up like there's more to follow, but nothing does and she runs after her sister.

"I was short-circuiting when I saw her," Corbyn says to their parents. "I thought she was gonna be the guy. I probably would've screwed things up anyway, but it didn't help."

Wyl says, "Everyone's alright. That's the important thing." And then he cracks, "Make sure you let us see that letter."

It's a joke, but his wife suggests, "That's not a bad idea."

They depart on more or less decent terms, as usual. Corbyn leaves and wonders what exactly brings people to believe he doesn't try to keep in touch with his daughter. He is mounting his bike when a child comes bouncing through the doorway.

Lia hops to a stop, to ask, "Do you want her email?"

He questions, "AnnaKays?"

She says, "Yeah. I can text it to you. Do you want it?"

He says, "Yeah. Yeah – that would be great. Hold on a sec." He creates a message thread and sends – reply here. He says, "Just in case – just – in case that might cause a problem, delete the thread after you send it. Alright?"

She already has and is running off when the notification arrives. She calls, "See ya, Unca-C," and disappears behind a door that's slammed, for which parent's voices can be heard admonishing.

The address is spoken and will never be forgotten: "AKRunner." It invokes a storm of thoughts and a strong desire to reach out instantly. But the words of caution shared by friends pushes that for later. Gives thought towards thoughtful consideration of what should be said, and how it should be presented, and so the long ride in begins in contemplation.

It is not the relatively casual ride envisioned when avoiding human contact was considered. There is a concerted push with gratitude there wasn't a morning run. It is a press that brings arrival prior to the start of operations, but only by minutes. Greetings are brief, and hurried. The door is swung, and everybody's watching.

Everybody greets him, "Corbyn," and Chel isn't the only one that's laughing.

Corbyn says, "Make my day."

Chel slaps him on the shoulder. He says, "Last man standing: Everybody's tables – you got crabs."

There's a groan as eyes turn to a large bucket. There's more laughter and hilarious chides mostly about his unfortunate condition: "A little cream'll clear that up."

"Last man standing," Chel reminds him – laughing all the way back to their station.

It is a station that won't be taken this day, because someone has ordered a large amount of crab. Crab that has to be cleaned, and cracked, and extracted. It is a one man job until the normal haul is processed. It means most of a day in relative isolation and a non-stop processing – cleaning, cooking, and cracking.

The one benefit considered is fewer distractions. The chance to think about what to say – what not to say – how to present what's important in a longer format. But the mind wanders, and mid-afternoon, others join to move the process towards an end.

By the time the final call is made, there is still a large mound of crab to process. The entire crew comes together for the final push, and Chel observes, "Look now: Corbyn went and gave everybody crabs."

Despite the extra time and work put in, conversation remains cheerful. There is an energetic push to finalize the effort as the clock nears four. It is slightly after when they finish.

There is relief as they all break free. A few continue walking. Most head towards cars. One heads to a bicycle, and Chel joins:

"You wanna grab one at Billy's?"

There's a soft chuckle at the denomination, but the answer's, "No."

"Come on, now: You know I didn't mean nothin'. I'm just not volunteering."

"Yeah – I know." Thumb and index finger are held close to demonstrate, "I was this close to being early. But Wyl caught me and reeled me in with an incredible breakfast. And then, yelling at me…"

Chel asks, "What'd you do, Corbyn?"

He shares, "It was just about my kid. I don't know why they're so worked up, though. His wife was really after me."

"Sounds like you need a drink," Chel suggests.

"Nah." He says, "One of the kids slipped me A-K's email, so I wanna get home shoot a note off to her."

Chel says, "Put your bike in my trunk."

"What?"

"Put your bike – in my trunk."

"For what," Corbyn asks.

He says, "You just got over a bad case of the crabs. Let me drive you home."

"Oh. No," Corbyn says, "You don't have to do that."

Chel insists, "I'm gonna drive you home."

"Chel," is argued otherwise: "It's way out of your way."

He says, "Least I can do. Gave it to you all day long, and ya took it like a pro. Let me drive you home."

Corbyn says, "Your wife'll be mad."

The man considers for a moment. He looks thoughtful, and says, "True. I'll see you, man."

"See ya, man."

The ride seems longer than it ever has. As legs burn as they push the wheels up another long incline, a vehicle is imagined a nice alternative. For a moment, the idea finds life. For a brief, energetic burst, the thought of reaching out to Tim is considered, but a clean idea grows quickly murky with thoughts of oil, gas and problems that will arise with anything that could be afforded. By the time legs rest on a too-quick coast down the other side, the idea of reaching out is buried.

There's no chance taken of being interrupted on the return. The drive down to the main home is passed, and a turn is made into the little store just before the campground. The cleared path is followed past the largest cabin, and a turn is made into the bramble. Wheels turn past the campfire clearing and brake shortly after at the tiny cabin. It is quickly scanned to make sure it's empty.

There is an immediate move to the table, and the computer is immediately booted. The browser's started, and Corbyn brings up email – four-hundred-fifty-two in the primary inbox. AKRunner is searched for but brings up nothing. New mail is clicked, and he starts writing:

Hi AnnaKay, this is your dad. Please read this: You are the most important person in the world to me and I will never be able to express how much I care about you.

I hope you at least read that, and if you don't want to read any more, that's fine. That's the most important thing for you to know. But I also want to apologize. I know, that could be for a lot of things, but I'm sorry I didn't immediately jump at your invitation.

I regret that I didn't, and I regret I missed your concert.

The only reason I hesitated is because the guy I had plans with is the guy that saved my life. I don't know if you heard what happened, but someone tried to kill me. If it hadn't been for Tim, I probably wouldn't have made it. I only hesitated because I owe him my life. But even Tim said I'm an idiot for not jumping at your invitation.

It's not an excuse, I just want you to understand why I needed a second to think about it.

I love you, and I hope you're doing well.

Love, Dad – aka Corbyn

There is an emotional overload, and in the flush that rises the message is sent. There is immediate regret. Immediately, Corbyn's hand mimics Corshae's from the morning, and he smacks his head. He says, "God. What am I doing?"

No review, no reflection – just written and sent. Disgusted, he shuts down the computer and leaves the cabin.

It is a beautiful night with clear sky and only a gentle wind. The sunset is exquisite and at the cliffline, the ocean largely washes out the passing traffic. It also makes the mind question if a notification was received, or it was merely wishful imagination.

The device is extracted and it indicates a message from AKRunner.

"No," escapes in disbelief, and the screen's unlocked with fumbling fingers. There is simple reply that only asks, "What happened?"

The video's uploaded, and Corbyn replies, "My inglorious moment. Tim's the guy that jumps in after me."

The screen's stared at as the sun closes on the horizon but it isn't even present in the mind. All that is – if there's another response. If what was sent was too much; too disturbing. The screen's watched as it goes dark, and eventually, it's considered the response already gotten is more than ever hoped for. But there's another:

A-K asks, "Who are those people?"

The answer is more complicated than can be quickly fat-thumbed on a phone, and so Corbyn runs back to the little cabin and lifts the laptop open once again. He types:

"It's what the belated birthday gift was about. It's sort of a fencing club, but there's also role playing. We have meets where we have mock broadsword battles. Everyone in the video is part of the consortium except the guy that attacks me – and me. We were both going through the initiation. I hoped you'd be curious and it would open up conversation."

Corbyn hits, send, but if feels like it's both inadequate, and too much. He begins to rise, to dig up something to eat for dinner, but the chain of email highlights again. It's clicked, and the response is a question, "Did they catch him?"

The response is opened, "It might be easier to explain everything if this was a conversation. Call if you want to know more, or details, but as of now they haven't found him.

We know who he is. We know where he lives. We know who he works for. We have no idea why he did it, but everyone's taking precautions, so please don't worry.

I watch everyone everywhere I go. I take protection, and I don't let my guard down until I'm somewhere safe and secure. For all we know, it was just some lunatic that decided he'd take advantage of the moment.

The police are looking and keeping everyone safe. They think they're getting close. They don't think there's an ongoing danger.

And it's closed, "Love you, Dad."

A minute passes, and there's no response. Fifteen later, and Corbyn is slumped and staring at the screen. As the time passes eight, it's accepted that the conversation has ended, but it's been more conversation than they've shared in years.

He is starving, but he walks up the hill, to the home, and he firmly raps against the door. A few moments pass without response, and he moves to knock again, but Corshae turns the corner and peers through the door.

She smiles as she recognizes who's present. She opens the door, and says, "It's good to see you. Do you wanna come in for a drink?"

He answers, "No. I still haven't had dinner. I just wanted to check in with Wyl – is he around."

"He went back to Portland. You knew he'd get caught up in this, right?"

"Yeah." Corbyn asks, "You're good? Girls good?"

"Yeah – everyone's good. Everything alright with you?"

"Yeah, Corshae – I need to thank you." Corbyn shares, "I finally got through to AnnaKay. And, I gotta admit, sometimes I get irritated with you constantly telling me what I've gotta do, but tonight, you were in my ear when I reached out to her. And, it worked. It ended kind of abruptly, but it was more conversation than we've had in years."

She offers the look of a mother finally seeing her child following her advice, and says, "That's really good to hear." And then she says, "Keep reaching out. You really need to keep impressing on her that you're there for her. But it's good to hear you're talking."

Something in the response – something in the press from the morning and days prior – something brings Corbyn to ask, "Is something going on?" She says nothing. She looks back like there's – disappointment. Disapproval – there' something. It's noted, "She was pretty upset when I saw her. And you've always bugged me – but it's been a lot more, recently. Is there something I should know?"

She says, "You need to know your daughter needs to know you care about her. She needs to know you're there for her. Keep reaching out and don't let your personal feelings or opinions interfere with the conversation."

"Yeah," He says. Corbyn says, "Of course. I mean, you'll tell me I need to call CPS. Tell me I don't need to."

There's hesitation, but she says, "No." She makes an effort to smile, to be casual, and suggest, "One drink? You can tell me about the conversation."

Corbyn says, "Nah. I've got things started at the cabin. I just wanted to let you guys know what happened – thank you, ya know. For keeping my head straight. I'm never gonna stop trying with the kid, but what you keep tellin' me – I think it was good to have that in my ear. So – thanks – Corsh: Thanks for keepin' me straight."

The best part of runs is their conclusion on the beach. It's a final stretch on flat, packed sand that is the perfect finish after ups, and downs, and obstacles. A cut down from the highway, the hills, or the trail, just south of the northern end impediments of no-man's-land. A final mile where muscles can be pushed to maximal limits without concern about the placement of a foot – wide open visual, except in heavy fog. But it's a bit less than a mile from that entry to the creek, and the sand doesn't stretch much further once that's crossed.

There is a stretch of flattened rock purportedly cut for wagons, but it's pocked with divots and only remotely usable for a short distance.

Most runs follow the coastal trail. It is redundant, sometimes challenging, and the cause of numerous injuries – primarily sprains. The other options are the highway which is unpleasant due to cars, or into the hills on one of several back roads. The latter quickly build a burn in legs as they are climbed, and then awkward stiffness against descent and gravity.

Gravitation is towards the coastal trail even with it's challenges, as, after decades, those have been catalogued and navigation doesn't even enter conscious focus.

Most of the time.

Occasionally there's another person, and they've always been watched warily, but it's more so since taking a swim. The trail has come to feel sinister. Anyone crossed is viewed with deep suspicion. Especially when someone's on the trail when it's raining.

A man stands on the overlook. It is one of several that have been built to give a clear view of the state-long trail's namesake. He's leaning against the rail and watching as Corbyn approaches. He says, "Good morning," as he's passed, and seems to follow.

Corbyn turns, ready to engage, wishing he'd brought something more than a pocketknife.

But the man smiles. He steps to the side, and questions, "Are you turning back."

He's answered, "Yeah," and Corbyn lopes down the slope to pass again. He's offered, "Thanks," in passing. He thinks to call, "Have a good one," and continues, back the opposite direction and completely ruining the run – carefully measured markers irrelevant after breaking course.

The claim that times aren't watched as closely is finally true, as the pace draws down, as the path is run back – past the point of entry. It's followed further, but not too far: Ten minutes in and retreat is taken.

At the highway, the pace picks up again as Corbyn sprints across the asphalt. The speed's maintained along the lot of the little campground, over uneven grass terrain and a leap is made into the opening of the cliff face, sliding down in the loose sand that's accumulated at the bottom.

The final stretch will not be as satisfying as it usually is since two thirds of that leg was truncated using the home-side entrance. It's barely enough to find muscle burn as feet carefully target the little islands of the river. The run concludes with feet slogging heavily as the rocky rises are approached.

Just like after every other run, fists come to the sides as Corbyn begins recuperating. As he walks casually back the little creek that once brought joy at a run's conclusion. One that was stamped, and splashed, and felt good against the naked back, even in the coldest days of winter.

The water trickles past – spread wide as it navigates the sand. It is a tiny delta changed with every tide, and also altered by an angry foot that crushes the river's work, angered at the stupidity of avoiding water.

The water is told, "Fuck that guy. Fuck that asshole – fuck him." Feet stomp through the water, splashing against the legs, against the back, and it feels good. To the air on the other side, Corbyn declares, "This is my fuckin' beach."

He retreats back to his little home, grateful no one saw his infantile fit. He quickly showers and dresses, and then begins thinking about what should be done for breakfast.

There is the thought, as there always is, to join the family. However, Wyl's inconsistent presence leaves the prospect of more haranguing from Corshae, and the ensuing silence since the day he'd finally exchanged emails with his daughter shuts down motion towards the joy that is the family.

Instead, Corbyn sits at the table and digs a hand into a box of cereal. He cannot help but smile at thoughts of the comments the sisters would rightfully make, that it was terrible and flavorless. It is consumed without inspiration and washed down with a glass of water as raindrops begin to speckle the view out of the window.

The though passes through the mind of running in the rain, and eyes close to imagine the sensation as the gentle plinks turn into a downpour: Water pouring down as feet cover the terrain with more caution, a sense of enlivenment when it does. Like a panther in the forest chasing prey.

One last handful of cereal is taken before it's put away. Set into the large duffle bag that contains all possessions. From which the rain gear is extracted with two protein bars. It is zipped closed and slipped back beneath the bed.

Riding in the rain is not appreciated like it is when running. Riding in the rain is unpleasant, and despite wearing rainboots, feet always become dampened, and in winter months – cold.

Gloves are slipped on, and the shield is lowered, and Corbyn sets out for an unpleasant trip into work. Where employees are expected to arrive in clothes that are respectable, despite the job leaves them fouled by the end of the shift.

The ride is unpleasant as expected. Despite all the gear, water finds a way. Water slips in around the wrists. It worms through the elastic on pants that seal the boots that themselves are intended to seal out water. Somehow, it slips through. Little by little, water finds a way to work into the shoes, onto fingers, and around the neck. Somehow, droplets of water have found their way around the shield to distort the view from the inside.

"Crap weather," greets Corbyn as he brings the bike to a stop.

He grumbles back, "Shoulda called in sick," and it brings laughter.

Those laughing are not stopped by weather. They continue their work through the worst of it, when any reasonable person would find it inadvisable to be on the water.

He enters, to, "Spot me, Corbyn," and the woman doesn't wait for him to respond. Corbyn is left dripping in rain gear with two potential customers at the counter.

He sloshes over and says, "I'll be with you in just a sec. I need to get the gear off."

The statement is ignored, and a woman says, "I need four pounds of the salmon, and two of the crabs."

Corbyn is stumbling around in battle with a bootie. It is refusing removal without taking a shoe. The woman asks, "How much are the salad shrimp?"

The answer is on the sign perched atop them, but Corbyn says, "I'll look it up," and he carries the gear to the end of the cabinet where he leaves it piled. Along with his shoe. He walks back, leaving a sogging path of footprints from the one foot left only with a sock. He says, "Everything should have the price displayed."

The woman waves a piece of paper, and clarifies, "How much with the discount?"

"Thanks hon:" Relief arrives none too soon, and she's told, "Not a problem."

It takes a moment to work the shoe free. The bootie stubbornly holds its quarry, but the fabric is peeled with fingernails, and it finally slips loose. It's expected that the gear, the disheveled appearance, maybe the quiet squeak with every footstep will be easy targets for clever quips. But the door's swung open, and all that greets Corbyn, is:

"Corb."

"Corbyn."

"Hey, Corbyn."

And Chel asks, "Hey Corb: What's goin' on?"

The other person in the space just watches. Watches from the group. A group standing around and gathered together.

It's not exceptional. People come together – usually at lunch. Usually around crab. But in the mornings, people are usually on their phones, drinking coffee, or sharpening knives. It is unusual for everyone to gather together before they get started.

So, Corbyn asks, "What's going on?"

He's told, "Your boy's leavin' us."

The man in question says, "Watch who you're callin' a boy."

In response, another says, "The old fart's leavin' us."

Corbyn questions, "What?"

"Hey, man." Chel says, "I came on this opportunity. I grabbed it and gave my notice."

Corbyn joins the others, and asks, "For real?"

The question's asked with great disappointment, and that only grows, because he says, "We're sellin' out. We're headin' to the city."

There are jibes taken about holding down the station, about being left behind, and Corbyn's the reason why. They're meant in jest, but they cut deep because it feels like more betrayal. It feels like he's being left behind, again.

"Corb," Chel says. They're elbows deep processing the haul. It's been quieter than usual – with everyone. The mood is grim and it's because moving on is something all of them should have done. "Corb," he says again: "Don't be mad. I'm old. I need some money in the bank."

"Yeah, man," Corbyn says: "I get it. Gonna miss the conversation – you'll be missed."

The man suggests, "Then, how about you join me – get a drink at Billy's after this."

Corbyn says, "It can't be Billy's anymore."

He says, "Don't start, man."

"No – no: It's on you. There's no one left to represent."

"It's Billy's," Chel insists: "One more time."

"Yeah." It's agreed: "Tonight it's Billy's."

They find it largely overtaken when they get there. A loud and boisterous crowd of bikers have gathered to enjoy good drinks and reasonably priced Italian fare. They have also discovered that the reasonably priced Italian fare is served on tiny plates or in cups. There is raucous humor regarding portion sizes and the secret unravels – it's not really that affordable.

But they are having fun and running with it as the pair take a place at the bar. Chel orders the usual; Corbyn opts a bourbon, neat:

"A double. I'll take a double."

His partner cracks, "They get you for BUI?"

"Probably," Corbyn says, and it's a direction they would have followed another time. But they came together because they're going to part, so Corbyn says, "So, what's this thing you got lined up?"

"You should check it out," Chel suggests: "Put a couple dollars in your pocket. Get you out from under your old lady."

There's a laugh of appreciation, and he jokes, "Yeah: That's what she tells me, too."

Chel says, "Ain't a joke, man. You're built for it and they're still lookin'. Your little shed'll still be waiting."

"Tell me about it," Corbyn says: "What's the gig?"

He shares, "Construction. Two years, and something. They got trailers waitin' right on the line: All you gotta do is roll outta bed and roll on board – takes you right in."

"Some kind of project?"

"Some kind of stadium," he answers. "They're lookin' for people."

"Yeah," Corbyn says, "I'll think about it. What about after?"

"After," Chel questions. "After I'll be sittin' on boatloads of cash instead of smellin' like boatloads of crap. Like the lady says, we get to know the place, find some connections, and we'll be movin' on and movin' up."

"Well," says Corbyn, and a glass is raised: "To a new city, a new job, and a new beginning. I truly and sincerely wish you the best. I might even stop by to see when I get up there."

Chel says, "Not if I don't tell you where I am."

"Wouldn't blame you. But I am gonna miss you. You even made crab days entertaining."

"Don't start," Chel says.

Corbyn claims, "I'm not," but his partner already heard the answer, and he says:

"You won't even consider it. I knew you wouldn't, man – I knew you wouldn't."

"You know," Corbyn starts, but the man beside him wants none of it:

"It puts dollars in your pocket. You would have cash to spend. And after two, you ask? Like you said, you're a free man in two more years. You'd be set up. And you'd also be livin' by your kid. Don't be an idiot, man – I can put a word in."

Corbyn rues, "They'd probably move again. Not that being close would make a difference."

"Here we go," Chel says, and downs the beer. He motions for another, but then turns to address Corbyn directly: "Why do you got to make everything depressing?"

“I’m not..” He claims, “I’m stating the obvious: The kid wants nothing to do with me.”

“I thought you said you were passed all that.”

“For a second,” Corbyn shares. “She responded to an email, but then she stopped. It’s been more of nothing ever since.”

Chel asks, “Did you email her again?”

“Texted,” Corbyn says, “I’ve left a couple messages.”

“Did I ask?” Chel says, “I didn’t ask about texts or messages, I said – did you email her back.”

“I don’t think it matters. She doesn’t respond.”

Chel becomes animated, and says, “Dammit.” He punches an open hand into Corbyn’s shoulder, and demands, “Email your damn daughter.”

“What difference,” Corbyn starts, but Chel talks over: “Send a fuckin’ email.”

Eyes roll, and, “Whatever,” blows off the order, but the device is extricated and a message is written:

Hi AnnaKay – it’s your dad. That is, Corbyn. Just checking in to see how things are going. I hope all is good. I love you, Dad.

As it’s done, it’s announced, “Email. Sent. I’ll pay your first month’s rent if she answers before we split.”

“I’m out the door when this one’s gone. You’ll pay my rent – she answers.”

“No deal.” Corbyn drains the remainder of his drink and motions to the man behind the counter. He asks, “Another?” But Corbyn answers, “Just the bill. I’ve got both of us.”

It earns a heavy hand of appreciation against the shoulder, and Chel admits, “I’ll miss you, man. You and your crazy-ass bicycle; livin’ out of somebody else’s shed. Any time I’d start thinkin’ it ain’t worth it, I’d look at you – I’d look at you, and I’d say – I could be

Corbyn. Corbyn and his messed up relationship with his kid." And he asks, "She answer yet? 'Cause I need that rent."

Corbyn was laughing from you and, and with the finish he moves to reciprocate the gesture – he puts his arm over his friend's shoulder. Chel pulls him closer, and the come together, A firm hug between them, and as they separate, Chel asks, "Well? Did she?"

The device is held to indicate there's nothing.

"I'd offer you a ride, but you're gonna tell my wife'll be mad."

"I will," Corbyn admits. "I'll see ya tomorrow."

When they go to leave, Chel repeats the offer, but the same excuse is made as always, and Corbyn heads back down the incline to retrieve the bicycle. He stands beneath the overhang of an adjacent restaurant to prepare for the return ride – gloves still damp from the morning.

The steady rain and sometimes drenching has given way to heavy mist that alternates with showers. It is not nearly as unpleasant, though the shield has to be cleared repeatedly, from the fog, and spray of passing vehicles.

It is a leisurely ride. There is no pressing urgency to return. No desire to push muscles to their fullest. On two occasions, turnouts are used to rest, as well – take in the view. It is likely the slowest ride ever on the return from work.

The destination finally nears with one last hill of significance to climb before descent to relatively flat, and straight highway. Gears drop and the body lifts away for better leverage. Gears drop again, and feet rotate many times faster than the tires. Once the crest is met, the seat's re-taken and gears shift up again.

It is still light out as travel comes towards an end. It is light enough to see someone standing beside the highway. The first thought that passes as that is noted, is that it's an assassin, awaiting his return to finish what was interrupted. But the shape, and size, and mannerisms soon reveal that it's only Wyl.

This is not a welcome sight. If Wyl is standing on the roadside and waiting for him, it indicates he means to intercept him. Likely, on orders from his wife. He is consequently greeted with a more curt than usual, "What's up?"

"What is up, Cardio? You seem a bit more sour than usual."

"Long day," Corbyn says; he shares, "Chel's leaving us – heading up to Washington."

"Oh," says Wyl, but this seems to cheer him. He says, "That's a bummer. But you know what will cheer you up? Joining us for dinner."

"Not tonight."

"Come on, Corbolla. Luscious lasagna and homemade bread: You can't resist."

The statement is accurate. Despite the pestering that will be likely, a good meal is difficult to decline – considering alternatives. So Corbyn says, "Yeah." He agrees, "That's fine – I'll join you guys. But," he pleads, "Can we go light on the hammering? I don't need to be reminded to talk to my kid."

"Do you," is answered, "No."

"It's really important to stay in touch," Wyl stresses. He says, "Coronado, you need to be there for her."

"I kind of resent," Corbyn snaps, "That you seem to think I wouldn't be. I call, I text, I email – nothing. She does not want to talk to me."

"Hey – Corbs." There is no hint of humor, as he says, "Just keep letting her know you're there for her."

"I do. I tell her constantly. Did something happen, because it feels like you guys are really hung up on this."

"She's sixteen, Curacao. She needs someone to listen more than she needs someone to tell her what she already knows."

"That is?"

"In general. Can I set a plate? I promise we'll only harass you for ninety-three percent of the meal."

There is reticence. The feeling of being an unwanted intrusion has been supplanted by the sense that he is viewed as incapable. That constant reminder is needed not to treat his only daughter badly.

"I guess. Let me get cleaned up. I'll be up. Just – chill: Okay? I will not stop reaching out. Even if I never hear from her again: All positives and sunny days. Ears are open."

"Good, Cobana: I'm glad we've cleared the air. You've got fifteen, and I send the girls for you."

"Yeah, yeah: Go take your bread out of its wrapper, Wyldberry."

It is, as noted, a sour delivery. The attempt to ignite the amusement and connection between them finds it's frayed. There is something ticking away at the easy friendship held for decades. Somehow related to communication. With no one willing to share anything and a daughter that is entirely disinterested it is presumed that new-found freedom with a vehicle and age are catalysts for friction.

The door to the small home is opened, then closed by a foot as the rest of the body collapses on the bed. The hood's pulled free, gloves removed, and the jacket is unzipped and wriggled from. All are tossed in a heap on the floor. Consideration of the girls that will be sent to retrieve their absent uncle brings Corbyn to sit upright and remove the boots. They successfully pull both shoes with them.

Keys, and wallet, and the always present device are pulled from pockets and set on the table: There is a notification – from AKRunner.

There is desperate fumble to unlock the screen. Email's clicked and the message is read. The reply is just a question: "Why didn't you call?"

There is panic, as indecision pauses the reply – to boot the laptop, or clumsily thumb. It begins to ebb as the initial shock wears away, and Corbyn takes a seat at the table. The irritating message constantly throbbed into his head by friends is present, and he is eminently grateful.

A moment is taken to collect thoughts, and a non-panicked response is typed:

"Hi, AnnaKay. I don't remember saying I would call, but if I did, I apologize. I don't remember. I'll give you a call right now. Love you, Dad."

The message is sent, and a call is immediately placed. As it always does, it rings six times and goes to voicemail. Corbyn says, "Hi, A-K, it's your dad. Call me if you wanna talk. Love you. Talk to you later." The call is regrettably ended and eyes turn back to the computer – to another response.

The message is an accusation: "You said to call if I wanted to know about what happened. I left a message but you never called me back."

Fingers scramble to check the call log, but there's nothing. Voicemail's called and there's nothing new, and the most recent is an old one left by Wyl.

He writes, “Hi AnnaKay. I’m not sure what’s going on, but I don’t show I ever got your call. I’ll check if something’s wrong with my account when I’m in town tomorrow.

I will always call you back as soon as possible if I get a message from you. Please don’t hesitate to call me at any time. I love you, Dad.”

The message is sent and Corbyn leans back and closes his eyes. He brings his hands up to his temples to massage the tension away and is met by a burst of cool air, and a burst of sound:

“Unca-C.”

“Unca-C.”

One more glance is taken at the computer, but there’s nothing new and it’s closed. Corbyn questions, “Has it been fifteen?”

Lia says, “We just wanted to bother you.”

15

The idea of losing Chel has begun to sit more easily. The idea is, he won't be lost. He is an excuse to spend an exorbitant amount of money to go to a game. He is an excuse to be proximate to a child and offers an opportunity for re-opening conversation. He can also be emailed, a suggestion had over drinks for a second straight day, as Corbyn reflected – it was his third drink which is probably too many – he said, "That's the only way I can get my kid to respond to me."

Of course, Chel had said, "And, you're welcome."

They'd spent too much time at Billy's and had far too much to drink, on a Tuesday. To the point that Chel's wife had to come get him. It was the first time that Corbyn met her, and she seemed like a lovely woman – she seemed to be very understanding. Corbyn had taken the blame for their condition, anyway, but she was offering regardless, and insisted that she drive him. With Chel in chorus and in rare form – an exceptional thing to say of a man that always was – Corbyn caved and accepted the transportation.

On arriving at their destination, his wife had asked, "You really bike that every day?" Astounded. Perplexed. Finding it incomprehensible that anyone would, or could, make that trip to work every day. She said, "You are wild."

But her husband says, "Nah: He's just crazy."

As Corbyn exits the vehicle, he tells the woman, "I am gonna miss this guy. It was good to finally meet you."

She says, "It was a pleasure."

"All mine," Corbyn says, and as he looks into a window of another life he's never seen before, he wishes he would have taken the offer to have one more drink with them. To hear their voices for a few more minutes and to watch the way they interacted.

He rolls the bike down the driveway, thinking about the people at the plant, thinking about how even Chel was mostly a blank page. How there was little known about his wife or children outside the jokes, or the disingenuous complaints he'd make while they worked. It wasn't until a bit more than a week before they left that Corbyn had even met the woman.

And Chel was considered a friend. Someone to whom he could confide personal information, and that went for both of them. Opinions that never could be shared were held between them: Thoughts about an ex and complaints about a child. Frustrations with a marriage and disappointment with his own. Honesty shared over the slaughter of sea life and yet the hour spent in the company of the man's wife, it was clear that the words were shared held little water. The truth was clear – he doted on her, and she did the same.

"Corbs," ratchets the brain around to the moment. The head turns back to find Wyl leaning through the door. He asks, "Wanna go for two in a row?"

He's given, "Ya know."

"Ya know," is volleyed back, because, "If you didn't want to, Cortipulator, you'd be skulking around the shrubbery."

"Wyllingness to call them shrubbery is – a word I can't think of. Let's just go with wrong."

"Ya know…"

"Yeah, yeah. Thanks for blowing up my delusion of artifice. But I'd call them prickly vines and weeds."

"Artifice," Wyl questions: "Are we expanding our vocabulary, Correspondent?"

Corbyn says, "It's becoming a regular part of the scenery."

"Ah." It's imagined, "Your submariner."

There's laughter, because, "Yeah. I'm gonna check out tonight, 'cause I'm wiped. When are you back in town?"

"'Til the weekend. Didn't want to stick everything on Corsch."

"Goin' good," Corbyn questions.

"Goin'," he answers.

It's not a positive, and so Corbyn turns and reassesses his answer. He asks, "You run into problems?"

"No. Not – problems, exactly. Some of the ideas I had are more difficult to pull off than I anticipated. It's moving along, but it just feels like I'm piling bricks."

"Hey, man," Corbyn says, "Step back and reset yourself. Ya know: Let that vision flow. Forget whatever it is that's got you stuck – remember what you envisioned. Look at that and you'll figure out how to get there."

"Yeah. I'm not taking another one under deadline. All they want you to focus on is the progress."

"Sometimes you need to let it breathe."

"Exactly. Exactly, Corbynara. That's exactly what I'm doing – taking a week to let it breathe. You joinin' us?"

"Not tonight, Wylabama. Before you leave, though."

"You mind I come down, later? Have a few and shoot the breeze?"

Corbyn says, "I'm good to shoot. Enjoy your dinner."

"Yeah. Enjoy whatever tasteless protein amalgamation you've got planned."

There's laughter, and, "See ya," is said by both.

The mood is lighter than it's been for a considerable time – especially after work. It could be the result of a peer into another person's life, a window that had never been truly looked through, prior. Or, it could be a conversation with someone with whom conversations had felt changed: It had been an open, honest, uninhibited exchange – it felt like old times.

Corbyn is walking down the slope, through the proclaimed shrubbery and his mood is high. He is feeling like he does when his legs are working perfectly, when his chest is open, and everything feels like it's liquid.

He rolls the bike, and comes to the little cabin, and all of that's left behind.

Paranoia reels, and his heart burns in his chest as he observes that someone is in the cabin. However, he doesn't fall to the ground, as he did before. He doesn't disintegrate into the paralysis that the push into the river has generated. He stands stiffly, and assesses what he's looking at. And what he's looking at is his daughter.

The bike is dropped, and Corbyn quickly strides, before stopping. He stands at the door and knocks at his own residence. He waits until AnnaKay turns, and only then does he turn the handle, and enter.

He says, "AnnaKay: It's great to see you."

"Hey," she says. She stands awkwardly, and backs away. She says, "I don't know what's going on, but you keep telling me to call you and then you never call me back. Did you get my message yesterday?"

Eyes grow wide as the device's pulled free and fingers fumble a quick search. "I forgot," Corbyn admits: "I was gonna see if something was up, but I've got a friend." There is nothing. No message, no evidence she called, and it's held to show proof that's the case. "I'm sorry. He's moving, and we went out after work. But I didn't get a message, A-K. Is that: Do you, I mean – do you still like A-K?"

"Yeah," she says. "I'm A-K." She holds her own device up to show numerous calls made to, "Dad."

Voicemail's called. There's nothing new, and the most recent of the deleted remains Wyl's.

"I'm not sure what's happening. Because I've got nothing. You sure you're calling the right number?"

"Dad," she complains. It is beautiful to hear and it strikes them both, and the complaint becomes filled with sorrow: "It's the same number I've always had. Did you get a new one?"

"No," he says. Corbyn tells his daughter, "I've had the same number for decades." He sees her again on the verge of tears. She is close to where she was the last time that she was present. Then, fumbled words and confusion watched as she ran away in anger. He says, "AnnaKay," and it is only to pull her attention. It is to gain a moment to restore balance that has been off since she was viewed sitting through the window. She is angry, and it is anger that he knows. She is throwing accusations that are his own. Very tentatively, Corbyn says, "Can I – ask – you something?"

"What?"

He asks, "Do you get my texts?"

"I don't get texts," she says: "I never hear from you. And then, you just send emails from out of nowhere. And then I call you, and you don't return my call: You said to call you. So, I did."

"A-K," he says. "I want to sit and have a conversation. Can we do that?"

She admits, "I don't know," indication she is ready to run away again. Acknowledgement there is anger, and it's spread everywhere.

Corbyn sits, and says, "I can offer you some protein bars if you're hungry. I was also invited up to the house, if you're interested. If not, it's the bars, some cereal and a couple apples. If you're thirsty, all I've got's tap water."

"No bourbon," she says.

It is a slicing question. Sheared from the accusations of prior years. Words used to claim unsuitability as a parent. One of many claims that was given traction despite no attachment to reality.

Corbyn says, "I already had three after work. There's most of a bottle under my bed."

She says, "I'll take that," and Corbyn laughs. It even tugs a slight smile from his daughter.

But then, he says, "Your mother would love that."

AnnaKay says, "I wouldn't tell her."

Understanding that she's serious, he says, "I don't approve of you drinking. And if I did make an exception – 'cause I know this isn't easy – I'd have to take your keys."

She digs into her pocket and throws them on the table.

Lips purse, but he meets her: "Not like you need it, but if you did…" He lets the thought trail away. He puts it in her corner, "Under the bed. Duffle bag – right side." And he jokes, "That's the pantry side."

She looks back, and there's distrust. She looks back, uncertain if he's serious, but she resolves and pulls the bag from beneath the bed. Two cups are extracted with the bottle and she takes a seat across the table. As she pulls the cork and begins to pour, her father holds two fingers close to demonstrate how full.

He watches as she leans back and raises her own. She takes a sip and wrenches forward. She cringes against the burn, and, "Uh," is followed by the question, "How do you drink this?" He laughs as she rises and proclaims, "This stuff is terrible."

Corbyn stops her from throwing it away, offering, "I'll drink that if you don't want it."

"I'm getting water," she says. She nearly doubles the volume in the cup and then tries again. By the expression given, it gains approval, and she takes a larger gulp.

"Easy," is warned as misgivings grow.

She looks back derisively, but returns to the table and teases with just a sip.

He says, "You understand – at this point: I'm not gonna let you drive."

She says, "I got it."

He suggests, "I'm sure the girls will love having you spend the night," but she insists, "I'm staying here."

Thoughts to a night with Chel come to mind, but he says, "Okay," and then, "I don't care, either way, but I do need to know if your mother knows you're here."

She says, "No."

"Okay." He says, "We do need to let her know."

He's answered, "Whatever."

He asks, "Do you want me to do that?"

He's answered, "I don't care."

"I don't want to," he jokes, "But I need to. She needs to know where you are. You get that?"

She says, "I don't care."

"Okay," he says. He opens contact and presses call. The phone goes immediately to voicemail, just like always. He leaves the message, "Hi Anika – it's Corbyn. I just want to let you know that AnnaKay drove down again. Considering the time, I thinks its best if she spends the night before heading back. Give me a call if you want to – ya know: Talk about anything." The call is ended, and he texts, "In case you don't get the message: A-K's here. She's planning to spend the night. Let me know if you want to coordinate to make sure she gets back safely." He turns attention back to his daughter, and says, "I'm open to anything you wanna talk about. If you wanna just hang out – that's also fine." Corbyn suggests, "We could take a walk down to the beach."

"I wanted to know," she reminds him, "Why you didn't return my calls. You tell me to call, and it goes to voicemail like you don't want to take it. And you never call back."

"I hear you," he says: "Something's going on with the phones. Before you go, we'll head into town and figure out what's going on."

AnnaKay lifts her device and then turns it to demonstrate she's calling, "Dad." Corbyn lifts his to show there's nothing, and both listen as it immediately goes to voicemail.

"That – is not – my message," Corbyn says. He asks, "When was the last time you got one of my texts, or calls?"

She asks, "When was the last time you did?"

He says, "Today," and she says, "Prove it."

They have returned right back to where they were the last time she drove down. The last time she asked for proof he was paying child support. Now, she is asking for proof he's been trying to contact her.

They are the same thing. She is saying she does not believe what she's being told. She has been offered words and found that they are empty. She is saying she will not accept any more without proof of their validity. Prove it was not faultline to be danced around – it is recognized that was a terrible misinterpretation: The line ripped open years before. She is asking if she can trust the path across the resultant gorge.

There will be no more coquettish dance around feelings. No more credence given to the words of others. Only, as Chel said: Speak to truth.

Corbyn pulls up messages, and then turns the device for his daughter to see. He begins scrolling, to demonstrate the vast number of messages that were sent, but she grabs his finger, and tells him, "Stop."

She takes the device and scrolls rapidly, and then stops and starts reading the messages.

She is quickly overwhelmed. Tears begin to flow, and she is shivering.

Corbyn says, "A-K," and puts an arm across her shoulders. She pulls him close, and they sit together as she continues reading.

She reads on through years of messages until the tears are no longer falling. Eyes are still damp but she has composed herself by the time she's finally had enough. She says, quietly, "You sent all those."

"Yeah," says Corbyn. "Even if I never heard from you, I was never gonna stop telling you how much I love you. You're my fuckin' world, AnnaKay." He says, "Shit. I love you more than anything."

She finds her father is also not emotionally stable, thought that had been demonstrated many times over the years. Usually when blowing up at her mother. But when she turns, she finds his eyes are also not dry, and she takes her fingers to wipe the water from them. And then, wipes them on his shirt.

It is the little girl from a decade before that would tell him, "Don't be sad, daddy." She doesn't say it, but it's spoken with the gesture.

"I can't tell you how glad I am that you came down here. We'll get this all sorted out, but I wanna make sure that we focus on just us. I was dead after you left the last time."

She nods, understanding they have many shared qualities, and she asks, "Can I see your phone again?"

He says, "Go ahead," as it sits before her on the table. He unlocks it, and she pulls up messages again.

She taps the icon, and she is perplexed. Anger grows, and she demands, "Why are you sending these to yourself?"

Corbyn looks, and it is his daughter. A picture taken a half-dozen years before, and the number at which he's always called her. The number that he texts. Where he once received messages in return.

He says, "That's not my number. That's yours."

"That is not my number," she insists.

She takes his phone and quickly jots a message. A moment later her own vibrates. She opens the message, and questions, "This is you?"

"That is," he agrees. She quickly updates contact information and then replies to the number that is now Dad.

His phone brightens with a notification, and she reaches for it. She hesitates, but he doesn't move to intercede, so she takes it and updates her information for him.

The phone is set back on the table, and she just stares at it. A shiver goes through her – her jaw is clenched: She is angry.

Softly, Corbyn tries to break the ice: "A-K?"

She says, "Don't tell me not to be angry."

He laughs, because, "I'm the last person that could say that. But this is what I'm afraid of. It's why I tried to balance the conversation, last time."

The anger spills, "You know it's her. You know she's the one that did this."

"I know," he says: "I'm not gonna tell you not to be angry. I'm not gonna tell you what to say. But I don't want anger to be what we have. I don't want our frustration with your mother to be what brings us together. I want it to be us – you and me. I just want you back."

She says, "Okay," and wraps her arms around him. She leans her head against his shoulder, and says, "I love you, daddy."

"I love so much," he tells her, and he has to hold his breath because he's losing his composure.

Fortunately, "Whoa," interrupts the moment with a burst of air. Wyl stands, holding the doorknob like he's been electrocuted. He says, "Holy Corbnolly: I didn't know you were here, A-K – is that still okay." He asks, and then notes the reddened eyes, and further questions, "Is everything alright?"

Corbyn says, "Yes. At this moment – right now – everything's alright."

"Okay," he says," I was coming down to bother your dad, but I can save that for later. Should I keep this quiet?"

AnnaKay says, "I don't care."

To clarify, Wyl asks, "It's alright if I tell the family?"

He's told, "It's fine."

"Any interest," he tries, "In seeing the rest of the gang?"

She says, "I don't know," and then, "Maybe," and her father adds, "Maybe in a little while."

"Okay." Wyl says, "That would be great. I know they'd love to see you. See ya, Corbubbles."

"Yeah, man – we'll see."

He leaves then and shortly after the door closes, AnnaKay asks, "Are you going to say something? To mom," she clarifies, "About the phones."

"Yeah. I'll say something. But I don't want that to be our focus – right now. We figured it out, and, ya know, we'll deal with it. But that's a conversation to have with her."

"I'm gonna say something. Because she lied to me, too."

"That's fine, A-K. That's your decision. I support that decision."

She shares, "They told me you didn't care. They said that's why you didn't call."

He tries, "A-K," but she isn't seeking calm.

She wants to stress, "I knew that wasn't true. I remember how mad you got when they said they were moving. I remember you said you'd never get to see me. I never forgot that and anytime they said you didn't care, I knew they were lying."

"I get it," Corbyn says: "You need to vent that's fine. I'm not gonna defend your mom, but I'm not gonna pile on. I'm savin' it for her."

It brings the first real smile since she arrived, and she asks, "Can we not stay long? I don't wanna be weird and not say hi, but I wanna come back and drink more bourbon."

Both laugh, and Corbyn says, "I never said I was a great parent."

The laughter grows, because AnnaKay says, "Neither is mom."

It is a release for both of them. Laughter fills the cabin, greater than it should, because it empties icy water that lives in both of them. Laughter begets laughter until tears are falling. It rolls in waves until it finally crashes with Corbyn almost slumped out of a chair and his daughter lying on the bed with her arms stretched out.

They are both at ease, and AnnaKay asks, "Do you know why I decided to come back down here?"

"Well," says Corbyn: "I'd like to think you just wanted to visit, but it probably has something to do with a sword."

"A sword," she confirms – and she's laughing. She says, "Mom would kill me if she knew I had it. What's it for?"

Corbyn pulls himself up, and shares, "It's for a group I joined." He pulls the chair around so that he faces his daughter. He explains, "The guy I work with thought if we made you a member and delivered a sword, it might break the ice." He takes a moment to pull himself together, and admit, "He's usually right."

She asks, "What do you do?"

He answers, "Sword fighting."

She's laughing again. She questions, "Sword fighting?"

"We do mock swordfights – which is what yours is for – and practice what we're gonna do with fencing swords."

"So," she says, "You want me to swordfight?"

He reminds her, "I told you, I'm not great at this parent thing."

She suggests, "Let's go up to the house for a minute. You can tell me about it when we get back."

"Technically," Corbyn says, "You're supposed to be with me most weekends. We'd planned to take out the submarine on Saturday."

Her eyes go wide, and, "What," is questioned, as if ears had failed. She asks, "Submarine? What does that have to do with sword fighting?"

Corbyn rises and extends a hand to help her to her feet, and says, "It's complicated."

16

AnnaKay knocks at the door and waits. Their eyes had met as she approached and there's nothing to prevent her from entering. But she waits, and the usual call of invitation is forgone: Corbyn rises and opens the door.

She greets him, "Hey, dad."

"You got something to eat?"

She says, "I thought you were gonna be there."

"I was," he says, and he admits, "I was thinking – I'm really struggling." She enters, and the door is closed, and she falls back on the bed. It's explained: "I was thinking. This thing with your mom. I think I'm not – really – angry because: You're here. But I'm gonna get pissed. Eventually, everything's gonna roll down – I'm gonna flip."

"Flip," she says.

"I'm trying to get my head where I can avoid that, but – I – just – can't. I can't get my head around it."

"Oh my God," she says, and for a moment, there's concern he's said too much and been too honest. But A-K says, "I thought you were blowing it off. I thought I'd just – whatever. But I was, like, how can you just let her do that."

"Yeah," he says, "Yeah. I'm just glad, I'm just grateful; I'm relieved you're here and we're talking."

"But it's awkward," she suggests.

"We just don't," he says, "Ya know: You were – a kid – last time we were having any kind of conversation."

She says, "Some people think I still am."

Corbyn says, "It's hard. To go from where we were to where we are." And in a moment of conciliatory empathy, he says, "It's hard for your mom, too."

She asks, "So, are we saying something?"

"Yeah," he says. "I'm gonna get pissed – I'm warning you. It's gonna click and I'm gonna lose it."

She says, "Just make sure I'm there."

He laughs, and says, "Come on – kid: Let's introduce you to the consortium."

They exit the home and walk through Wyl's shrubbery. They move past the cabin and for the cliff line and as they near, the large rock embedded in the sand comes into view. There is one person on it, one leaning back against it, and two girls in a race around.

"You told them," Corbyn asks.

There is accusation in her reply, "You didn't say not to."

"No," he says, and worries, "I probably told them more than I should've. But they know about it. I just don't know how Awrol's gonna take it."

They slip down through the break in the cliff and cross the loose and piled sand. A-K hops on a driftwood log and walks it to its conclusion before hopping to the matted sand.

"Unca-C," blows in a wavered call from distance, but they are too involved in their diversion to break away. They continue around the rock and parents.

"Was it supposed to be a secret?"

It's a question that wasn't ever asked, however, "We're doing this around – everyone. I never asked, but I don't think so."

She says, "They know about it, you know."

He says, "I know. I told them. Your mom also knows. From what I heard, she thinks it's stupid. But I've really enjoyed being a part of it. I really – really – like fencing. I hope you'll try it."

She says, "Okay," and they continue until, "Unca-C" is greeted with an impact.

Shey, then Lia run to hug, and then run away to resume their game encircling their parents.

Corshae greets them, with, "I thought you were joining us."

"Yeah, Crabapple. Ditching your own kid?"

"Yeah – I know, Wyltherine: I meant to. Got caught in my head. Ya know, this – thing – with Anika."

With disapproval, Corshae asks, "Corbyn: What did you do?"

"What did I do," he snaps. He catches himself. He feels the red burning in his neck, and it's never served him well. Usually, it hadn't been useful to dip into that fiery well of anger. Regardless, those in front of him didn't deserve to be the target. He answers, more tempered, "I've been too patient. I've been too considerate – I've been an idiot."

Cautiously, Wyl asks, "Care to share?"

AnnaKay quickly says, "I didn't tell them."

He decides, "It's not worth it. Me and A-K need to figure some things out. We'll get to it later."

"If you need," Corshae volunteers, "Someone to act as a moderator, we can do that."

He says, "No. This will be us having a very blunt conversation."

"Okay," Wyl agrees. He is of cheer and happy to move on, and addresses the reason all are present: "So, do we get to meet the pirate?"

"Can you show some respect?" Anger is leaking out. It is not in the forefront of the mind, but it is boiling deep within it. It is exactly what Corbyn didn't want to happen, but he knew it would. It's why he didn't call – it's why he hasn't texted – because, it will erupt. It is only simmering as he points out, "The guy saved my life. I have no idea if he'll even show with everybody here."

It's observed the girls have stopped their game. They have climbed atop the rock, and they are watching: They have seen this before. They know what will follow.

And Lia asks, because she's blunt, "What's the matter, Unca-C?"

"I'm angry," he admits. "And I don't know how to fix what made me angry."

"Mom," AnnaKays says obviously.

"We'll explain it. Just not now. Maybe at dinner." There's a look exchanged. It's curious, because it appears there's some knowledge. Corbyn is beside himself, and asks, "You know about the phones?"

"Phones." Wyl is perplexed, and it's obvious – Corshae is shaking her head. "What's up with phones?"

"Look," Corbyn says, "I'm gonna lose it at anything that sounds off. Maybe by tonight I can try to explain it."

"Okay, Corbs. You wanna see if your – guy's – around?"

"No promises," Corbyn tells him. He walks to the water, and calmly says, "Hey, Awrol: You got a crowd of millions waiting to meet you. Hit the exhaust if you don't wanna deal with it."

There is nothing. Seconds tick by. What feels like almost a minute passes, and the older pair conclude it's because the person does not exist. The three young women wait with anticipation, and uncertainty. Corbyn steps back to watch, because he expects a man to walk out of the ocean.

The sight of the water spraying – almost like a wave, if not looking directly at it – it brings a smile. The heaviness that had accrued during the week feels like it's immediately peeled away.

Of the others watching, time had passed enough that thoughts had turned to what they were going to say: Derisive, alleviating – some were working on jokes. In fact, all of them were thinking of amusing things to say. But just as they begin to say something about the prospect of a man joining them from the ocean – within that spray that seems to form an arch, in fact – a man begins to emerge from the water.

A series of sounds and exhortations are made as he walks out of the ocean, and it appears he's completely dry.

He is a large man. He is tall, and broad, and he's wearing a hooded cloak – a dry cloak that turns as it catches wind. He has a thick, full beard, and his eyes are just glints of light as they peer from beneath the hood. He walks from the water and other than the cloak he is not in uniform. He wears jeans, and a shirt – a weird, puffy shirt – and boots that come nearly to his knees. He walks from the water, and moves for Corbyn, directly.

They come together in embrace. They hold each other fondly, and Corbyn asks, "How's it going?"

He pulls away, and notes, "Evidently – superior to yourself.

It brings a laugh, because that is something that he'd say under any circumstance. But it is also to inform him that the man's aware of what's going on. Awrol does know about the phones.

"This is Awrol," Corbyn announces. "Amazing guy, and – ya know: Personal hero." He says to the man, "My daughter – A-K. These are Wyl and Corshae, and the rock climbers are Shey and Lia." He shares, "This is the guy I've been working with."

Wyl is the first to speak, and he attempts to make light of a suddenly weighty introduction. He says, "I didn't even think you were real.

Awrol says, "I am – unreal. However, corporeal. It is a tremendous pleasure to finally meet those that are most significant to my associate: I am honored."

Shey asks, "Can you do magic?"

He says, "Of course. Did I not just emerge from the ocean waters?"

It is a good point, and she says, "Cool."

"What else," Lia asks.

Awrol says, "My gifts are the tools of my trade. They are not for entertainment. They are powerful, they are extraordinary, and they are dangerous."

Lia says, "I still wanna see another one."

"Another time," he suggests. "That is not why we have come together on this day."

"Girls," Wyl says: "I think that's our cue."

But he's told, "Stay. If," Awrol says, "You have interest in what we do."

"Yes," says Shey, and in syncopation Lia follows, "Yes."

"We would certainly," Corshae says, "Love to know," she wonders, "What that is."

"AnnaKay," he calls, and she stands stiffly at attention. Awrol asks, "What has your father told you?"

"Om," she says, "He said sword fighting." It had not been heavily discussed – there were distractions. There were phones, and there was a father open to conversation. She remembers, "He said something about costumes."

"AnnaKay," the man pleads: "You have been givin membership to the consortium. If you choose to continue your membership – promise me: You will work with your father and help him articulate explanations more thoroughly. It is an area where he is severely lacking."

"Facts," Wyl seconds, but A-K says demurely, "I'll try."

"What do we do," Awrol bellows.

Lia calls, "What do you do?"

Both girls are excited and anxious to be part of whatever it is – there are swords and costumes.

Quietly, Awrol asks, "Is this a secret?"

Three faces look back, frozen with gravity. One is toying with a rock in the sand, and the two girls are dying to move again. Towards that end, Shey confidently says, "Yes."

Awrol bellows, "No." He says, "Do you see me here?"

Lia shouts, "No."

"Hilariously," he says: "We're supposed to pretend you can't see us when we're encountered during a conquest or a challenge. It is absurd, but that is the point of all of this. But a secret? Corbyn: What do I always say?"

"Speak to truth," he answers.

Awrol bellows, "Speak to truth.

"We actively engage within the public purview. We are a shocking vision to those we encounter. We have had the authorities called to address our activities more than fourteen-thousand times. We are not – a secret.

"What we are, AnnaKay, is a group of individuals that hold the rules, regulations, and activities of the consortium with an inordinate degree of importance.

We are a band of brothers and sisters that will do anything we can for another member. The secret that we hold is that every member is our kin, and we will go to extreme lengths to help, to protect, and to care for one another. Despite that we go to great lengths to bludgeon one another, if you choose to stay with the consortium, you will discover it is a vast and close-knit network."

"You ask," says Awrol, "Because you still do not understand, what is this, and where did it come from?

"The consortium originated at a fencing club, and at its heart, that is what it remains. Every member of the consortium knows how to fence, and it is through that we practice and perfect our broadsword work. Broadsword battles occur during challenges, but these are choreographed, and not actual. The sword you were given is not intended to kill, not easily, it is only intended to look beautiful.

"We take great pains to ensure these are not damaged during challenges. There is no intent to cause damage to the weapons, not to our uniforms, and most importantly – not to our members. I stress this because I am aware you have seen the video. I know your father told you what happened when he attended his first challenge, and I want to assure you – it is unequivocably unacceptable. We protect members of the consortium – we do not bring harm. We will uncover who was behind what happened, and we will hold them responsible.

"But moving on," he says: "A challenge can be brought at any time by anyone."

"In uniform," Corbyn mentions.

Awrol says, "A challenge can be brought by anyone at any time while members are in uniform. These do not need to be accepted. However, if they are, the victor has the option of bringing the vanquished under their orders, and orders cannot be questioned. Alternatively, the victor can propose a conquest. This can be anything at all, and if you lose a challenge and a conquest is delivered, you must take part in the conquest.

"As your father has discovered, conquests are typically heavily weighted to favor the person, or team, that created them. Consequently, most of our time is spent trying to locate the victor while in uniform so they can be challenged. A successful challenge will negate the conquest. Corbyn will answer any questions."

There is quiet. Corbyn says, "Anyone?" But even the younger girls are overwhelmed: They are students in school where they are required to be still and pay attention.

Their parents are not far from that, and Corshae admits, "That's – pretty much – what Corbyn told us."

Her husband says, "That's – a lot."

"How many challenges." AnnaKay asks, "How many conquests do you have to do at a time."

Awrol explains, "This is not meant to add stress to our lives. It is meant to do the opposite. You challenge as you want to challenge, and you can decline. The vast majority lead to nothing, usually secondary challenges between those that assist others: Members of the team. The primary challenge is between those that are on the conquest. Generally, those that work with them challenge one another solely for the challenge. It is rare another conquest comes from those – however, it can. You do need to be in uniform for at least five hours every week, but if you are overwhelmed, you can petition to have a conquest dissolved."

Corbyn adds, "If you wanna be a part of it, I wouldn't even worry about conquests at the start. Just get a feel for it: That's what I'm doing."

"Two can be overwhelming. They can be tremendously involved."

Wyl says, "If no secrets, can ya tell me – what's your conquest."

"Stupid," Corbyn says.

"Absurd," is agreed, however Awrol explains, "It is typical of El-Assissi. He is clever and insightful."

"He found a thunderegg," Corbyn explains, "That looks like some nebula. If we wanna win, we have to find one that's a closer match. Basically impossible."

"Did you tell me that? Cobunkanegg? I feel like you might've told me that."

He's answered, "I don't know. I think I might've."

Corshae says, "It was nice to meet you. And thanks for, kind of, filling in. Like you said, Corbyn doesn't always give us the details."

"The pleasure is mine," Awrols says, and shares, "I have the advantage as I feel I know you already. Our mutual acquaintance speaks of you often and with great love. Your children are as exuberant and delightful as Unca-C has claimed."

This brings the two mentioned to fall out in hysterical laughter, finding it beyond hilarious that the big man in the cloak, the mysterious, bearded man with glittery eyes would invoke the name.

He tells them, "Next time, I will prepare something for your entertainment," and to their father, he says, "I believe I am supposed to address you as Wylicopter. I am grateful he has a friend as loyal and willing to expedite his well-being. One day, we will break bread together."

"Hey," Wyl says, "For sure. Any time."

Corshae calls, "Let's go, girls."

"Bye," Lia says.

Shey says, "Bye, Awrol."

"Awrol," her sister howls.

They walk away, but though the wind distorts the sound and waves are crashing, both can be heard repeating, "Awrol."

Observations and calm are broken as the namesake questions, "How long have you known them?"

The anger that might have mistakenly been believed to have resolved, is present, as, "Forever," is said, and, "Why do you ask," holds evident hostility.

Awrol says, "There is a pill in the cushion."

"What the fuck does that mean?"

It's admitted, "I don't know. I don't know the relationship."

"She's friends with my mom."

"Ah," says Awrol. "Perhaps that is it." He asks Corbyn, "Do you wish to continue?"

To his daughter, Corbyn says, "There's a submarine in the water." He says, and knows, "This is a leap of faith, and I don't want you to feel like you have to, but you've gotta walk in the water. You'll have to hold your breath for just a bit – and it's cold. But then you get on board, and you're hit with heat and fans, and the water's gone. No one else in the consortium has a submarine, so, you don't have to – to be a member."

"You've done it," she asks.

"Yeah," he says. "Many times." And he knows, "You're gonna have doubts as the water starts going over your head, but right after – you're on board. It's not something we have to do today."

She looks at the large man standing in front of her, and she remains uncertain what to think of him. But she then looks to her father, and she has decided she can trust him: He has been open. He has spoken of failures. He has not attempted to present himself favorably, in contrast to her mother: He has avoided saying anything about her, despite the many reasons that he could.

She says, "I want to."

Awrol is already heading to the ocean. He marches directly in. He submerges himself to his ankles, to his knees; to his waist. There is a more determined press as he moves his chest against the water, and his shoulders go under. A wave crashes in and submerges him entirely, and as waters recede, there's no sign of him.

"He walked out," A-K says to herself. She says, looking for confirmation, "He came out of the water."

Her father says, "The first time's scary. You don't need to go in."

She asks, "Will you hold my hand?"

He says, "I think it'd be better if you go first. I'll hold your shoulders. If I push – just let me. That'll get you in."

She says, "Okay," and it's a moment of trust that she gives him, that he gave Awrol, and that he gives him again: Trusting the design to protect his daughter.

She hesitates at the first wave that fills her shoes, and Corbyn assures her, "We can turn back."

She doesn't answer. She stands for a moment as another wave crashes, and then follows it out to the water.

She presses as the water hits her thighs, and it is surrender to fate as it covers shoulders. She pushes, and feel hands against her shoulders, and for a moment, the words of her mother are flashing red against her mind. For a moment, she wonders if he is killing her.

The world is dark, the water's cold, and then A-K gasps as she enters a space with air. She is blasted and the warmth that was promised encapsulates her fully. She is standing in a space with the large man that is Awrol, and pushed forward as her father enters.

She looks back at the void through which they seem to have entered. She looks around the small space and it is odd, and looks old, and there is nothing particularly interesting other than a wheel that seems to be attached to a door.

She wonders, "This is a submarine?"

Awrol says, "One built for fewer numbers," and Corbyn instantly snaps, "You invited her. You don't want us here – we can go."

"Settle yourself, Unca-C: We are congested. A different protocol will be needed going forward." To A-K, Awrol says, "If you will do the honors – wind the dog."

"I don't," she says, "I don't know what that means."

She is alarmed. She is distressed – she is uncertain. She offered trust but it emptied in the water. She has walked into a world where she has no bearing.

It is a moment that is recognize and understood, and Corbyn tells her, firmly, "You're good." She looks to him, and she doesn't believe it. He shares, "Behind you is an optical illusion: We'll explain it. The dog is the wheel on the door. You turn it clockwise to open."

"You want me?" She asks Awrol, "To turn it?"

He says, “I would mention situational proximity but I am afraid it would instigate further remonstration.”

Corbyn admits, “I’m really wound tight, right now. Everything feels like an attack. I apologize – if – you weren’t trying to be a dick.”

“AnnaKay,” Awrol says – it is an order: “Wind the dog.”

She looks to her father, and he agrees, “Yeah. Turn it clockwise.” He looks beyond his daughter, and acknowledges, “It’s tight – okay? It just sounded to me – like – you resented us being here. I know you like working alone.”

“Do you want me to,” A-K asks.

Her father says, more calmly, “Yeah. Go ahead.”

She begins turning the wheel as Awrol says, “I have enjoyed the camaraderie and coordination. I have come to think of you as someone that is interesting. However, I will not continue to do so if you react in this manner. I am not responsible for what you are dealing with, and I do not deserve the accusations and bile you are regurgitating.”

The door pops free, and A-K looks to her father, uncertain what to make of anything, of anyone, and feeling entirely uncomfortable. She is more so as Awrol says, “Enter.” She hesitates, and he explains, “Despite your father’s ill-tempered reaction, my observation that the quarters were unsuitable for three is warranted: He cannot enter until you and I have – he can then close the door to move around it. As I stated, the submersible was not designed with numbers in mind.”

“Skewer me,” Corbyn says: “I already told her, I’m in a terrible place.” He says, “Go on, A-K: You’re gonna love this.”

She pulls the door open, and tentatively enters, and she is enchanted. She hardly hears, "You know about the phones…"

Awrol is following, and says, "Only that there was something with them. What I heard of your conversation on the beach."

"Wow," is a welcome derailment of the conversation – for both that follow.

AnnaKay enters and is awed by what she finds: By the entirety. By the controls, the wood, the brass, and that there are bunks. She is enlivened as she enters into a space that is remarkable, and markedly old: It appears to be ancient.

She asks, "Where did this come from?"

Awrol tells her, "This is my creation."

She looks back, and he is not that old – maybe younger than her father. She says, "It looks old."

Awrol says, "The aesthetic that I aimed for." He says, "AnnaKay – and not Corbyn: Tell me why your father has become more irrational."

She looks over, and he admits, "The freakin' phones."

"My mom," A-K says. "She had us thinking a number was each other, but it's probably her. We'd call, or text, and there wasn't, you know, any answer. It's the same number: It's the same number. I thought it was his – he thought it was me. But it's just my mom. This is what she does."

Corbyn adds, "I used to get responses that I thought were from AnnaKay, but – she didn't. It was probably Anika."

"You have – different numbers?"

"Yes." It is answered irritably and anger is ready to boil over. Corbyn says, "She gave us both the same number. To call each other – not either one of ours. It's probably," and he checks himself because blood pressure is erupting. He takes a deep breath and tries speak calmly his suspicion: "Probably a second phone she has."

Awrol questions, "How long have you used the number?"

"Oh," Corbyn reflects: "It's been six, eight years since we got you a phone? That's the number I've always had. Apparently – never actually hers. Just a." And he stops. The words that were about to come out of his mouth are words that spilled freely a decade prior. In the quiet that awaits continuation, he reflects that they served him poorly. They played into her hand and demonstrated exactly what she'd claimed.

"What do you intend to do?"

That answer is complicated by the young woman that is examining the vessel that they've entered. She has slowly moved forward and peers throughout the cabin. She is nervous, and uncertain. She's unsettled, and it isn't only because of the submersible she's standing in.

That's why Corbyn answers, "I don't know. A-K doesn't need me screaming at her mom. Like I told her, I want us to be about us – not anger, and not piling on her mom. I need to talk to her, but I'm not ready yet."

"Corbyn," Awrol says: "I advise you to seek the counsel of an attorney."

He answers, "Don't have attorney money."

"El-Assissi is an attorney. He will work with you."

Corbyn says, "No." He looks to his daughter, and she's watching him. She is just learning who he is – understanding how he reacts. He says, "She'll say it was to protect AnnaKay: I'm a hothead – I blow up. She just went too far. So, we'll talk – maybe the three of us.

Once you're back, A-K, tell her we need to talk about the phones. You can conference us in together and we'll have a conversation. That sound alright?"

She says, "I guess?"

"Corbyn," Awrol says again, "You need to speak with a laywer."

But he's told, "My kid needs a relationship with both her parents. I'm not calling a lawyer, or the court, or cops, or – whatever. We all need to do better. So, we'll talk – after I stop thinking about how much time I'm willing to spend in jail."

AnnaKay smiles, understanding it's a joke, and that's what he wants. But Awrol still warns, "You need to put this on record. At a minimum, do not delete the messages, nor call logs. This was not merely excessive, parental oversight. She knew how much you wanted to reach your daughter. That, is something else."

He's told, "We'll handle it."

The subject is dropped, and Awrol says, to AnnaKay, "Welcome aboard. We are the only house of the consortium with a submersible. I wanted it to reflect how I felt as I was building, consequently – it appears to have been across a great journey. It appears old, as you said. It is tarnished, but it is hale and ready for adventure."

She asks, "Does it have a name?"

"Ooothodaipsa," he answers.

AnnaKay is laughing because she spelled it out as she tried to gain understanding of the certificate received. She asks, "Is Apothocles someone from mythology?"

She is more relaxed than she has been. She finds the name amusing and is becoming more comfortable.

She is told, "No. That is my wife's name from her days in the consortium."

"Do we need names," A-K asks.

She is answered, "Yes." Awrol instructs, "Beyond working with your father to improve the content and delivery when communicating with others, you both need to submit names for approval. I have been trying to irritate your father by calling him Unca-C, but he embraces it."

She is looking at her father and smiling, because she appreciates, "He likes being Unca-C. We'll come up with something."

17

It is the first time in a long time that the sound of feet splashing through the creek brought the tsunami of dark water. It had been weeks – months had passed since the incident. And yet, as the run came to a conclusion, as feet pounded against the sand and muscles burned – as the deeper parts of the little creek were targeted – the sound of the first step felt like a sledgehammer to the chest. The sound of the step was the body hitting water.

The second nearly brought a fall as the panic that ripped into him stopped feet where they were. Brought Corbyn to a halt in the water. The sweat that poured became clammy and cold, and minutes passed as the dark water slowly slipped away. As the deafening water gave 'way to the kettle drum pounding in his chest.

The sound of the shoreline waves crashing barely registers above the throbbing. Corbyn stands in the water, and the feet that moved so fluidly moments earlier, are leaden weights that can barely be pulled to dry ground. He slogs from the stream and moves to the rocky outcrop, staggering forward to find support.

The heart is slowing. The throbbing in the ears becomes a background drum against the rhythmic ocean waves cascading against the shore. There is a grip against the rock that holds the body steady. That finds an anchor to the present that can look back on the past and know it's gone: That the sound was a foot splashing into a tiny river, and that the night that fell out of it has moved on.

Corbyn rests against the volcanic rock that flowed from ancient mountains that are only hills, any longer. He watches the waves rolling against the sand, and the sheet of water that recedes against another that follows in. Eyes look into the distance at the thin mist that softens the shoreline.

That suffocates vision. A mist that swirls in and drowns the landscape. He breathes deeply to fill the lungs and feels the water filling them.

A wave crashes – a foot splashed: A moment of silence.

As he'd fell into the water, there'd been a moment of peace – a moment of relief: He missed the dock. He avoided catastrophic injury, but then – panic.

He was tumbling. The water was dark and there was no way to determine orientation. And as that set in, the cold began to bite into his flesh.

Eyes look into darkness. There is cold, and there is only black – dark waters, muddy and suffocating. There'd been a surge to fight for survival: Legs kicked, arms pulled – but there'd been nothing. Nothing to indicate the direction moved was towards preservation. It had been desperate, and helpless, and is understood as the last-chance effort to continue living. It is understood, that if another hadn't risked his life – he probably wouldn't.

Sweat has become a grimy film that is the paint of paranoia and anxiety. It sits uncomfortably on prickled skin that remains sensitive to stimulants. There is an air of uneasiness that had been a constant until recently. Until AnnaKay was found sitting in the cabin.

In the ensuing weeks, dark thoughts and glances over the shoulder had been replaced by something more familiar: By anger.

Anger at duplicity and maniacal behavior. Anger that the last years of his daughter's childhood were lost. But mostly, anger at himself for not having pressed the issue sooner. Anger at anger that erupted and precluded any semblance of conversation. With a footstep in the water, that anger was gone.

With a footstep, the uneasiness and sense that nothing sat properly in place returned.

The tiny islands formed by the creek water seeking a way across the ever-changing seashore, are carefully tiptoed across. It brings the memory of a woman whose name he no longer remembers, and the promise of a call if his assailant was caught. He cannot remember the last time he saw her, but it could have been that day, and Corbyn wonders if she stopped running because of what he shared. If she's worried about the predator still amongst them.

Corbyn glances over his shoulder as if she might be running towards him. As if someone might be approaching. The cliff is scanned, but there is no one. The beach is empty, and he continues back. He walks just beyond the water's longest runs and climbs on top of the large, embedded rock once it's met.

There, he stands and faces the ocean. He watches the clouds slowly roll in above the crashing waves. He watches the waves. He watches as water flowing back largely cancels the next that follows in. They are watched as a rhythm seems to build until one fortuitously has the timing to fully run.

Only after watching shadows grow shorter as wave after wave crashes against the shore, after letting the sounds of the seashore soothe the mind, only then does he think to check the time. The stopwatch closes on an hour, but it's still early enough there's no urgency.

"Cornbread," breaks the gentle peace and sends a chill across the spine. Corbyn turns to find his friend approaching, and he's called, "Corberant."

Corbyn steps down and greets him, with, "Morning."

"Morning? That's all I get?" And then he asks, "Is everything alright?"

There's muted laughter and Corbyn shakes his head, because there's a catalogue: A potential killer on the loose, his child back up north, and of course – that child's mother. But that's all obvious, and as for which one has brought concern, he asks, "Why wouldn't I be?"

Wyl hops on the rock, just so he can sit and face the ocean. He says, "Ya know – with the kid going back. You seem to get a little down."

"Ah," says Corbyn, and he admits, "Yeah. It's been great to spend time with her again. But I'm good – I'll bug her later."

It's explained, "I saw ya here. Standing. On a rock. Corsh thought I should maybe check on you."

"You checked, Wylbeing. All's good. Thanks for checking."

"I mean, you were just standing out here. Forever. That's not very Corbynesque."

"It's incredibly stupid."

Wyl suggests, "Try me."

"I was running – just a normal run. I can't tell you if it was a good run, 'cause I didn't stop the time until after I was standing out here – forever."

Wyl guesses, "What's her name?"

"No. I was just thinking about her – Jesty: That was her name. But no. I was at the end, and I hit the water."

"Corbyn…"

"It just hits me. Like I'm hit by a wall."

"You gotta get over it, Corbs."

"You don't understand. It hits me, and I am – there. I'm underwater. I can't breath. Everything's black –

I'm frozen. My foot hit the water, and it was me going in."

"Corbs, man: You've got to accept it was just a fluke thing."

"Fluke thing?"

"Yeah. I mean, you guys are out there doing your thing, and a new guy takes it too far. The guy saw you go in and panicked."

"For three months? He's completely disappeared."

"At some point, he's going to track you down and apologize. He's gonna explain it was an accident."

"That's an interesting theory you have, Willfully-errant. But the guy drove his shoulder into me. And when that didn't work, he used the momentum of my turn to push me in. Nothing about that was an accident."

"It's been how long now? And nothing since. You've gotta stop dwelling on it."

Corbyn looks to his friend, and it's said irritably, "I'm not dwelling on anything. I've been focused on my kid. That's what I've been dwelling on, recently."

"And that's good," Wyl says. "You know, I try very hard not to be an intermediary, but I think its fine to share that even Anika thinks it's beneficial."

"Bull – shit – Wyl."

"This is why I don't."

"I have a – direct – intermediary, now. I know exactly what Anika thinks. And especially about the consortium."

Defensively, Wyl replies, "I didn't say anything about that – and, let's not. I was trying to be positive."

"To me, it feels like you're always advocating for her. Can I tell ya what she did with the phones?"

"Stop – please," Wyl begs: "I'm not advocating. I learned to tune out most of that conversation, but with you and A-K kind of re-connecting, ya know – I've been paying attention."

"How about, when you're not sharing what I'm saying or doing, Wyleaker – tell her she needs to face up and have a conversation."

"You're not gonna want me to say this."

"Then don't."

"You gotta move on, Corbs."

"It was mental. I'm just supposed to let it go?"

"You're gonna have a stroke, man. I'm not saying it wasn't bullshit, I'm not saying it wasn't wrong, I'm saying – appreciate what you have. Concentrate on that."

"Are you nuts?"

"Probably. But A-K can see you whenever she wants now. You know: Just move on."

"Move on, huh – I'll move on. One of two ways, Wyllem: Either she grows up and has a conversation with me, or I have my attorney file a complaint with the court. Either way, and I'll be happy to move on."

It's a joke, that he questions, "You got a lawyer?"

He's told, "Randall Syrianni. He thinks filing a complaint's a better option than buying a car."

"What," Wyl asks, "A car?"

"Yeah," Corbyn says: "To run her over." There's laughter, but only by one. Corbyn remains too irritable to even pretend to be sinister. To even joke it's an actual possibility. Instead, he says, "Tell your wife, I'm fine."

"Come on, Corbs. I'm just saying, things are better than they've been in a long time. Stop worrying about people attacking you while you're running on the beach – worry about being a better father."

"Dude: The fuck."

"Not what I meant – it came out wrong. I meant, Corpuscule, focus on how to keep building that relationship. We all need to."

"I'm gonna focus on what the fuck is up with us?"

"Listen: Corbyn. I just see you in a really good place right now. I see right now as a place that you can build on. I just want thing to continue to be good – for you."

"Talking to you used to be a break in the clouds. It was sunshine breaking through. But recently, you irritate the piss out of me. What the hell is going on?"

"Okay. I get it," Wyl says contritely: "We've noticed you seem down after A-K leaves. We just wanted to make sure you're alright."

"I've gotta get to work. Tell your wife I'm fine, but I'm not. I just saw myself in the fucking water again, and my psycho ex pretended to be my daughter for the past four years. That is fucked. I'm fortunate I'm alive and I'm talking to my daughter again, and that's where I'm focused. But I'm not letting anything go."

"You're gonna stroke out, Corbo."

"Probably won't kill me," Corbyn suggests. They begin heading back, and he imagines, "Probably turn me into a vegetable."

Wyl wonders, "How will we know?"

"That's the thing. I'll just be sitting there in the cabin. Doing nothing. Could be years before anyone knows."

"Just pointing out: I left my comfortable slippers behind to check on you."

A hand falls against the shoulder of a friend, and Corbyn says, "I'm okay. You guys don't need to worry I'm gonna take a swim."

"Just making sure. You got time for coffee?"
"I got time to shower and to haul ass into work."
"Want a ride?"
"Nah. Hey – Wyl."
"Hey – what?"
"How's Portland going?"
"Portland – is gone. The grand reveal will occur on the first."
"A work?"
"A work."
Corbyn says, "Can't wait to see it."
He holds two fingers up as an offering of peace, but departure is paused, because Wyl says, "Hey – Corbs?"
"What's up?"
He groans, and rubs his hands into his face, and regrettably, Wyl says, "I know this is gonna come back and bite me in the ass, but let's just say you heard about the first. Let's say, you decided on your own you wanted to be there. As a surprise." There's a pause as he looks over, caught between a bad place and nowhere good. He shares, "Anika and Plinio are planning to be there."
"Oh." It's a sound that's made in reaction to the tremendous amount of information that was shared. Of secrets held, agreements made, and opinions held out of ear. Corbyn says, "I don't wanna cause any problems."
But that's countered, "No. No, no, no. I'm putting my foot down. You're my best friend – my oldest friend. It isn't right not to invite you: I want you to be there. I don't care if things go sideways."
"They won't," he's promised: "They won't go sideways."

"Please be there if you can. I would really like to have you there."

"I'll talk to A-K. If she's okay with it then I'll be there."

"Fair. Fair," Wyl says. He nods, and says, "I've gotta go eat shit, now. Hope your day goes better than mine's about to go."

"Just blame me," Corbyn suggests, "Wyllakers. Tell her I pestered the shit out of you. Tell her, I wouldn't let it go – ya know: I have that problem."

"True," he says. He shakes his finger the man's direction and nods thoughtfully, and says, "Or, I can own up instead of being a sorry-ass weak sauce. See ya, Corbs."

He's offered the same, and nothing needs to be observed to know there's no more time for delays. Corbyn quickly showers and dresses, and breakfast is just a protein bar. Two more are tossed into the sack, along with a sad banana.

It is the first day in several where the threat of rain is not predicted, however, that wispy fog that made the morning so ethereal continues to cling. It is not heavy, but it does leave a damp that folds over everything. It softens distance and grows thicker up the foothills. It shades the landscape into clouds. It is a frame that encircles everything. A grey cover over the world, but it is light gray. There is a sense that sunlight might find a way through at any moment. However, it doesn't.

The ride in is typical, if more pressed than average in light of all the conversation, of all the standing; of all the staring at the ocean. Vehicles careen along the highway, swerving wildly where there are views of ocean. They drive onto bike lanes that are a casual suggestion, that are often viewed as shoulders by those that are passing through. Traffic is light, as it always is in the morning, but there is one trailer that has to be navigated – the most dangerous of the coastal highway vehicles. There are multiple logging trucks that seem to time the Jake brake with proximity, like they always do. But the ride is eventless. Hills pressed, and down-slopes pedaled on account of time, but it is a welcome reprieve. The wrap of fog brings a peaceful sensibility that is welcomed after the near heart attack when a foot splashed in the river.

The ride down the final ramp is taken at the extreme edge of control, and brakes aren't hit until wheels have crossed the sidewalk: Bike and rider come to an abrupt stop only inches from the water.

The store is entered and it's busier than it has been in a while – a sign there's hope the weather won't be miserable. Corbyn enters, and asks, "All good?"

The woman says, "We're good, Jimmy."

He stops, and turns, and says, "What the fuck?"

"Jesus. There are," she points out, "Children."

"Corbyn," he says. "I'm Corbyn."

She reiterates, "There are children."

He walks on, through the swinging doors and there is rage burning, and he knows it shouldn't. The anger is unwarranted. But it is just like the footstep against the water. It is an old friend telling him to let go. It is more than ten years working together, of taking heat for giving relief while she takes a break. It is Chel no longer at the counter.

Corbyn walks through the space, to, "Corbyn," and, "Morning," and, "What's up bro?" None of it is Chel and his sardonic, sordid vitriol. Corbyn walks to his station, and stands alone.

"Empty," announces the end of the day.

It is not only Corbyn that feels the loss of Chel. The entire operation has changed with his departure: It is quieter. It is less engaged. It has become a slog through the butchering of seafood.

Corbyn walks through the swinging door to the front of the store and through the window – it continues raining. Hope for respite drowns with the observation. The hopelessly optimistic backpack is taken back to processing where it unfurls the gear to return home.

The swinging door is passed a third time, and – one of the few pieces of the experience that remains appreciated – Corbyn says, "See ya, Shirley."

She answers, "Get lost, Jimmy." There is feigned hostility, but both find amusement: It has brought them closer.

She's left behind for rain that continues to fall steadily. It is the third straight day of rain and there has been little reprieve.

It is a slow roll home. It's a day where stops are taken, and shelter's sought just to get a break. It's a rare day that one is made about halfway back, to rest the legs, get a bite to eat – to get out of the rain. It would not have necessarily been the destination of choice if he hadn't been half drenched; didn't need to strip the gear. But the overhang in front offers just enough space to remove it, shake off the rain before stuffing it in the bag.

The strength of the business is what they brew. The food is creative, but it's limited to soup and sandwiches. All of that would make it an option, the overhang keeps it as one of few, but it was chosen, because walking in disheveled, wet, and tired doesn't raise an eyebrow.

Corbyn heads straight to the bar and sits heavily – bag falling beside his feet. It is a unique space, but comfortable. Worn, wooden floors, a store, the bar, and a few tables – each one is unique. Some are simple, but others are works of art. None of that's absorbed as eyes are on the menu.

And what they find, is, "No soup?"

"Aw." The big man behind the counter says, "All gone. Ridin' into the weekend. No corned beef or Totinas either."

"I'll go with pretzels and the stout."

The boots are finally peeled away, and like always, the left shoe is pulled with them. Fingernails dig in to the fabric to extract it and it's finally worked free. As it's set down to slide back on, it's observed there's big, wet footprint where Corbyn was standing: It is one more degree of irritation.

But he returns to the seat as the beer arrives, and the man delivers with it, "Bravin' the weather?"

"All I got," Corbyn says, "It's what I do."

The man says, only, "Enjoy."

It is a fine beer, and the pretzels are good – served with a very good, house-made honey mustard. Pretzels weren't what was hoped for but they were the best option remaining on the menu to compliment the beverage.

There's little left when the man comes back, and says, "Looks like your boots aren't working."

Corbyn turns back to the sodden footprint that's still present. He shakes his head, and says, "Sorry, man. After a while, everything's wet."

"No sweat." He says, "Can I get you another?"

"Yeah," Corbyn agrees, "I'll take another one. And then the bill."

He says, "You got it."

The second is sipped slowly, delaying return to the everlasting rain. He is skimming through short videos when a notification pops up from AKRunner.

It is a question: "What do you think of Elkilia? I think it's funny."

Corbyn smiles, and quickly types in reply, "I think it's great. I'm still working on mine."

Another message is quickly returned, and it asks, "Will you come to my meet on Saturday."

Corbyn doesn't hesitate, he types back "Yes. Send me the details."

One more message is received, and it says. "I sent an email. Don't forget."

He types, "I swear on the blade of my sword." It earns several small pictures in return, and with them, the brief conversation comes to a conclusion.

It is how most conversations are carried out – over text. It is immediate, and almost always brief. Messages arrive randomly throughout the day, cover a topic of passing importance and find conclusion with a little picture. The meaning of most remain lost on Corbyn.

But they are always buoying. There is excited anticipation with every notification. It is a connection, again, with his daughter, and she seems to be embracing it – sharing details of her life, ideas for their characters, and invitations to spend time with her.

It brings something that Corbyn finds little of – it brings him joy.

"Be safe out there." This is called after the raincoat's pulled back on. After rain pants, boots and gloves have been adorned. There was a turn towards the exit, and the proprietor called.

Corbyn turns back, and says, "Hey – ya know: Always a good stop."

The man says, "We'll have soup on Friday. Stop back in."

"Yeah," Corbyn says: "Maybe I'll do that."

The stop was a ray of sunshine on a cloudy day. A break from the rain. A respite where he found continued conversation with his daughter, while enjoying a stout that would exceed anyone's expectation. And while, like all the food offered, the pretzels were slightly above average, the mustard excelled, and it paired perfectly with the beverage.

With renewed vigor and determination, Corbyn mounts the bike and sets off to attack the rain and the back half of the return. It is not an enjoyable experience, grinding down the spirit after days of the same, but the spray from passing vehicles, the continuous distortion on the shield serve as motivators to push harder and shave minutes off the journey.

He arrives fairly exhausted – after the exertion; after the beer – and thoughts to stop in to see the family are superseded by the thought of a hot shower. A hot shower, and then toweling off and being dry.

He heads down around the cabins side of the property, despite new awareness that the approach is not as surreptitious as he'd previously thought. But it does signal he's avoiding human contact and conversation, and he wends through Wyl's shrubbery, along the path that's manicured to the fire pit, and out the other side – where the bike is stopped.

There would be panic, but the number of people observed through the window brings something else.

It brings a heavy weight that crashes on the psyche, as the attempt to calculate the number, fails, but one is broad and familiar enough that it's certainly Timothy Brandt.

There are now faces peering out the windows; through the door, as Corbyn brings the bike around. He jumps off and lets it fall to the ground, marching to the door that is opened for him, and he stands in the entry to survey those present:

Eleven.

There are eleven people packed into the tiny cabin. There is scarcely room for another one to enter, and the door isn't pulled completely closed, as he does.

Most present are unfamiliar. There is Tim, and there is Randy, but they are the only ones that are known.

Corbyn is aware their presence and the presence of the many is indicative of a problem: It is an intervention. Something has happened, and Corbyn demands, "What's up?"

Tim rises, and he is Awrol: Standing to defend. He says, "There have been developments. Please take my seat."

Corbyn does not. He stands in the door, and anger is in the air. He demands, again, "What the fuck is going on."

He's told, "There have been some – unfortunate – and disturbing developments," by Al-Assissi.

Corbyn doesn't bother asking again. He stands in the doorway and looks at them like they are the enemy. All the anger that boils in him is focused on them until they change the target.

Awrol understands the situation, and says, "You will be angry." He explains, "We are trying to protect you."

There is still no further entreaty, as the first question remains unanswered, so Al-Assissi says, "You are going to need representation. I will provide that. We will work out how you can repay me, later."

"Tell me," Corbys says, "What the fuck – is going on."

Awrol does. He says, "Based upon information that you shared with me, I suggested the investigators look in a specific direction. As a result of what was uncovered, they obtained a warrant to listen to the calls between certain individuals. This confirmed what we had come to suspect."

"We is who," Corbyn asks. "You guys are fucking doing this, or it's the sheriff?"

A person that isn't known, says, "I am the sheriff. This is a courtesy that we're letting you know."

Before Corbyn can protest, Awrol clarifies, "We – both – have been investigating. As Cartwright says, he is a deputy sheriff. Our investigation provided information to the sheriff's office and based upon those findings, phone surveillance was approved by the court."

"Corbyn." Al-Assissi is trying to reach through the lava that is only rising. He says, "I know this isn't easy, but we need you to understand: What we are telling you is based upon recorded conversations."

"Who," Corbyn asks, "The fuck is it?"

"Anika," Awrol tells him.

"Anika?" There is complete disbelief. Corbyn asks, "What the fuck would she get out of that?" He says, "No – no: You got it wrong. Sorry, man – bullshit. That's not Anika. What would even be the point of it?"

Awrol shares, "AO9S is a corporation used to transfer funds and property for Plinio Gauff." On the chance it wasn't clear, he bluntly states "Agreave Topel works for Plinio Gauff."

"Maybe Plinio," Corbyn considers: "Maybe he did – for some reason. I mean, I still don't get it. Maybe this guy's a wildcard and it's random. It's probably just coincidence."

"Corbyn." Al-Asissi is again attempting to gain attention: "This is why we tried to stress that we have these conversations recorded. This is not conjecture – it is on the record."

"Corbyn," Awrol says, and his name is called with sadness, and it is deeply sympathetic that he shares, "We wanted to let you know before the warrant is issued for their arrest. Cartwright will give the word and that will happen."

"You want me to believe," Corbyn asks, "That my ex-wife that I have zero relationship with asked some guy that works for her fiancé to kill me? That's what you're asking me to believe?"

Al-Assissi says, "Again, this has been recorded. It is on the record."

"Anika said she wants to kill me…"

Awrol says, "It has been mostly concern about what happened reaching your daughter."

"That isn't all, Corbyn." Al-Assissi tells him, "She has irrevocably implicated herself in the attack."

"Why," Corbyn asks, because, despite the animosity. Despite everything that's happened over the years, "She's got me by the throat. What the fuck does she gain by having me offed?"

"We don't know." Al-Assissi says it, and Awrol adds, "That is a question that remains unanswered." However, he says, verily, "Her involvement is without question."

Corbyn is still dripping with rainwater and disbelief, but he finally wonders, "This was phone calls? Who the fuck was she talking to?"

Al-Assissi says, "This will not be easy."

Come have a drink" Awrol suggests, but Corbyn takes a step away.

His hand remains on the doorknob and he is now completely exposed to the rain, as he demands, "Who?"

Those in the cabin recognize the unfortunate positioning. That their wish to escape the elements has completely compromised their intentions. That their attempt to intervene has been subjugated by the weather and left them with little recourse to move against anger, rage, and potential violence. Everyone watching Corbyn back away knows the answer could potentially ignite an undesirable response.

Awrol accepts the circumstance, and says, "Corshae, and – Wyl."

"Wyl," Corbyn asks in disbelief, and he devolves into laughter. Because, "Wyl doesn't have a violent bone in his body. You all are full of shit."

A person starts, "Let me," but he isn't allowed to share that information, because Corbyn continues, "You're fuckin' with me." Anger, rage, and desire for violence drain, because it's accepted, "This is some kind of test. You want to see how I'll react. No go, fella's: You fucked up bringing Wyl into the conversation."

"Corbyn," Awrol attempts: He is trying to manage the situation, and says, "Come speak with me. Come sit with me: Let me explain."

"Don't ask me to fuckin' sit down again. There's no way Wyl had anything to do with this. If anything, all of you did. I'm thinking this is some kind of freak cult and you're trying to cut me off from the people I know."

"Corbyn." Al-Assissi pulls his attention, firmly. He states, "This was not our investigation. We provided information to the authorities, and they came to these conclusions based upon what they discovered. We've pointed out: This is based upon what they heard."

"I know this is hard," Awrol tries, but Corbyn is unassailable and fires over him, "You want me to believe that Wyl had anything to do with it? You're out of your fuckin' mind."

"Corbyn." Al-Assissi again insists upon taking center stage, and states firmly, he states loudly, "Arrests are happening – today. We are only here because we feel you deserved to know what's happening. But this was not simply an attack against you. It was an affront to our community."

"Corbyn," is said with sympathy. Timothy suggests, "We don't know exactly what Wyl's involvement was. They're only going by what they've heard. But he is – at least – aware that Anika was behind it."

"You want me to believe," and there is a clammy sweat that begins to complicate opinions. He says, "You want me to believe Wyl knows anything about it."

It is Al-Assissi again, and he state firmly, "He does."

"Wyl knows," Corbyn questions, and it is a derailment of everything believed. It is every last bit of faith and trust being shattered. He says, voice wrenching on the edge of full emotional disfunction, "Anika? He did this?"

"He knows," Awrol clarifies: "It is only an opinion, but I do not think he was involved. Only that he is aware she was responsible."

Al-Assissi is less forgiving, and makes clear, "We do not know everything. We do not know the degree of his involvement."

"My Wyl," Corbyn asks, and he is falling into crisis.

Tim, and every other is aware, and he tries to sympathetically begin, "Corbyn."

However, Corbyn is beginning to see red. He asks, with anger behind the words, "He knows? He knows Anika had this guy come at me?"

"Please." Tim is both himself and Awrol. He says. "Please come with me. Let me help you connect with your daughter. We need to help her understand what's happening."

But Corbyn is in no place to rationalize a path forward. He is still at, "Wyl?" He cannot believe, "He wouldn't tell me?" He screams the question, "You want me to believe Wyl knows who tried to kill me?"

"Corbyn," is said in synchronicity. Al-Assissi says it firmly, trying to gain attention – trying to rationalize. Awrol, in contrast, said it with sympathy. Hurting for a friend that was seeing his world shred to pieces.

Corbyn disregards them both. He tears away and storms up the hill through the pouring rain without regard. He pounds his fist against the door and tries the handle, but it's secured. He shouts, "Wyl," and resumes pounding, punching against the wood until a worried face peers around the corner.

As soon as Wyl recognizes who's present, the concern is immediately alleviated, and he smiles. He moves to the door and unlocks it. The door is opened, and he says, "Hey," but his shoulder's punched back immediately.

He is confronted by anger: "You knew it was Anika? You knew she hired some asshole to kill me?" Corbyn stomps forward and strikes his shoulder again.

Wyl questions, "What the fuck," but Corbyn yells, "They recorded your fucking calls. They know everything. They're issuing warrants for your arrest."

The look that he watches tells him everything. It tells him that the claims that were made were valid. It tells him that his lifelong friend that he trusted more than anyone betrayed him.

Wyl says, "Fuck," and he is under assault, immediately after.

Corbyn charges and strikes his cheekbone with a fist. It sends him reeling, and more is coming, except a thick arm intervenes.

It is not enough. Despite the strength that Awrol carries, the rage and years of fitness overcome his attempt to stop the attack.

But others follow. Awrol grabs him by the arm again, Al-Assissi steps in front and presses his chest against him, and others move to hold him back, to prevent the continuation of the attack.

Corbyn warns them, "Take your hands off me, or I'm gonna take out all of you."

Two of those that are holding him are much larger, by appearance. Both are strong and more muscular on first glance. However, neither takes his statement without merit. Both understand he has the ability to cause significant damage. It's why the numbers gathered.

But there is one thing Tim knows the man holds with more importance than satiating anger. One person more important than retribution, and he tells him, "This will affect your daughter. Think about your daughter." It brings a wash over the burning rage, and brings Corbyn to turn his head, to see the person speaking, and Tim tells him, "You need to let her know what's going on."

Corbyn says, "Take your fucking hands off me."

Awrol nods, and the others accept his assessment, and back away. Most believe the man they've freed will use the opportunity to attack again, but Awrol believes the point is made. He believes that the message was received: Others will be hurt by the revelation.

Corbyn walks past them and exits the home into the rain. He calls his daughter, and she answers, saying, "Hey. What's up?"

He has no way to soften what will follow. He has no way to fix what will happen. But in the seconds that he hears her voice, there is a panic, that the behavior that's led to the moment could also put her in danger.

He asks, "Where are you?"

She says, of course, "At home," and she wonders, "Why?"

"A-K," he says. "I've got no way to fix what's going on. I just need to make sure you're safe."

"What," she says: "What do you mean – safe?"

He says, "A-K: Can you go to a friend's? Just for a minute. I just want to make sure you're safe."

"What is going on," she asks.

Corbyn begs, "I need you to trust me. Go to a friend's and let me know when you get there."

She asks, "Why," and Corbyn says, "Please go to a friend's. Let me know when you're there, and I'll explain."

"Dad," she says. "You're scaring me. What is going on?"

He tells her, "It's probably nothing. But I need you to go to a friend's house to make sure it isn't. Will you – please – do that. Let me know when you get there."

She answers, "Okay," but questions, "What should I tell mom?"

He suggests, "Tell her your friend just had a breakup. Tell her you need to be there."

She says, "Okay. I'll let you know when I get there."

He says, "Thank you," but the call's already ended. He looks to those standing in proximity, and none of them are Wyl, so he continues down to the tiny cabin.

He stuffs the few possessions that he has that were not already contained into his duffle bag. What doesn't fit is left behind, and he straps the handles over his shoulders, and exits the small cabin to the almost dozen waiting.

He has nothing for them and moves directly for his bike. As he begins to leave, Al-Assissi attempts to step in front of him, but Corbyn crunches down and then hops wheels to the side. He punches hard against the pedals and accelerates away.

19

A large man walks through the forest. He wears boots that come nearly to his knees, and he is notably covered by a cloak. The hood of that garment is pinched near it's apex by what might be considered a crown. It is nearly the same color of the fabric, if more tarnished – more worn. But the clothing also holds experience: Nothing on the man is recently fashioned.

The pants he wears balloon slightly above the boots. A burnt sienna color that might be velour.

He is an imposing figure, crashing through underbrush, up a significant foothill with an incline that is not easily surmountable. As he climbs, he does not think that the person that he tracks is unsalvageable. The thought that person is beyond rescue is not what he reflects upon: He believes the person he is tracking down is the ideal candidate to help him unseat the far, west coast member of the consortium from his absolute control of the territory. He is someone that is uniquely capable, fit, and learning quickly. It is recognized that he is already a capable ally. But he's also a complete disaster: On that, Awrol does not bother wasting his thoughts.

He walks up the steep incline of a coastal foothill. He has crossed paths with four others on the trek, and every one has reacted negatively – there were concerns. Those grew as the odd – and the man is a large man – cloaked, person was observed to have a long sword strapped to his side. To those he passed he appeared to be an ancient knight on a conquest, perhaps, as one said to another that wondered who and what he was – perhaps, to slay a dragon. This was said in nervous jest, but even another of significant girth considered the man to be a concern.

Each was left with, "Peace to you, brother." Or, "Peace to you, sister." Or, "Peace to both of you. Be well."

All were left wondering exactly what they'd encountered.

But their concerns and questions are of none of either to the man that continues to climb. The man that continues onward until he arrives at what he's come looking for. And what he is searching for, is an encampment that has sprung up recently.

When he finally comes upon it – no accident: He has been tracking the man. He has been monitoring his activity. But what he finds when he breaks through to a small and natural clearing is that the space is antiseptic. It is immaculate, other than a small, beige tent that has been erected. This is not surprising at all.

He says, "Corbyn: It is Awrol." There is no immediate response, but he doesn't bother repeating what was said. He has stated what needs stating and waits patiently.

After – approximately – twenty seconds, the zipper is pulled around and the tent is opened. The person that emerges – and, this is also not surprising – he emerges well-kept, well dressed, and hostile.

The man's told, "Get lost."

He says, "You are stung. I have no argument, however we had no involvement. I have merely wasted an hour of my life to inform you that activities will resume at oh-six-hundred-hours on Saturday. We have all pledged our availability."

"Listen," says Corbyn: "I appreciate you – I do. But I'm done. I'm in a vacant place right now: No idea where I'm going."

"Understood." There is no argument. Except, Awrol says, "As an incorporated member of the Consortium and a comrade of the Official Order of the House of Disorder and its patron Saint, Apothocles, I have also notified your daughter, as required." He waits, and he can see that Corbyn is seething. He can see that the anger that has overtaken him is burning and waiting for the opportunity, for the outlet to erupt. And he says, because of this, "This is a courtesy. By the bylaws, I am not required to inform you of what I share with another member. But I do understand – she's your daughter. I understand you are both working through difficult circumstances."

"Yeah," says Corbyn: "Understatement of the year."

"You speak with her?"

He's answered, "Yes," angrily. There is an opening to fire back, and Awrol's asked, "Why the fuck would I not be?"

He says: "I know she is also struggling. I hope you both keep communication open."

"Yeah," says Corbyn: "Communifuckincation."

She texted and inquired his opinion. As he always had, he had qualified what he thought – he had hedged on absolute honesty.

She had asked, do you really think she meant to hurt you, and he'd answered, I don't know.

She'd said, "Mom says she didn't want him to really hurt you. She just wanted you to stop being part of the Consortium."

He hadn't answered. He didn't respond, because he'd watched the video ten-thousand times, and it showed him what he'd experienced that night: The man had intended to inflict harm. He had meant to knock him in the water, and when the first attempt had failed, he'd tried again – and been successful. To Corbyn, there was no question the man had carried out the orders he'd been given, and he'd almost been successful. The only reason that he wasn't, was because of the person that was presently interrupting the bitter vitriol the man he came to find was wallowing in.

Corbyn tells him, "I'm sorry I got all of you dragged into this. I'm an albatross on everyone I come across."

Awrol ignores the self pity, and asks again, "You're talking with AnnaKay?"

Corbyn says, "Yes," but the conversation has diminished. Again.

She had texted, "I believe her."

And he'd answered, just, "Okay."

The words that Anika and Plinio were saying to acclaim their innocence were irrelevant. They were distractions. They glossed over the fact they'd hired someone to attack, and he did: Just like they wanted. Corbyn had answered, okay, to his daughter and left it at that.

"I have discussed," Awrol begins, but Corbyn looks up with hostility, and states, firmly, "No."

He's asked, "Have you developed the ability to read minds? Or, perhaps you have developed technology you would be willing to share."

It is said in jest, but no humor's found. Corbyn predicts, "You're gonna say – if I need somewhere to stay." It's what cuts the deepest, and so he answers the offer never given, "I'm done with that. I'm not taking anything from anyone."

"I understand." He regards the man and the anger at the revelations shared has not abated in the least. Corbyn stands tensely, he is hostile, and he is still looking for an outlet for the violence that is wracking through him: He is looking for a target to inflict it on. It doesn't help that Awrol shares, "Your daughter asked to your well-being and accommodations. I have not yet," and he is interrupted again:

"If she wants to know, she can ask."

"I'm telling you this," and he is Tim. He says, "This is a courtesy: Telling you we're resuming activities, and telling you your daughter's afraid to have a conversation with you. You feel like shit, and I get that. You're pissed off, and that makes complete sense. But how do you think your daughter feels? She's living with a person she has a complicated relationship with who has possibly tried to have her father killed. Where do you think she is? Your child needs you, Corbyn: That kid needs her father.

"You want to walk away, then walk away: From us; from your kid. But you have worked hard to hold onto the few threads that remained of the relationship with your daughter, and because of that, you have managed to build those into a rope. But those threads will fray away again if you do not continue to work on that relationship. And it is the same with us.

"You are an able accomplice. I have enjoyed our work together. But I will not give you membership. You will have to earn it. Like the relationship with your daughter, that is not a door that will remain open forever. I hope you will move past the anger, and hurt, and recognize that there are many people that surround you, that care about you, and want to help you.

"The path down that direction is not clean. It is not the break and buffer that anger – violence, perhaps – will give you from what has happened. From connections – your relationships. It will be sticky, and you will not pass through without damage clinging to you: It is necessarily, and unavoidably messy. But I know you can, and I hope you will.

"I have said a thousand times, and I say again: Speak to truth. With us – myself – and especially: Your daughter."

He says, "Brother," and holds his arms open. He holds them wide as he regards the man across from him. There is the slightest breaking of the hold hostility had staked. A slight cracking of the anger.

It's what's expected. That what will follow will be the collapse of spirit. An outpouring of sorrow for all of what unfolded. But the thin shell that holds it back is well defended, and Corbyn doesn't break.

He says, "I appreciate what you're doing." However, "I'm not ready to move past wanting to kill her."

"Be honest," Awrol says, "In conversation. You will find it is not always rewarding, but it can set you apart. Disagree if you will, but I believe that is especially important with your daughter."

He's told, "I'll make a note."

"Fair enough." Awrol moves to retreat, with the parting, "I hope to see you Saturday, if not sooner. Al-Assissi has called the conquest, and we will either need to challenge him in the next two days, or find a geode that looks anything close to a nebula. I will also be sharing this information with your daughter, as required."

"Right," Corbyn says. He is still hostile but it's cooling. He manages, "I – appreciate – the offer. Thanks, but – I'm not gonna." And, he also says, "I'm not gonna be there."

"I understand." Awrol bows deeply and then turns, and he begins his way back down through the forest.

There is a moment of guilt that grips Corbyn. He feels it would be decent to call out and stop him, because if he continued up the slope another several yards, and then turned east, he would soon come upon a road.

But, of course, Corbyn remains in the last position he was seen: Still standing. Watching after a person departed that should probably be considered a friend. Someone that went to great lengths to find him, and then hiked up the hills and through the forest to share information, opinion, and consolation.

He also brought the slightest fracture to the shell, but he remains partly unknown. Both have shared deep secrets with one another, but they were feelers: Tests of trust. It feels as if the trust's deserved, but because of who he is and everything that's happened, it opens the door to the punch of betrayal, and the shrinking of humiliation.

Speak to truth with the man that calls himself Awrol is recognized as a conversation that will set emotions loose. That would see the anger, but also the wounds inflicted by a friend whose trust was never questioned. It would bare the shame that interruption of the consortium's activities was the result of his own problems.

It would mean looking in the mirror and recognizing he had many failures. That he had failed most of his closest relationships. That he had spent the past decade living in a shed, and that predicament had only gotten worse – a reflection that sees the same happening with his daughter, once again: Wanting to believe her mother, and asking Corbyn to accept the excuses given.

There is nothing but smoke from the fire that tore through and left nothing in its wake but smoldering ruins. A euphemistic rope that had only recently grown stronger, left burning and envisioned, again, separating entirely. An experience that held great enthusiasm, buried past a bridge so ruined with embarrassment that not even the foundation is discernable. An anchor that had always tethered life experience, and in the moment he was needed most, it was an anchor that pulled him underwater.

The only islands are numbness, and anger. Everything else is a thirsty ocean, reaching against those plateaus to pull the psyche under.

There is no one to trust, no one to turn to, no one to help navigate a way forward.

Even Chel is gone.

"It's Corbyn," he types, and says to Chel, "I don't know if you heard what happened"

Shortly thereafter, it is indicated the message has been read, but there's no sign Chel will respond. The thought crosses through Corbyn's mind that he doesn't want to. That Chel left to be done with everything, and everyone.

But he follows up, and says bluntly, "I need help."

It's not expected there will be an answer, but seconds later, the phone is ringing, and the caller is Chel:

"Hello?"

A familiar voice brings warmth with the question, "Why would you text me? You know my hands don't work."

It almost brings a breakdown, except – Corbyn doesn't know. Eyes turn from inward to an old friend, and he wonders, "From the new job?"

"No, asshole." He's told, "From goin' to war against the sea world. I can hardly hold a fuckin' fork."

"I'm sorry, man. I…"

"Whatever. What the hell are you goin' on about?"

Corbyn says, "I don't know who to talk to. I don't know what I'm supposed to do."

"Corbyn," Chel says: "I hear you're in a mood, but I gotta get back to work. Tell me what the fuck is going on."

"You know," he begins, but it's the beginning of reflection, and Chel knows it, so he stops him, and says, "One, two, three: What has happened?"

Corbyn shares: "You know I'd been doing better with A-K. And you know that guy dropped me in the water. It turns out, the ex hired him to do it. Now, everyone wants me to accept excuses – including the daughter. I'm in a bad place, man. I need someone to talk to – maybe I could come see you."

"Sure, Corbyn. Anytime. But why aren't you having this conversation with your artist?"

"That's the thing," Corbyn shares: "He knew."

"Knew? Knew," is questioned. "Knew what, Corbyn? He knew she got some guy to come at you? What are you tellin' me he knew?"

"He knew she was the one behind it. They've got recorded conversations of them talking. He knew it's Anika – and didn't tell me. And A-K's buying it was just a prank that went too far. I feel like everything's falling apart."

Chel asks, "Was it?"

There's conviction behind, "No." He admits, "I questioned it. Before I knew anything, I thought, maybe the guy just went too far. But I've watched that video a million times, and that's not an accident. He did what she hired him to do, and that's – get rid of me. He worked his way onto a team, convinced them to set up the meet, and then he took his shot when he had the opportunity. That's not a spur of the moment decision."

"There you have it," Chel says: "That's what you tell your daughter. If she don't like it, remind her there's a video."

"You ever seen it?"

"Yeah, dumbass: Why the fuck'd you let go of the crane? That's the only thing that saved you on the first shot."

"I grabbed the crane?"

"A million times you watch and you don't know? You're gone, but then you grab the crane. And then, you let it go. That's a nice somersault you take goin' over."

"Ya know, I didn't know what was going on. I thought it was part of the game."

Chel forcibly sighs, and says, "I know I'm gonna regret this, but why aren't you talkin' to that guy?"

"Because. We've got people all over the country, and because of me, they suspended everything until we knew what happened. Because of my stupid ex-wife, everyone knows I'm the idiot that got dumped in the river. I screw up everything."

"Alright." Chel says, "Corbyn. I do admit – I find all of this very amusing: Ex-wife, hires an – assassin – to kill you while you're prancin' in the dark. It's hilarious watchin' that video, but I know, because I know you too damn well: Your artist was not behind this."

"I don't know." Corbyn says, "I just need to get away. Can I come up for a couple days? I just wanna get away."

Chel says, "You may not. Not 'til you hear your friend out. You told me how many times that man's been there for you? Countless, Corbyn. Probably on a weekly basis. That's not obligation – that man actually cares about you. You find out what the hell was happenin' and get back to me. You still wanna come up after that, then – maybe."

Corbyn admits, "I'm still too angry. But I'll talk to my daughter."

Then," Chel fires back, "I don't gotta warn the wife that Corbyn's coming."

He says, "I guess not."

"Oh, Lord," Chel complains: "You put your head in the sand, and there's always been one person could get you to pull it out again."

"Yeah," Corbyn suggests, "You."

He's answered, "Bull – shit. That's the only person in the world sees something in you. Find out why the hell he didn't tell you, but I think 'cause something else – and, after. Your guy's not on the plot."

"I just can't understand why he wouldn't tell me."

"That's why you ask him, Corbyn. Talk to your kid, talk to your people and you'll get to where you need to."

Corbyn admits, "I know you're right. It's good to talk to you."

There's a muffled, "Shit, Corbyn." Chel says, "You'll be alright."

He's given, "Thanks," but Chel's already gone.

The chink that was started with Awrol's arrival, allowed for some honesty with an old compatriot. Allowed words to find some merit and acceptance there's work to be done. It allowed the shell not to shatter, but to soften. An opening to operate outside of the emotion that had consumed him. To not hedge words because he knew that anger would flood out. A chance to begin addressing what had happened, and that would begin with his daughter.

He texts, "I know you are upset. I know you are hurt, and angry, and scared. I am also angry, hurt and scared. I'm humiliated and I feel betrayed."

Almost instantly, ellipses form, but just as quickly, they disappear. Corbyn continues, "I want you to be okay. I want to continue talking. But I need to be honest with you."

There is nothing, and he knows it's because she knows what he's going to say and doesn't want to see it. He continues, "We are both trying to process a lot. Your voice is the most important voice in how we do that. I promise to listen to you, and I will work with you."

He sends the message, and then another: "I know you don't want to hear this, but I do not believe your mother."

There is an immediate response, "She says she didn't want you hurt. He was only supposed to scare you."

He answers bluntly, "Your mother hired someone to assault me."

She stresses, "Not to *kill* you."

He says, "I am very sympathetic to what you are dealing with. But the man was hired to attack me."

Ellipses form, but he doesn't wait: "Corshae told your mother about the consortium. She used that as an opportunity to have the man attack me."

"She had this person ingratiate himself with Al-Assissi, earn his trust, and he convinced him to hold a meet."

"He took the first opportunity he had to attack. The first attack was unsuccessful, so he attacked again. He did what he was hired to do. It was not an accident."

There are no ellipses; no response. Corbyn points out, "This was planned for months. They plotted a strategy to attack me. I know that is not easy to accept, but you have seen the video."

He planned to end his point with that, but he can't help to add, "I'm sorry. For you. I wish we could talk in person."

He knows she's scared. He knows she's probably crying. He know she feels helpless and feels her world crumbling around her.

His own eyes are blurry as he receives notification of a message. He slides it open, and his child's greatest fear is revealed: "I don't want her to go to jail."

He types back quickly, "I know."

He takes more time to add, "Help me figure out how we get through this."

He sends, "I want you to be okay, and I want to do what's best for you. Work with me."

There is still no reply after several minutes, so he reiterates, "I'm not letting your mother walk away with no repercussion. But I think we can find a solution that will work for both of us if we work together."

He receives, "How?"

He types, "Your mother is going to have to accept responsibility. She is going to have to accept responsibility for the phones, and the crap she's pulled for the last decade."

He quickly adds, "I don't need her to go to jail. But she needs to be held accountable."

A quickly issued message questions, "How?"

Corbyn replies, "I don't know. I am still too angry to start that conversation right now, but I am trying to get there."

He quickly adds, "I hope you will help me. And I hope you will let me help you. If we work together, we will find a way to move forward."

She says, "Okay."

Corbyn sends the message, "I love you, AnnaKay. If you need to talk, or vent, or anything: Do not hesitate. Any time of the day."

Several minutes pass, but the sound of notifications has become a source of joy, and Corbyn is already smiling as he reads, "Love you, dad. I'll call you later when I'm at a friend's."

"Final run," is called like the trumpet of victory. Fish are sent sailing to the stations, and every one is caught and quickly brought to cutting boards to be processed.

The sea-life victims are quickly scrubbed down through the wash. Their bodies slap against the stations in quick succession as the scaling knives are pulled, and the ratching of the process fills the space. It is after this there is a difference of opinion on how to proceed: Some opt for a chopping knife to remove the head, while most move directly to the fillet. Both are effective, but one resounds more notably.

The latter is all that's used to spill the guts, and the fish are moved into the rinse, again.

There is a second, rhythmic slapping of truncated bodies against the counter, and knives split against the spine. The implements move quickly to separate the bodies into two, and to trim, debone, and remove the fat lines.

There is a third wash, and the fillets are moved on to the elder statesmen and women, who will evaluate the product and determine what will move to the front of the store, what will be locally distributed, and what will be quick frozen for further distribution.

Corbyn is the first, to call, "Next," and another of the catch is sent his way.

It brings the comment, "Damn, Corbyn: You're goin' at 'em like it's your ex."

It is a conversation that is not uncommon, as every iota of information discovered by those involved becomes: A point of ridicule. A point of embarrassment. A point of humiliation. A point of dismissal. A point of amusement. A point taken: Corbyn says, "I wish."

It brings laughter, as those around him understand the stress that he is under. They commiserate, because none of them would be there if their lives had worked out as they'd hoped. They are derisive, and empathetic, because every one of them have felt the sting of failure.

The resonance brings another to say, "Fuck that woman," and to that, Corbyn says, "Don't."

He's ignored. Yet another says, "You need me to take care of her – I'll take care of her." He pauses for a moment, and then follows, "You know I'll take care of her."

"Yeah, boy," is said, before the foreman drops the hammer:

"Stop talking and pay attention to what you're doing. Focus on the product."

He walks over to the only station that has only one, and says, "I know you're going through some things. If you need a break, I can spot you."

This is viewed as a challenge. It is a challenge that is a trap. It is a trap that is intended to show an inability to work at the level that is demanded. And that level has increased since Chel left.

No replacement was brought in, but the level of productivity as a whole has been expected to continue. It's expected that the same amount of product will be processed in the same amount of time that it was before he left.

It hasn't – but it's been getting closer.

Corbyn says, "Show me you can do better. You and me: Head to head. Have the old guys judge who does it better."

The man says, "If you can't handle a little conversation, we can find someplace where you can work alone."

It's a strange comment. Even with Chel gone, the conversation's what makes the operation tolerable. It's sometimes brutal, but there's camaraderie. There's appreciation for each other. At the end of the day, there's sympathy for experience, and happiness for others that move on, or have a child, or, get married – find a drink they really like. A recipe – a place to visit. The conversation's raw, but it keeps minds sharp and nothing's said with real hostility.

Corbyn ignores the comment, and instead brags, "Even with – all – the distractions: These guys comin' at me; my life crashin' all around me – I still push more product through than the young guys."

The man says, "You're not helping yourself," and Corbyn is now irritated, and there's hostility in the question, "What does that mean?"

"I'm leaving," he's told.

Corbyn asks, "So, what the fuck are you goin' on about?"

"Look," he says, "Losing Chel – you know: He was slow. He could hardly handle a knife, anymore. They're worried about pulling you off the line."

"What?" Corbyn asks, "What the fuck are you talking about? I'm gettin' canned?"

Heads turn as voices escalate, and the man says, "No one's getting canned: Get back to work." More quietly, he says to Corbyn, "Can you keep your shit together for a minute?"

Corbyn says, "If you can tell me what the fuck you're talkin' about."

"They're talking," he explains, "About moving you into this role. But they don't want to take you off the line."

"No way." Corbyn says, "Fuck that. No way I'm workin' two jobs."

The man asks, "Do you need a valium, or something? Take a deep breath, Corbyn."

"I'll take the bump," Corbyn agrees, "But we'll need two more on the line. You tell them, that's the deal or I'm out of here."

"Why," the man questions, and his voice rises as he asks, "Are you such a fucking knot head? They asked me to float it by you. I told them you're a piece of shit – they didn't listen."

Corbyn says, "This piece of shit wants an answer by the end of the day."

"Oh," he says, "Okay. I'll hand over Corbyn's demands. Get ready to walk, 'cause they're gonna laugh you out of the building."

Corbyn shrugs, and says, "Last day, either way, unless I get your job and two more on the line. We can negotiate the rest."

"You're an idiot." The man says, "They asked me to put it out there – it's not an offer. And I wasn't leaving today."

"In case I didn't make it clear," Corbyn tells him, "I am. Unless they give me the job, and two more down here."

The man shakes his head, and leaves him with, "You're a fucking idiot."

The moment he's gone, from across the room, he's called, "Hey: Fucking idiot." The man shares, with his attention pulled, "Appreciate you."

Another say, "Yeah. Fuck this shit."

"Keep pushin' us for more. The fuck they think they're payin' us?"

And the fourth of four swears allegiance, vowing, "You walk outta here – I'm walkin' with you."

"Hey, man." Corbyn says to all, "Take care of yourselves. And don't follow me, dude – I never make the right decision."

One pushes back, "They've been pushin' us since we lost Chel."

"We should all walk out," finds agreement, but Corbyn says, "Hey – idiots: How ya gonna get your fix if you're not workin'."

He's asked, "What are you gonna do?"

"Either give y'all shit or take an offer up in Washington."

"No shit," is said with respect and surprise.

Chel had been an outlier amongst those that worked the line. He'd been there for decades. Corbyn was close to ten, but the closest after that was under four. The other three were two or less. Most didn't view the job as a career, but Chel and Corbyn were considered constants. Two that were there when others arrived, and two that were there if they stopped by after moving on.

"Never thought you would," is the common sentiment.

The heightened mood that had overtaken the crew after hearing demands, after watching one of their own go toe-to-toe, after hearing Corbyn advocate on their behalf, it plummets with the realization that what was asked for will probably not be delivered, and the one that asked will probably be leaving – not why they soured: It brings reflection on their own circumstance.

Longer hours, a constant push to process faster – stagnation at a job they didn't want. Reflection there are better things they should explore.

Yet, all but one are filled with unease when the foreman returns, and calls, "Hey shithead: Old man wants to see you."

Corbyn is not uneasy, and says, "Lead the way."

Sounds fill the space like children who watch a peer get in trouble. The others call, "It was good to know you," and, "Can I have your knife?" Another asks, "Can I have your paycheck?" Corbyn offers them a parting gesture, and moves to follow.

He is led quickly and without explanation. He follows up the stairs to a second level he has never seen before, and they walk past a small seating area – there is a door and window on the inner wall, and through it there is an office – to the hallway that leads from it. It is lined with several doors, and they move to the last one on the left – every direction but the one they came from is sealed by doors. The door is opened, and they walk into a conference room where three are seated: Elwhinnie, who is the woman often called by other names when she's greeted in the morning, a man that is only known as Mr. Dinwhistle that regularly oversees processing, and an older gentleman that appears to be related.

The woman says, "Hi, Jimmy: I understand you might be interested in becoming our operations manager."

He agrees, "I might be."

She says, "You know my husband, Arthok Dinwhistle Jr." He stands, leans forward and extends a hand, to greet, "Corbyn," as his wife continues: "And, of course, his father – Arthok Dinwhistle Sr."

The man smiles brightly as he stands, and says, "It's nice to meet you, Corbyn."

"Nice to meet you," Corbyn echoes, and he shares, "I know I've seen you, but I couldn't have matched the name."

The old man says, "I wish I could say the same."

And as he chuckles, Corbyn understands, "The video."

He laughs more fully, and admits, "I wish I could tell you I didn't watch it multiple times."

"And, it gets funnier every time," Corbyn suggests.

And he agrees, "It does. Not the first few times, but after watching it many times, I can't help laughing. No offense."

"I don't know if you heard," Corbyn shares, "But the funniest part is my ex was the one behind it. She hired the guy to toss me in the river."

"Oh," the man says, and there's an exchange of glances. Elwhinnie asks, "That's being handled?"

He says, "I guess. They're making excuses and trying to bribe their way out of it, but we'll see what happens."

The woman motions, and it's the cue for the foreman to leave them behind. He closes the door, and Elwhinnie says, "Part of the reason he's leaving is we want to expand the role."

Junior adds, "I want to reduce mine. I'll still oversea operations on your days off, but we want you to be the primary contact for the company."

Corbyn says, "I don't want to waste your time, so I'm gonna repeat what I said: I'm not interested if I'm still expected to put in hours in processing. And I need two more guys on that line."

The old man says, "It was a thought. We agree it would be too much."

His son adds, "We've already started interviews. We'll have one on board before you're gone, and then we'll see about adding someone part time."

"Full time," Corbyn insists. "These guys are putting in way too much time since Chel left, and he can hardly use his hands after all the time he put in here. I've gotta have two, full-timers added to processing, or I'm not gonna take the job."

"Honey," Elwhinnie says, "It's not a career for most of them. It's a summer job, or a year or two. You and Chel are the only ones that stuck around."

"I'm not gonna ask people for twelve-hour shifts. No one complains when we've gotta put the time in on extra orders, but that's gotta be the exception. I'm not doing that to guys."

Junior suggests, "Why don't we come back to this, after you decide if you'd be interested in the job."

"I'm not if we don't have six."

"He's a good man," Elwhinnie says, "If he says we need six, then we need six."

Corbyn clarifies, "We need ten. We can get by with six."

"Okay." The old man relents, "We'll bring another person on."

His son takes over, "You'd be our operations manager. You'd help with marketing, oversee sales, operations, and make sure orders are filled. You'd be responsible for keeping the store stocked, payroll, and coordinating with suppliers and the boats. We'll need you available twenty-four hours a day to meet them at the dock."

"Whoa," Corbyn says, "How many days?"

There is another exchange of glances, and Junior suggests, "Five?"

Corbyn says, "I need weekends for my daughter, so, Monday – Friday?"

"I can't do Sunday," Junior says. "That's my non-negotiable."

Corbyn considers, "I don't care about Sunday. I could do Sunday. If you take Saturdays. I could do Sunday through Wednesday."

"You've got to be here Thursday-Friday. Those are the busy days. I'll need you here."

Corbyn suggests, "Sunday, and Wednesday, Thursday; Friday. Do you just hang out in the office?"

The old man looks to his son, and asks, "Is that acceptable?"

He says, "I guess." He considers, "We could see about shutting down Monday, or Tuesday. I know guys hate giving up the weekends, but we could see if they'd come in Sundays."

"Corbyn," the old man says, "We'll let you broach that topic."

He agrees, but asks again, "I've got a bicycle. Am I rolling in when a boat gets here, or am I stuck sitting in an office."

"I'm sorry." Elwinnie says, "We're jumping around pretty fast. But on the days you're working, you'll need to be here. You never know when crabs are coming in. But you'll have an apartment."

"An apartment? I'm – gonna live here?"

"Days you're on," Junior confirms. "If you have another place, you can be wherever when you're not."

Elwinnie explains, "They're decent places. I'm not gonna lie – we've got the nice one. But the one down on the end's the one you'll probably want. That was Artho's place when his parents were here."

Corbyn summarizes, "Four days on and you're giving me an apartment. Is that the offer?"

"I want to stress," the older Arthok says, "You will be the primary contact for the company. Even on days off, you will take calls and deal with problems."

"It'll be a lifestyle," Corbyn jokes. "Does this come with benefits? Paid vacation?"

"Yes, to both," Junior says. "Two weeks paid vacation to start. If you last five years, we'll start adding days. But full benefits – yes."

"Fifteen, to start," Corbyn counters, and the old man and Elwhinnie begin laughing.

She says, "I told you."

He agrees, "You did."

The younger Arthok says, "My wife said you'd be the perfect fit. She called you tenacious."

"And kind," she says.

Her husband says, "If fifteen days is what it takes to bring you on, then consider it done."

"I get my guys?"

"One," the old man says, "Until you're transitioned off production. Then, we'll bring another on."

"I get to bring them on," Corbyn says, and it's not a question. He says, "I need a guy – I get 'em."

Arthok Junior says, "Six. If you think you need more, that needs to be approved by us. But up to six – you fill as needed. I think we agree – we would like to formally offer you the position."

"Agreed," his wife says.

"Yes." The old man smiles, and says, "I'm glad we could bring on one of ours. It will still feel like family."

Corbyn says, "I'm in. I mean – there's more money, correct?"

Junior says, "Of course."

His father steps in and says, "I am inviting you to join us for dinner, this Friday. We will modify the contract to reflect the changes we discussed, and we'll go over the details while we eat."

"I – can," Corbyn says, "But there are two things: I might have my daughter on Friday, and also, I currently live in a tent out in the forest. Any chance I could move into that apartment – soon?"

Junior laughs, and asks, "The forest?"

"Corbyn," Elwhinnie says, and like the others, she's laughing. She says, "You lead quite a life. And of course – you're daughter is aways welcome."

"Until Friday," Senior says. He rises, extends a hand, and says, "Welcome aboard."

It is the second time in seconds that Corbyn has bit his tongue. Firstly, so as not to mention certain aspects of his life, and again as the thought crossed through his head, he already was aboard. But he only says, "Thank you."

There is a feeling of elation as he bounds down the stairs, but he's disappointed to find that processing's done, and all have left. He follows, through the swinging doors into the store. He's whistling as he exits but stops as the front door's opened. As he pulls the door, he finds that Wyl is standing just beyond.

He greets him with, "Ah – fuck." Corbyn says, "You sure know how to ruin everything."

"Corbs, man," Wyl starts, but he's told, "If I saw you an hour ago I'd have punched your face in. Get lost before I get pissed again."

"Give me five," Wyl pleads: "I'm begging you, Cor – Corbyn. Just give me five minutes."

"Can you tell me why the fuck she did it?"

Wyl answers, "Yes."

"You'll tell me?"

"If you give me five," Wyl agrees. "You know I hate being in the middle of that conversation, but I'll tell you – everything – she said. Promise Corbs: I promise."

"Why do you even fucking care?"

"Why do I care? About us? 'Cause you're the best friend I ever had. I need you, Corbal – Corbyn: I'm sorry."

He's dubiously asked, "Need me for what? I spent the last decade leaching off you. What the fuck do you need from me?"

"Corbyn," he says: "Everything. You're the only reason I ever push back and argue I should keep doing what I'm doing. If it wasn't for you, I'd be knocking on doors selling bogus life insurance policies."

"Nice. I get what you're doing."

"I need you back."

"Bull," Corbyn says, "Shit. You want me to sign whatever Plinio's throwing at me. Not gonna happen."

He moves to leave. He reaches the bike, and Wyl continues, "I never would have shown anyone my work if it wasn't for you. I never would have thought it was something I could pursue. I never would have opened the gallery. It was only because you kept telling me I was doing something I should share that I did any of that. Because you kept telling me my work was good. You bragged about it to our classmates. You know, I've got Corsh telling me we've got to do something different, and it's only 'cause sometimes, I hear that in my head I argue back. You're why I applied for the job in Portland. If I didn't hear you, I would've folded while I was filling out the application. Just give me five, Corbs. Let me try to explain why I didn't say anything."

"You knew she was gonna do this?"

"No." Wyl answers emphatically, "We found out the day it happened. She called Corsh – hysterical."

"And, you know why she did it?"

"Fuck, Corbs: I'm not gonna pretend it makes any sense, but yes."

There's a breaking: The shell is collapsing, and it's a dangerous moment. However, there are voices in Corbyn's head, as well, and he shares, "Everyone tells me I gotta talk to you. Awrol says talk to you. Chel said talk to you. My kid says talk to you. I still wanna punch you in the face, but I also – really – gotta get an understanding why she did this. Tell me why and we can go get a drink at Billy's."

"I need five, and then I'll tell you."

"Fuck you, ya Wylting willow. Why the fuck would Corsh want you to walk from the gallery? You got a house, you got a wall in Portland: Everybody knows Wyllem. You got some sort of habit I don't know about?

"Corbolla: You've got no idea. I get that commission in Portland, and it sounds like a windfall. But I've gotta supply materials. I've gotta pay for travel – room and board. And, you know how I get on projects. By the time I walk away, it's about twenty-grand."

"Oh," says Corbyn: "Twenty K for a few months of work – terrible. Can't imagine how tough that is."

"One commission, Corblivious. I might get another one in three years. In the meantime, I might sell one thing at the gallery in a month, or I might sell twenty. When Corshae's trying to pay the bills and it's one a month for half the year, it get's tough telling her she's wrong."

"She's wrong," Corbyn says. "I'm not an art guy, or sculpture guy, but you're better than ninety-nine point nine percent of people out there. People are gettin' that. You'll probably be a billionaire in another year."

"Corbal," he says," You make my point. Please – I'm begging you: Give me five."

"Are you gonna tell me she didn't try to kill me? I explained it to my daughter, and I can do that for you, but it's the last thing I'm gonna say to you."

There's a moment of quiet, before Wyl replies, "I can only tell you what I hear. I tried to balance the conversation over the last ten years, and I thought I did a decent job. That's where I was when Anika called, that morning."

"You're gonna tell me why?"

"I'll tell you. But I want you to understand where I was: That was never against you."

"Alright." Corbyn agrees, "I'll give you five. But you better tell me why the fuck she did it. And you need to tell me now if she had a reason, or if it was one of the stupid ideas she gets in her head."

"Corbynastra: I'm melting. I've been dying. I've been so – fucked up. Thank you. I didn't understand how bad shit was, and it's the last one. It's completely fucked up, but I've got to talk to you before I get to that. Will you let me do that?"

"Fine. Wylshire. But I wanna let you know, when I found out you knew, it was like when I thought A-K didn't want to talk to me. You fuckin' stabbed me in the heart."

He says, "Corbs: I am walking a line. I'm trying to remain married, and I'm trying to take care of the best friend I ever had. I'm not trying to make excuses; I just want you to understand where I was."

“You gonna let Corsh know she’ll need to get you, or you gonna crash here? ‘Cause I think we’re gonna kill some alcohol.”

“Come on,” Wyl says. “I’ll drive us up to Billy’s.”

21

"It wasn't even six, and the phone starts ringing. Corsh is, like, it's freakin' Anika, and she knows it's something, 'cause it's early. So, I took the bullet. I took the phone and I was gonna tell her Corsh is in the shower. But I never got around to that because she's absolutely hysterical. She crying, and screaming things I couldn't understand. I told Corsh right away it was bad. So, she took the phone.

"At that point I was already shaking, 'cause I'm thinking it's the worst with AnnaKay. So I left to make coffee, thinking we're gonna be on the road and it's gonna be a day.

"Here's what I want you to understand, man: I hear things all the time from Anika, and sometimes through my wife. I also hear you say things, and I don't always know where it comes from. I know you were dealing with a lot of frustration, and I know a lot of things Anika did pissed you off."

"Rightfully," Corbyn says. "The woman's a psycho."

"Alright. But here's the thing: Corshae hears the things she's saying, and then she hears you admit it's at least as bad as what she claimed, and I can't tell her Anika doesn't have anything to be upset about. And that's been the case since you started seeing each other. So, the way I dealt with it, to keep my wife happy, to keep you level, I try to point out whatever it is I think's the crux behind whatever. That usually gets you pissed off. Corshae just rolls her eyes. But I felt like it kind of balanced the conversation. What I didn't do, is tell you what Anika's saying, and I don't share the things you say with my wife. That way we're not having conversations we don't need to have."

"The conversation I wasn't having, Wylgrettable, was the one with my daughter. Because that nutbar woman was pretending to be my kid."

"Corbs: You just told me that. I had no idea what was happening. All I heard is what Anika was saying, and what you were saying. That's why we kept telling you to keep trying. 'Cause she'd been having a lot of trouble with AnnaKay, and she's complaining you checked out completely.

"And, again, she's saying things that kind of align with what we see: The running, the biking, the gym, and then – the thing. And, you know: Avoiding us. Any time I'd tell Corsh you're trying, she'd ask, when's the last time I saw you. And it'd be days, or a week."

"I was living in your fucking shed, man. You got a family, you got a life: I was trying to keep out of your hair."

"You don't need to, Corbo. We want you to be part of our life."

"You got two minutes left."

"Come on, Corbs: You interrupted and distracted me. What I was trying to get around to, is I'd been dealing with this for more than a decade. Anika says something, Corshae gets upset, and I've gotta put the fires out – it was just always something. And it wasn't only Anika. I had to constantly fucking work on you.

"Thanks."

"Everything just went to shit, man, and I watched this unflappable guy fall apart. That guy that pulled me out of the darkest worlds was wallowing in them. You had me scared, Corbs. There were times I was really scared you were gonna do something."

"Well, Wyl: Last time we talked I was gonna kill you. But then, I thought the ex should be the first one on that list. But you're both on it. Corshae gets a pass for now – depending how deep she's in."

"No one's in on anything. Both of you are friends that both of us care about. We tried to keep conversation as civil as possible. But then, this thing you do."

"The Consortium."

"Yeah – that. That sent her over. Anika completely lost her shit when she heard about it."

"Yeah? That's fantastic. That really cheers me up, Wylopopulis. Tell me more."

"I can tell you I thought you went Corlooney. I didn't even think the guy was real. Remember that day we were out there on the rock?"

"I remember."

"Corsh convinced me we needed to stage an intervention. They'd decided you'd completely lost it – like, having delusions. I suggested we try to meet the guy. And then, your wizard walks out of the ocean."

"I think that's five."

"You keep distracting me."

"Not my problem, Wylbur. I gave you five and all I've heard is what a pain in the ass I was to deal with. Tell your wife she won't have to deal with me anymore."

"Corbyn: Fucking listen to me. I did not say you were a pain in the ass. I said there were challenges balancing the conversation. And, if you'd paid attention you would have understood, that's why I try to filter what either one of you tell me. And that's where I was coming from that morning.

"By the time I got back in the room, Corshae had got Anika calmed down and she tells me – it's okay. I made sure it wasn't AnnaKay, and that everyone was okay, and then, I walked away. I figured – just another Anika freakout: They happen.

"So, I figured everything's fine. I shower, I dress, I make breakfast for the kids, and then, I realized everything wasn't fine. Corsh put on a show, but I could tell something was going on.

"After we eat and clean up, she tells me we need to take a walk without the kids, and I freaked out. She tried to tell me everything's fine, but it's you, and I was thinking you jumped off a fucking bridge, man. You'd been so despondent, and I was thinking the worst.

"She tells me, you're in the hospital, but you're going to be fine, and I'm still thinking you did it to yourself. But she gets me to go on the walk, and that's when I hear what happened.

"You understand, that was the first we heard about it, and what we heard came from Anika."

"Right, Wylmission: I'd been chucked in a river and was lying in a hospital."

"I know."

"Paid for by the Consortium, by the way. Something else I can thank you for: Making them think they were responsible. I felt like such an asshole."

"My point is, Corbstructor, we have more than a decade of dealing with shit between you two, so it sounded like more of the same. My point is, what we heard came from Anika. And what she told us, was she was pissed you were spending time and money with this thing. Prancing around the beach in costumes. Sword fighting – submarines. She told us, she was mad you were wasting your time with them, instead of making an effort with your daughter."

"When am I supposed to get interested?"

"She claimed she asked a guy in the consortium to scare you, so you'd have second thoughts about joining."

"See, this is where it's bullshit: The guy wasn't a member of the Consortium – he works for Plinio."

"Corbyn: Shut the fuck up. I didn't say that's what I believe – right now. I'm telling you, that's what she told us. She said you got together for a sword fight in the middle of the night, and the guy tried to scare you. But she said you fought back. She claimed you broke multiple ribs and shattered the guy's orbital. She told us the guy was fighting for his life and you tripped going after him. She told us you lost your footing and went in the water."

"And, you bought every word of it."

"If you weren't being a dickhead you'd have heard I don't believe anything either one of you say about each other. I'm just telling you what she said. What she told us was the guy was supposed to injure your leg, or your foot. Because if there's one thing that's gonna piss you off, it's gonna be something that interferes with running."

"Glad I'm a simple."

"I'm telling you where I was."

"When do you get to where you didn't tell me?"

"I'm trying. I'm telling you, there's been a history we've been dealing with – with both of you. I knew there was gonna be more, but all we had was what Anika told us. And like I told you, when I answered the phone, she was – extremely – upset. Corsh said she was devastated something happened to you. She claimed she just wanted the guy – who we were told was part of the thing – he was supposed to stomp your foot, or smash your shin with his sword. You supposedly blew up and went after him, and then tripped, and went in the water. She was afraid it would get back to AnnaKay, so Corsh asked me not to say anything until we got more information."

"There's not enough alcohol…"

"I get it – Corbo: I understand that's not what happened. They clearly didn't realize the events were recorded. But that's what we were told, and I agreed not to say anything because she was already struggling with your daughter. We already have to avoid crossing paths with you when we're with Anika. The last thing I wanted was you going off on her again."

"Again, it's more deserved, the more I know."

"Yes, Corbyn. Anika has done some things that are inexcusable. You've also been an incredible dick to her at times. And the person that gets caught in the middle of that's your daughter."

"Uh-uh."

"Yes."

"No. You listen to me, Wyllem: I sacrificed my dignity, and nearly my relationship with my daughter – trying to defend her. When A-K asked me to prove I paid child support, I didn't do it. Because I knew they were having difficulties, and I didn't want her to go back and call her mom a liar. I told AnnaKay, I was not gonna pile on her mom, because I didn't want that to be the basis of our relationship. So, no, Wylpo: That wave was coming from one direction only."

"The mall."

"Deserved it. And she knew it then."

"Your daughter was right there, Corbyn."

"Maybe you should ask my daughter what she thinks."

"What does she think?"

"She tells me, Wyl, that she never believed what her mother told her about me. She told me, that she knew I loved her. She said, when I lost my shit – that proved it. No regrets, Wyllifucker."

"You're talking to her?"

"Now that I have, ya know – her actual number. Me and the kid are in a really good place. We're working through this together."

"Is it alright if we reach out to her? The girls, especially?"

"I've been blunt," Corbyn shares: "Chel always says, speak to truth. Tim always says, speak to truth, and that's what I've done. So, she's aware of exactly what happened. Call her if you want."

"I didn't set out to not tell you. It just kept getting worse. And at a point, I didn't know how I would."

"Maybe, hey – just a little heads up: Your ex hired a guy to take you out."

"That's what I'm trying to explain to you: We didn't know that. That's not what Anika told us. You – didn't know. By the time I saw the video, I already knew this wasn't gonna end well. But that's where I should've told you. Corsh was in my ear telling me I can't because of AnnaKay, but at that point I should've pushed back against that argument. I fucked that up and I've got no excuse. Maybe, everything just felt like shit by then."

"I've gotta tell you, Wylberness, I was hoping for something solid. Something that would make me say, ah: That makes sense. But I'm not finding this very compelling."

"I've been sick, man. For months. I've felt like shit, trying to figure out how to fix everything. When we found out that guy wasn't from the consortium, I knew there was a problem. I knew her story wasn't gonna hold. But I was still in the mind frame of protecting everyone."

"You missed one. So, why'd she do it?"

"Uh – Corb. It just kept getting worse. She said she hoped it would bring her and A-K closer. That if she saw you get hurt doing something stupid, maybe they could find something to agree on."

"Let me," Corbyn says – and flabbergasted: "She hired a guy to off me so she could commiserate with my daughter? Are you seriously telling me that's why she did it? I am done."

"Corbs – please."

"Wyl: That is fucking insane. The woman is batshit crazy. I'll see ya."

"Wait." He reaches out and pulls Corbyns arm – he turns, and there is anger:

"Take your hand – off of me."

"I'm sorry, Corbyn. I don't have a good reason for not saying something. I started out believing it was no big deal, and it just kept piling. It got to a point I was afraid how you'd react. If you found out that I knew. I didn't accept that she might have actually wanted to hurt you until recently. Corshae still refuses to believe it. I am truly sorry – for everything. And, mostly for myself because I've lost my closest friend. Thanks for letting me talk, Corbs: I'm not asking you to forgive me – I just wanted you to have an explanation."

As he'd started, there was a look that was remembered: The quiet boy in the corner that slammed his notebook closed if anyone got too close. And then, he'd finally admitted why he hadn't spoken.

Corbyn shares, "I got a promotion today."

"We're talking?"

"Ya know – Wyediator: Sometimes I forget who you are."

"Are you leaving, or no?"

"No. I only had a single drink. I'm here to celebrate."

"What – happened?"

"I saw you," Corbyn says. "I remembered who I'm talking to. You kept telling me to listen and I wasn't. 'Cause I'm still fuckin' pissed. But that's because of Anika. She screwed up everything. You were just doing what you always do – trying to fix things for all the screw ups. I understand it: You were afraid to tell me."

"Corbs, man, I was so afraid of what you might do. It wasn't even about me and you. I was really afraid you might do something you'd regret."

"Still an option, Wyllis. But probably not because my kid doesn't want her dead. Or in jail, unfortunately."

"What are you going to do?"

"Work with AnnaKay. Talk with Randy. Figure it out. I've gotta have something. After the phones, after the bullshit the last ten years."

Wyl vows, "I'm pro-Corbyn, after this. I'll do whatever you need me to do."

"Don't do that, Wyltastic: Be yourself. If the rest of us were like you, the world'd be perfect."

"Come home, Corbal. We all miss you. The girls even offered to give up a room for you. Please accept that we want you there."

"Can't, Wylbeing."

"You can."

"Can't – Wyl. I'm the new operations manager at the plant."

"What? The… Oper? Manager? What's that mean?"

"It means, the old man's coasting on what he built and Junior's looking to live the good life. So, they're moving me in to oversee operations."

"That's," Wyl says, and there's a pause. He thinks carefully, and decides on, "A lot."

"I know. It's gonna be a headache. I already know it's gonna drive me nuts. But I've gotta meet boats whenever they arrive, so I get an apartment on the second floor. It's gonna wear me like the smell of fish guts, but this is the job I was made for."

"You're stoked, aren't you?"

"I am, man. I am fuckin' stoked."

Wyl smiles – lips pinched: He nods. He says, "Good for you, Corborate manager, good for you. You deserve it. You're gonna blow it up."

"I am gonna blow it up. I can take care of my guys, and I got a chance to grow a decent business. I've had ideas forever how that could happen."

"It's funny – how you said you saw me. 'Cause all night, I've been thinking, that's the Corbs I knew. The guy with all the answers. The guy that lifted everybody up. I seen you, tonight, Corporator."

"It's been a good day."

Wyl says, "Let me ruin it."

"Why?"

"Cause there's something else I've gotta tell you."

Corbyn asks, "How bad?"

"Looks bad. Sounds bad. It was never a factor in my decisions."

"Clean slate: Speak to truth."

"Plinio," Wyl confesses, "Offered to endow the gallery. That was part of the conversation with Corsh. Part of, if I want to keep doing this, that gets us off the ledge. I always hated it, but she's not wrong. That would've taken care of my family."

"Drinks, Wylbonkulus. We need another drink. Your soul was splitting and there were no good options."

"I should've told you."

"That's done," Corbyn says: "Same as I said to A-K: We move forward. What's done is done, and all we can do is figure out how we get to tomorrow."

"I want you to tell me we're good."

Corbyn says, "Give me a name."

"Corblessed."

"Shitty. Very unfitting. But Corblessed gives Wylfuckerall his vindication."

"Corbs." There are tears in the man's eyes. He is looking for validation that the forgiveness he claimed he didn't want is being given. He has nothing more that he can offer, except an arm that reaches out.

Corbyn pulls him close and wraps his arms around him, and tells him, "I'm sorry you got stuck in the middle. I should've pulled you outta there a long time ago."

22

The vehicle pulls into the lot, and it's absurd that the driver's sixteen. But there's a conversation, and conflict, and an attempt to offer appeasement that's yet to be discussed, and so it brings a smile as Corbyn watches her carefully back the vehicle in.

She steps out, and forces a smile that becomes honest when Corbyn asks, "How much fun is it driving that on the Coastal?"

She's still smiling, but knows, "You hate it."

Corbyn says, "If you made Plinio pay for that, then I love it." She laughs, and it's pure, and free – shed of all the stress that weighed on everyone. She's asked, "You chose silver?"

"I like silver," she says. "I like how everything matches."

He agrees, "Looks good."

"Do you want a ride?"

Corbyn smiles at his daughter. He smiles because he knows AKRunner likely pushes the car to its limit. He tells her, "If you drive like you're alone: No pulling back – no pushing it. Just like it's a good day and you love driving."

"Okay. Are you going to the meet?"

"Your call, A-K."

"Do you want to?"

Corbyn says, "If you want to, then I want to."

She says, "I'll go if you want."

He asks, "What do you want to do?"

"I want to go," she says. She shares, "I want to show you something. Can I show you?"

"Of course. What've you got?"

"Hold on," she says. She returns to the car and pops the trunk. She retrieves a bundle of clothing, and Corbyn asks, "Doing laundry?"

She is breathless with enthusiasm, as she shares, "I made these." She fumbles with the pieces but hangs pants enough to offer an impression. Apologetically, she says, "They're simple, but we can do more with them later. This is yours."

She offers over gray pants, a long, blue tunic, two sleeves, and, "A purse?"

"You tie it around your waist. It's like a fanny pack, but you wear it on your hip."

"You made this?"

"Yeah. It's nothing, really. I just thought it would be fun if we had uniforms, too."

"We match," Corbyn says, and he's fighting tears. He says, "It's amazing," and truly means it. He holds his daughter and hugs her tight, and tells her, "Thank you. This is amazing – you're amazing."

She asks, "You like it?"

"I love it. I love it."

"Do you want to try it on?"

"Yeah. Absolutely. Come on. Let's get dressed and go see Wyllem. He'll get a kick outta this."

Corbyn turns and begins walking towards the store, and his daughter asks, "Why are you going to work?"

He says, "It's where I live."

She asks, "You live at the fish store?"

"Above it," he says, and explains, "That's where my apartment is."

"Oh," she says. She says, "I thought you were going to see Wyllem 'cause you're back there."

"You know," he jokes. He pulls the door, and says, "After you." As she enters, he says, "I thought it was time to get my own place."

She asks, "Are you still mad at him?"

"I'm not. Wyl is Wyl. He was trying to make everyone happy and failed very badly. Did you guys go to the unveiling?"

"No," she says. She follows her father through the swinging doors and up the stairs. She shares, "Everyone's weird."

Corbyn asks, "Am I?"

"Will you talk about mom?"

"If weird means no, than yes I am." They pass through the small waiting room into the hallway. At the end, Corbyn unlocks a door, and instructs, "Push it closed behind you." There is a door on either side, and one down further to the right. Corbyn heads to that, and says, "Welcome to the new digs."

He holds the door as she enters, and it is not remarkable. It is a very simple space, entered through a short hall that passes a bathroom. The wall on the right is a wall of louvered closets, and the living area is as furnished as it can be by just a sofa, a chair, and a table.

There is just a single window that lets light in further down the wall, and as AnnaKay walks through she finds a small, u-shaped kitchen tucked into the recess at the back. There are two stools at the counter, and through the back – two doors.

Her father says, "View's better from the bedrooms. I took the one on the left – a little bigger. You can call the other one yours."

She walks through the kitchen and opens the door to the right. She takes one step in, and Corbyn says, "You can see the bay, anyway. There's crap on the dock, but – ya know – that comes and goes."

She's not impressed, and makes the observation, "It's pink."

"Yeah." Corbyn laughs because he knows she hates it. He says, "This was the owner's son's. They had a little girl – their little princess."

A-K says, "I'm not a princess."

"You've got a heck of a chariot."

Her head snaps around, and under angry glare, says, "No."

It's a flash of anger and reaction that's very familiar. It shows a hint of why there's discord in her other home – conflict that was present prior to events unfolding that gave a reason. Yet, there was the car:

"It is a – very – nice car, AnnaKay. I can make that observation. How'd you manage to finagle it?"

She walks in the room, to take in the view, and says, "Don't ask."

The silent sound of eyeballs rolling is deafening, and Corbyn suggests, "How about I agree to talk about your mom, if you agree to tell me how you got that car."

"Ugh," she groans: "It's so stupid." It is a point of irritation, and unpleasant to think about, however, "You promise you'll talk?"

"Promise."

Eyes roll, but she shares, "He said he'd buy me any car I want if I call him dad. I didn't think he'd really buy it."

"Ah," says Corbyn."

"It's so gross. Anytime I say anything to him, mom's, like, call him dad. He always says, call me dad, like an idiot. He's not my dad. He's gross."

"Yeah. That's always been my impression: Greasy sleezeball that gives the cologne industry a bad name."

She stifles a laugh, but shakes her head as she remembers, "You promised."

"You made it easy. First thing that goes in the agreement, is you don't have to call him dad and you're keepin' the car. How's that sound?"

"Okay." She says, "I wanted to talk about mom going to jail."

"I would also love to talk about your mom going to jail, but I know that' isn't what you mean. So, what're your thoughts?"

"They're already going to court."

"It's an arraignment," Corbyn says. "They'll read 'em the charges, they'll plead not guilty, pay their bail, and walk away. No one's going to jail."

But there's worry in her voice – she says, "She could."

"She won't," Corbyn assures her. "Not after the arraignment. And I'm sure Plinio's got his lawyers on it."

But AnnaKay explains, "They're worried she might go to jail."

"Yeah," Corbyn says, "I know. Can I let her think that for a while?"

"Why? What do you mean?"

"I talked to Randy."

She asks, "He can help?"

"He said, the only way he can see her getting out of it is I eat shit."

A-K asks cautiously, "What does that mean?"

"It means," he explains, "I go along with her little story and say I tripped. If you watch the video, it looks like I might catch my foot on something. So, I get to eat shit and your mother walks away."

She asks, "You'll do that?"

"Will I do that," Corbyn ponders. He shares, "I've been asking myself that question. And what I can tell you, A-K, is I really, really, really don't want to."

She asks, "Will you?"

He asks her back, "Is that what you want?" He watches as a hint of motion becomes a nod. As, more certainly, she affirms it is. He says, "I can't just let that be it. I can't let her just walk away with nothing. Not after the phones – not after all the crap the last ten years. I've gotta have something, so, if you've got ideas, let 'em go."

She suggests, "What about counseling?"

He laughs, and questions, "Counseling? You want your mom to see a shrink? I mean, she probably needs it."

"We all could," AnnaKay suggests. "We could go together."

There's more laughter, and it's bitter, and Corbyn says, "I'm not going to a shrink." He watches the wash of darkness, and anger, and disappointment cross his daughter's face, and realizes it wasn't a spontaneous, nor random solution: There's thought behind it. There's experience behind it, but he says, "I don't need a fucking shrink. I know my head, and I know where I gotta do better. I'm working on it, and no shrink's gettin' me there faster."

She tries to throw a bone, and suggests, "We could make that part of the agreement. The judge makes it that she has to."

"You know: I understand," he says. Corbyn forces the fire down, and attempts to be understanding. He tries to be sympathetic, by saying, "That might be helpful," but a flame licks up, and there is fierce anger barely muted, that brings, "And, I get nothing."

Annakay suggests, "They could let you know how it's going. Like, give you updates."

Fires rage, but Corbyn says, "I eat shit, like always."

"We could try," AnnaKay suggests, and he asks, "This is what you want?"

She answers, "Yes."

He says, "I eat shit for one person only, and that's for you, kid. We make the terms, and she agrees, and – that's it. There's no negotiation."

She says, "Okay."

"You're part of it," Corbyn makes a point to say: "We – make the terms: You and me. But I'm giving your mom a – huge – fucking pass. You understand how ridiculous this is I'd consider it? She doesn't take what we give her, there's nothing else."

AnnaKay says, "Okay."

"I need you to understand, she accepts what we offer, or she goes to trial. That's it: Take our deal, or she's probably going to jail. I need you to understand that."

AnnaKay says, "I do. I know you don't want to – to let her..." She is falling apart, and it's because she knows she's asking for something unreasonable: More unreasonable than a ridiculously expensive car. She falls into her father's arms, and there's no way to stop the tears that follow. She says, knowing it will not be well received, "I don't think she wanted him to really hurt you."

"A-K," he says, and he lets her go to emphasize, "She hired the guy to assault me. Do you understand that?"

The tears fall harder, and she is miserable, as she says, "Yes." She says, "I know." She admits, "I just don't want her to go to jail."

Corbyn shares, "A friend of mine always tells me, speak to truth. And the truth is, your mother hired someone to assault me. If you want to work towards a solution where your mother doesn't go to jail, you need to start with accepting – truth: What happened is what she wanted."

"Okay." AnnaKay says, "Okay. But I don't think she really thought it would happen. I think, like, they were just talking. Like, what if they could."

Corbyn says, "A-K." He says, "The man was paid." He states, "The man did what he was paid to do. You want me to eat shit, you need to accept that."

She says, "I do," and he pulls her close, because he understands, "You love your mom. All the crazy shit she does – you still love her."

"Yes," she says, and she pulls against him, feeling her world imploding. She says, "She does what we want, or she goes to trial. But that would be her fault."

"We'll talk to Randy." Corbyn says, "Tell him what you want, and that's what we offer. Whatever you need me to do – I'll do whatever."

"Okay." She says, "Sorry."

"Nope." Corbyn says, "Don't be sorry. I'm doing this for you. That's what I want to do, so, you can't be sorry."

"Can I say thanks?"

"Wait 'til we see what happens. But he said with, ya know, their money – their attorneys – that'll probably keep her out."

"Okay. Do you wanna try the uniform?"

"Yeah, A-K. Let's see how we look in these."

She smiles, and gloats, "I look good."

He laughs, and says, "I bet you do. Let's see if I can match ya."

He's still laughing quietly as he pulls the pants on – thin but rough fabric with elasticity. He's beginning to recognize traits that are very familiar, traits that are certainly irritants to her mother. But they're also traits Corbyn knows aren't always beneficial.

He pulls the tunic on and it drapes down to his knees, but as the purse is tied around his waist, the costume feels more comfortable. He examines the tubes and wonders what they're for, but considering their size, he slides them over his forearms.

He walks out to find his daughter's door still closed, and calls, "We're gonna have to get some boots. Something different than running shoes."

She calls, "Do you like it?"

He says, "It's perfect. Perfect, A-K. You nailed it."

She emerges in the same uniform, except she does wear boots, and the first word is a disappointed, "Dad."

"Shins," he observes. The tubes are pulled over her shins.

She says, "That's what the other guys do. You didn't see?"

"No. Apparently I missed that."

She ignores him and walks across the room to the swords that have seen better days. She explains, "We can do something different if you don't like it, but I saw people doing this." She demonstrates by pushing the sword through the buckle at the tie, and says, "I think it works okay."

"You wanna drive?"

She says, "I'm not riding."

"I could call someone. Or, I could drive, if you don't want to."

She says, "I'll drive. You like it though?"

"Yeah, A-K. This is great. I mean, it's spotless but that won't last long."

"I just wanted to make something I could do fast. We can do something else later, but I wanted to get it done. So, it's simple."

"Hey – I'm telling you: It's perfect. It doesn't have all the layers Awrol has, but it's in the same – we fit together. You nailed it."

"But I can do more when you, ya know – go out on your own. When you have your own team."

There's clear disappointment as she's answered, "I'm not gonna have my own team."

"Why not?" She asks, "Don't you want to? Like, not have a king?"

"He's my king," Corbyn says.

She says, "We could make a team," and he replies, "I'm working with Awrol. I'm not doing this on my own. That's my guy."

She asks, "'Cause he saved you?"

He answers, "No. He was my guy before that. I'm working with him – you don't have to."

She says, "I'm working with you. I just thought, maybe we could do our own thing."

"Yes," he says: "We can do our own thing – but not in the Consortium. I'm part of Awrol's team. You don't have to be."

"Fine." She rolls her eyes, and it's clearly because she had ideas. She clearly was envisioning a father-daughter duo, but the loyalty that was pledged with mockery has become actual. And it isn't only because the big man pulled him from the river.

Her father says, "Let's roll down to Wyl's and see what's going on."

She says, "And you'll talk to Randy."

He pauses at the door. He says, "Yeah." There is a thought that crosses his mind, but he holds it, and only says, "I don't know if that'll happen today, but I'll talk to him. I said I would."

But then, she presses, "Before the arraignment," and the thought spills loose:

"Did your – mom – ask you to talk to me?" The answer's given away by the way her body stiffens; by the eyes that widen, but she stays silent. Corbyn says, "I'm asking for the truth, A-K. Did she?"

She is shaking her head, ands says again, "I don't want her to go to jail."

"You said that – I heard you. That's not what I asked. Did she tell you to talk to me?"

She nods, and she is becoming upset. Quietly, she answers, "Yes."

Corbyn is also quiet, and responds, "Okay." He says, "Let's get going. I'll try to talk to him. But these are supposed to be a break from reality, so I can't guarantee."

She blurts, "I'm not taking her side."

"It's okay, A-K. I understand."

"I don't wanna leave my team," she says. "I don't wanna be this far from my friends."

"I get it," he starts, but she says again, "I don't want her in jail."

Corbyn says, "Hey: I hear you. I want your life disrupted as little as we can."

"I hate the things she does," AnnaKay shares: "I know this is worse, but she does this kind of thing all the time."

With concern, she's asked, "How – so?"

"You know, doing something, or saying something and then saying it's a joke when someone gets mad. She does it all the time."

"What about Plinio?"

"What? Like does he do it? 'Cause, no, but he thinks it's funny."

Corbyn moves them forward, and motions, "Let's go. I wanna talk more, later. But I'm really in the mood for stabbing."

She says, "Me too."

The humor shared between them gives both momentary hope they'll move on, but neither knows where that will go, beyond an attempt by Corbyn, as he takes a seat in his daughter's vehicle:

"Nice car."

She says, "Yeah," and it lacks enthusiasm, because she knows her father sees it as exorbitant.

Thought towards what else to say bring nothing because she feels underwater – her father's own are stifled by the anger and resentment he doesn't want to share.

They are nearly to their destination when AnnaKay finally succumbs to the pressure of the conversation weighing over them, and asks, "Are you mad?"

"I'm not – mad: At you. I'm glad you told me. I am – I am mad, A-K. I'm pissed. I am really pissed. And it's not that, or one thing – it a fricken thousand things. I'm really pissed, and I'm trying – really – hard not to let that out around you."

"Well, I am too," she says. "I'm pissed at her, too. And stupid Plinio. So, like, you don't have to pretend you're not."

"I'm not gonna pretend I'm not."

"It's not like she came and asked me to. You know: They're always talking. About it's your fault, or they're gonna blame the guy. She said something about paying you off. You know how she gets. She gets an idea and then she can't let it go."

"And here we are," Corbyn says, and he laughs, because, "Ya know? That was something I really liked about your mom."

She says, "What," with disbelief, but he confirms:

"She gets ahold of something and she makes it happen. I think that was our connection: I'm chasing times – she's chasing ends. That's where we connected."

The look returned shows that doesn't sit well, and she questions, "Did you think she'd want to kill you?"

He laughs, because, "Yeah. There were a lot of times she probably wanted to kill me." He points ahead, and says, "Pull in the driveway. You can just park it there."

She says, "Okay," but wonders, "So, why did she want to this time?"

It dawns on Corbyn, "No one told you?"

She says, "No," and slows the vehicle to turn off the highway onto the familiar property.

He says, "Listen – A-K: I need you to understand something."

She says, "Okay."

"Okay," he echoes, and tells her, "I can't guarantee anything keeps your mom out of prison. A lot of that's out of my hands."

"Why?" She asks, and it's an accusation.

He says, "'Cause there were a couple months I thought some random guy tried to kill me. We had to convince people it wasn't part of what we do. Now I have to convince them it's a prank: They're gonna question it."

"Okay," she says, but she's not okay.

Corbyn tells her, "It never crossed my mind your mom had anything to do with it. If I'd known it was her, I'd – maybe: Ya know," he says, and he laughs bitterly as he turns to his daughter. He says, "I'd have lost it – I'd have gone off. Ya know? It's what I do."

She says, "You know why she did it."

"I know," he says, and asks, "You want me to tell you."

She says, "Tell me."

"Okay." He sighs and speaks to truth, with zero faith it's the right move. He tells her, "You mom thought if something happened to me – if it upset you – she could move in and be there for you. She thought it would bring you closer together – help the relationship."

A-K cries, "What," and she is beside herself: "There's no way. There's no way that's why she'd do it. Who told you that?"

He answers, "Wyl."

"Wyl? Wyl told you that? I'm asking him."

She is out the door, and there is anger. The door slams closed behind her and she is up the walk before Corbyn can unloose his belt. He moves quickly, but she is already in the home, and she is yelling.

She is her father's child as she stands in the kitchen of another's home, seeing red and demanding answers. She is demanding confirmation, and those receiving her are reeling: Two girls, years younger, watch with wide eyes and concern, while their mother watches Corbyn enter – she is horrified. The roiling mess she has fought to beat back from her doorstep is standing in the family's home and spreading it across her children, while her husband looks helplessly to the man that entered.

Corbyn says, "Ya know: Speak to truth. That's the road I decided to follow."

"Well," AnnaKay demands. "Is it true?"

"I mean," Wyl says. He looks to his wife, and she stuns everyone by saying, "Yes. That's what your mother told us. But she also said," and she stresses – said to Corbyn, "It wasn't supposed to go that far."

"That's just great." Anger spills over, but it dies as it hits the floor. AnnaKay says what resonates with everyone, "It's just like what she always does. She does something dumb, and when someone gets pissed off, she says it's a joke. It's the same thing she always does."

Corbyn tries to lighten the moment, and jests, "Usually – less attempted murder."

"Now she'll blame me." And she recognizes, "She'll say it's 'cause the Consortium. That's what she's gonna say."

Across the room, two girls are watching, and Corbyn calls, "You girls – all good?"

"Okay," is said very dubiously for a nine year old, and her sister tries to elevate the conversation by pointing across the room, and saying, "Unca-C." But the joy is absent.

Wyl explains, "We've been trying to keep most of this out of their ears.

"It's fine," his wife says: "They've already heard most of it."

Defiantly, AnnaKay says, "I like what we do. I am not stopping."

Wyl asks, of the costumes, "Part of the thing?"

"Meet in no-man's-land, Wylbo: You're welcome to be a victim."

He turns to his daughters, and asks, "Wanna check out a sword fight on the beach?"

"Yeah," is filled with the exuberance that was missing, and Lia echoes, "Yeah."

Corbyn extends the offer, and invites, "Corshae?"

She continues to surprise everyone, and says, "Yeah. I could use a sword fight."

23

The door's opened, and Wyl says, "Come on, Corbs." There is exhaustion in his voice. He has driven five plus hours to bring a friend to a meeting he likely would avoid if he wasn't forced. He is tired of being an intermediary. He is tired of the never-ending conversation that has only gotten exponentially worse after the trial. He motions with an arm to emphasize, "Let's go."

He's told, "I really resent this."

"I know."

It's said again, to emphasize, "I – really – resent this."

"I got it," Wyl says, and he is at his breaking point. He says, "I've heard it for the last five fuckin' hours. Get out of my damn car."

Corbyn turns to view his longtime friend, and he is filled with so much anger. There is hatred in his heart, and he says, "I really resent you. You and Corshae always pushing like I'm an incompetent idiot. Like I'd just blow my kid off. I really resent you buy everything she tells you."

"You wanna know what I resent," Wyl asks: "I resent you think we don't push back what she says. We pushed you to keep in touch 'cause we heard how bad things were getting with her mother. So, we told you to be there no matter what – for you. You are fucking welcome."

"And I'm sure dragging me up here," Corbyn says – and cynically, "Is for me. I'm sure she's got a plan to manipulate this shrink just like she does anything."

"Corbyn…"

"She made you bring me here for something."

"Corbyn," Wyl says, but he's told, "Fuck off."

"Listen, man." Wyl says, "Your daughter called me directly and begged me to have you here. I did this for AnnaKay. She was in tears. Now get – the fuck – out of my car."

"A-K?"

"Yes. Your daughter. She said don't tell you, but I'm so sick of you and Anika I'm ready to move to another country."

The mind starts calculating: When AnnaKay told him Anika had asked her to work on him, he'd blown it off. He'd considered it an evolution of conversation, and ideas, and desperation, but it wasn't. It was an intentional ploy to gain a written statement to support her claims.

The offer given, insisted on family counseling. It had insisted on individual counseling for the mother, and it was proposed that evaluation and progress should be reported to family services for monitoring. It proposed that regular updates would be given to the court, and to Corbyn. In exchange, Corbyn would agree that the intent was not murder. All of this was agreed upon.

All of that was used in court as part of a campaign to demonstrate that Corbyn had a malignant plan to use a cosplay event to stage the appearance of attempted murder. The charges of abuse from a decade prior were resurrected and hyperbolically embellished, and witnesses that had never been met had been brought in to claim they were part of an elaborate plan to steal primary parental rights.

Nearly all of that had been dismissed, but the onslaught had been effective, and the most serious repercussion was that the issue was referred to family services with oversight by the court. The recommendation had been counselling for everyone, with a monthly congregation for all involved. With the bitterness and anger from yet more betrayal, the inaugural meeting was one that Corbyn did not plan to attend. It had taken extensive effort to move him to the parking lot of that location, and despite revelations shared, he remained planted in the car.

"Corbyn."

"Just go." Corbyn stands and moves to walk away, but Wyl steps in front of him – inches taller, but no physical match for a man that's spent his life in training for a match he'll never get to run.

Corbyn says, "Get – the fuck – out of my way."

He's told, "Dude: It's a court order." He's told again, "You don't have a choice."

"My choice is to walk away. I don't – give a fuck – anymore."

Anger rises, and the response is yelled, "It's your daughter. Did you forget I told you she's the one that called?"

Yelled back, is, "Did I forget to tell you: She's the one that convinced me to sign that agreement."

It's an admission: That there are thoughts she's been complicit. That her admission she'd been pressed should have been a warning. That the claims of discord, the claims of interest in the Consortium – in a relationship – were red herrings. Thoughts had fallen to the Mercedes and the possibility it was payoff for collusion.

Wyl says, "Presume it's not."

"If it is?" It's asked with the anger rearing. It's asked with the passion that pushed legs to find another gear. To ignore exhaustion, to ignore pain, and push to a higher level. It is the suicidal drive to move the body past resistance, for a time, a distance; a win.

Wyl says, "If it is, I'll punch 'em both in the face."

A hand's held forward, and Corbyn says, "You better make that a promise."

His hand's taken, and Wyl says, "Trust your instincts. You know what's true."

"I want your word."

He gets, "You got my word, Corbustible. But I think you know she's got nothing to do with it."

"Yeah," he says: Hours on the road is not a good way to approach a meeting that isn't wanted. It's a long time to sit and stew, to imagine scenarios that only feed the anger. It's a long time to imagine being stuck in a room with the person that has given true insight into the meaning of hatred.

"Corbyn." Wyl calls, but there's no reaction: He stares at the building with anger boiling. Wyl tries, "Corbs," and is at least able to turn his eyes. He says, "Tell me you think there's any possibility AnnaKay had anything to do with it."

He's told, "No," because there was already regret that passing mote of vitriol was allowed to slip. As it did, the thought of his daughter dressed in her uniform flashed in his head. Memories of conversations, and the emotion that had flowed were in his ear. It is enough to dampen the fire, and he extinguishes the thought: "I was being an asshole. She's got nothing to do with any of it."

"You're here for your kid," Wyl reminds him – knowing what wasn't said, was the child had also been manipulated. A point from which anger could explode, and Wyl hopes to cap it, by stressing, "Your daughter wanted you here. For whatever reason, it's important to her that you're here. So be here for your daughter, Corsplosion."

"You gonna drive me back, or do I need to find a ride?"

He's told, "It depends. Keep it about your daughter and you'll have a ride."

"You think it would be justifiable? I mean, would anyone blame me if I killed her?"

"Corbs…"

"I'm gonna imagine an axe embedded in her forehead."

"Corby," is said firmly: "That's not focusing on A-K."

Corbyn says, "I'm going," and begins to walk away.

Wyl moves to catch him: "I'll walk you in."

"Don't trust me, Wylicer?"

He's told, "No."

They enter directly into a seating area that is filled with toys and books geared towards young children. They move to the window at the back, and a woman greets them cheerfully:

"Good afternoon. Who do you have an appointment with today?"

Wyl says, "Corbyn's supposed to meet his family here."

"Oh, yes." She says, "Sign in here and I'll buzz you through. It's the first door on the left."

Corbyn watches as Wyl takes the pen, and says, "I feel like hell."

He's told, "Focus on AnnaKay."

He nods agreement, and offers, "Thanks," before moving to the door.

It is into an open space, where the woman they were speaking to sits at a desk. It is encircled by three walls that have two doors on each. The thought to continue though and escape through the back can't even be entertained, and so Corbyn turns, and lightly taps against the door.

It's pushed open, and one step in, the sickness that had begun to grip him is overwhelming. He stands just inside the room and watches Anika dismissively laugh, but she's unimportant. He turns eyes to his daughter, and she is clearly tense. She is evidently stressed and distressed, and any iota of doubt as to her involvement is forever erased from consideration.

"Welcome Corbyn," breaks him from the fog he's fallen in. It turns his attention to the woman at the right that is sitting astutely on an antique, leopard print chaise. She says, "Thank you for making the trip. I know it wasn't easy."

It's unclear whether she means the trip or being present, but Corbyn moves further in, suggesting, "I'll presume the empty one's for me."

There's no appreciation for sardonic humor, generally, but it's met with silence as the door is closed and he begins to pass his daughter. Their eyes meet, and he says, "It's good to see you, AnnaKay."

Her lips are pinched and she nods – she lifts her hand and offers a slight wave.

He asks, "How are you?"

She says, "Good."

He asks, "How was the meet," as he takes a seat, and she says the same. He asks, "Good?"

She quickly answers, "Yeah."

He says, "Okay. Will you tell me more about it later?"

He watches her glance over briefly, and she quickly nods before turning her attention back to the doctor:

"I'm Doctor Bundizer. It's nice to finally meet you, Corbyn. I know you aren't happy to be a part of this, so thank you for making the effort. It's important to your daughter."

"That's," he says, "Why I'm here."

"'Cause the court," Anika points out, "Made you."

Plinio laughs in the childish, and faux-haute manner that he's practiced, but it's quickly shut down:

The doctor states firmly, "We have discussed this." And to all, she says, "I'm going to repeat what I've said to Anika and Plinio, so all of us are clear on why we are here, and how we are going to proceed." She asks, "Are you doing okay, AnnaKay?"

She answers, "I'm good."

The doctor says, "The reason you're here is AnnaKay. We are meeting to discuss her well-being and what's best for her. That's it. This is not a place to trade insults. This is not where you're going to make accusations. You are not scoring points – you are taking care of your daughter, and that's it. Are we clear?"

"Yes," Corbyn answers.

Anika says, "Got it," and rolls her eyes.

The doctor continues, "I know there's a tremendous amount of animosity between the people in this room, so it's important that you understand that we're here by court order. Based upon what was shared during the court proceedings, the judge became concerned about AnnaKay and what's going on around her. That's why we got the referral. Furthermore, because this is court ordered, I have the authority to file charges of contempt if you do not do what I tell you to do. You can be fined, and you can be given jail time if I feel that is necessary. If you do not follow the guidelines I have given you, I can assure you – you will find out very quickly that I am not your friend. I am not here for you. I am here for AnnaKay, and only AnnaKay, and that is also the reason that you are here. We are here to take care of your daughter. I want you all to tell me you understand what I have told you."

"Got it," Plinio says, and his wife seconds, "Loud and clear."

"You've got two strikes already," the doctor warns her: "There will be no snide, or side comments during this conversation. Is that clear, Anika?"

"Yes," she says: "It's clear."

"Corbyn," the doctor says, "You understand the guidelines and the penalties if you do not comply?"

"I do, but I gotta."

The doctor says, "No. Yes, or no: That's what I'm asking you to tell me. Do you understand we will only be talking about AnnaKay? This is not a forum to share the grievances with your ex-wife. This is not where we will be discussing what has happened in the past. We are discussing what is best for your daughter, moving forward. Are you clear on that?"

"I lose my shit," Corbyn says. He adds, "I'm sure you've heard lots of amazing stories."

The doctor says, "That's strike one. We are not doing that."

"I dispute it." Corbyn says, and anger fires, "I was owning up. So, I've got zero strikes. I'm telling you, if I lose it, just throw me out."

"I like that idea," says Anika, and she's smiling, barely able to keep herself from joining her snickering husband.

The doctor says, "It stands. I don't have to give you a warning, but I just did. And Anika," she says, "That's the third time you've spoken out of turn. That will result in a fine, and that fine will escalate every time I hand out another one. I'm not here to judge what's been done, I'm here to look after the best interests of your daughter. I need all of you to let me know you understand."

"Yes," Anika says, "We understand, doctor."

"I'll take that as an answer for both of you. Now, I need to hear it from you, Corbyn. Are you clear on the reason why we're here?"

He glares over, and the hostility even allows him to look at Anika and her preening husband. They are smirking as they watch, as they are both keenly aware he would love to run across the room and attack them both. Anika's smirk stretches into a malignant smile, as Corbyn tells the doctor, "Got it."

"Great," she says, "I am so pleased we are able to move on. Now," she says, "Corbyn: You have chosen not to participate in the recommended counseling. I understand that was presented as voluntary, but I can make that a mandatory aspect of the process if I do not like how this proceeds. I know you have been notified, but in the interest of absolute transparency, everyone else has participated in individual counseling. I have spoken with Anika and Plinio on two occasions, and I have met with your daughter several times. I am reiterating this so that you are aware I am familiar with their perspectives. I also want to stress, I have read the statement that you submitted. Most of that is not what we are addressing, but I do give you credit for being very thorough."

"I thought it would be cathartic," Corbyn says bitterly: "It just pissed me off more."

The doctor says, "Wonderful. The point of explaining that to you, was to make you aware that I have already been in conversation with the other people in this room. I have heard their perspectives, and I am aware of – at least some – of their motivations. As a matter of fairness, I would like to give you the opportunity to make a statement, or share your thoughts with regards to improving circumstances for your daughter. Is there anything you would like to say?"

There had been a song playing at some point on the ride north – a march: Brass forward. It had been syncopated and harsh, and it had felt like a push in the back. As the question's asked, Corbyn hears the music playing in his ears. He can see the trombone slides, he can see the horns swaying; he can see the trumpets punching up with emphasis.

He looks over to Anika and Plinio, and they are watching back with matching sour smiles, and he knows they expect him to explode – to start softly, but on shaky ground, and that instability will lead him to an earthquake. They expect an eruption will follow – and, they are not wrong. It is a failing he has worked hard to address, and he continues failing.

He pulls his eyes away and looks to his daughter, and she is still extremely tense. She looks back at him with eyes wide, eyes blinking harshly, and she looks like she is close to breaking.

"Yeah." Corbyn says, "Yeah." He looks briefly at the doctor and she sees the anger that's been advertised. She is poised to intervene and is reaching for the alarm as Corbyn rises.

But he doesn't rage across the room. He walks to his daughter and leans down. He pulls her close in his arms, and tells her, "You can say whatever you need to. You know I love you. All of us are here for you. Don't be stressed, A-K: Give us all the shit you've got to."

She turns red as she laughs quietly, and Corbyn returns to his seat, collapses, and says, "Yeah: I do have something to say."

He surveys the room again, and the smirks across have been replaced by stone faced worry – for everyone, except Annakay: She is watching back – much more relaxed: Relieved.

Corbyn says, to his daughter, "Whatever you need – we'll get it done. I'll do whatever I have to."

The doctor says, "I had not mentioned this, but everyone should remain in their seats for this session. I will call security if anyone leaves their seat again."

However, Annakay looks to her father and quietly says, "Thank you."

A concession, "It was fine," is made by the doctor, however, she reminds everyone, "There is a lot of tension in this room. Remaining where we are will help everyone feel comfortable. Did you have anything else you wanted to add?"

She's told, "Nope. If we're here for A-K, then I'm here for A-K."

There's a moment of quiet as the doctor awaits to see if more will be said, but it isn't, so she says, "Very good." She says, "AnnaKay, "You've mentioned several things that you feel need to be addressed. Would you like to open with one in particular, or would you prefer that I begin the conversation?"

Annakay leaves the script, and says, "I wanna know what happened."

She's questioned, "Regarding what," by the doctor.

She looks over to her mother, and there's hurt recognized, and it's the last thing Anika ever wanted. A-K says, "I wanna know what really happened. I wanna know what you told Mr. Topel do."

Corbyn begins to move, and says, "A-K," but the counselor says, "Seat it," and – reluctantly – he does.

He watches as his daughter looks back at him with tears in her eyes. He watches as she looks back the other way, and he knows that the instincts that compelled him to undermine his own relationship with her – they were not mis-aligned: She has a relationship that has many challenges, but it's one she clearly wants amended. The relationship is deeper than the conflicts. There is a conversation and history they hold that their child is desperately hoping can be salvaged.

Corbyn looks past her to Anika and Plinio, and they are the landmines of the conversation. They are the obstacle to resolving any disagreements because they are the core of the anger that burns, and the slightest draft ignites those flames.

There's no intervention by the doctor, so Corbyn says, "A-K: We've talked about it," however she shuts him down:

She spins her head and there is anger in her eyes – there is anger as she harshly tells him, "No." She tells him, "I was there. I saw how upset she was. That's – not – all.

To the doctor, Corbyn says, "I thought you were gonna shut this down – keep us focused on the topic."

"Yeah," she says – she explains, "I was watching. AnnaKay? This isn't what we'd discussed. Would you like to discuss this privately?"

She answers, "No. I want to know what really happened."

"There's a video," Corbyn points out. "A guy that works for Plinio assaults me. There are recorded calls. I get you don't like it, but they put your mom behind it. That's the end of it: Your mom hired a guy to try and kill me."

"Oh," Anika complains, "Shut up.

Corbyn finishes, "And he did."

"If only," Anika says, and then she claims, "All of this is your fault, anyway."

"My fault?" Corbyn is on his feet and there is only red – as the counsellor tries to intervene, but they are past a point she can: "How the hell's it my fault? You had your thug attack me out of nowhere. I hadn't even talked to you in months." The alarm is pressed, as Corbyn starts across the room. Plinio quickly moves to step between, but he's casually tossed aside, and he stumbles to the floor. Corbyn's red as his vision as he sticks a finger in his ex-wife's face and yells, enraged, "You hired a guy to kill me, and then manipulated your daughter to weasel out of it. You are a fucking psychopath."

He is just beginning, but the one person capable of diffusing the explosion puts a hand into his chest, and quietly says, "Dad."

Anika takes the moment to claim, "No one hired anyone to kill you." She rolls her eyes, disgusted as Plinio re-joins her side, and says, "Sit down. Your making an ass of yourself."

He begins by shaking his head, but the response is thwarted by another, "Dad."

"Please take a seat," is an order from a man that Corbyn hadn't noticed enter the room. The man elaborates, "You can either take a seat, or I'll escort you from the room."

"Escort me," Corbyn suggests, but he isn't because Anika admits, "I asked him to look into whatever the hell this bullshit you've gotten into is. That you're dragging my daughter into. That's what I asked him to do."

Corbyn says, "He got a different memo."

"Because of you," she says, and he explodes, "Bull: You hired him to attack me, and then manipulated your daughter to get out of being charged with conspiracy. And let's not forget about the phones."

"Oh, my God," she says. "Please escort him out of here."

He charges, "Can't deny it, can ya?"

"Deny what," she asks. "I hadn't picked up that phone in years. And I didn't manipulate my daughter. We live in the same home – we have conversations. You might think about trying it sometime so you don't look like a complete imbecile."

"Oh – here we go," Corbyn begins, but he's stopped again, because the man says, "One way or the other."

He is ready to leave, but AnnaKay says, "Dad," again.

He retreats, but makes the point, "There's a video, Anika: The guy attacked me."

"'Cause you're such a God-damned asshole."

He doesn't sit, because, "I'm an asshole? Who kept me from seeing my daughter for – how many years? Who hired some guy to off me and then – used – her own daughter to get me to give you a way out. Who's lied to the court for ten, fucking years to milk me for every penny I make while you're travelling the globe on a billionaire's dime. Which one of us is the asshole?"

Anika says, "You are."

"You're too much." He is leaving.

Corbyn is walking towards the door, but Anika says, "It only happened because you attacked us at the mall. That's how come he went after you. Because you're a fucking asshole."

Corbyn pauses, but not for contrition. He says, "I apologized," and it's reflection. He recalls, "I told you – no excuses. I told you I was out of line." The anger returns, as he spits, "I shouldn't have. You deserved every last word."

"You humiliated me." She is shaken, as she was that day. She shares, "You attacked us in front of everyone – in front of people I know. You didn't stop. I was trying to get us away, but you wouldn't let us. You kept chasing us down and screaming."

"I feel like it was very much deserved. Especially – since you tried to have me murdered."

She claims, "That was your fault."

"Oh," Corbyn says: There is anger. He shakes his head, and bitterly says, "I can't wait to hear this one."

"It's because you joined that stupid – thing. And then, AnnaKay got interested. We'd asked him to find out what it was because the way it was described to us sounded insane. But we met him that night after you lost your mind and he saw how upset I was. I told him it was you, and I said something about I expected you'd have an aneurism. He made a joke about it, and I said, maybe we'll get lucky the next time. He said he could make it happen, and I told him – I said no. I told him not to. But I did tell him to punch you in the face."

"Nothing changes."

"You're an asshole. I wanted him to give you a black eye so you'd have to explain to everyone what an idiot you are."

"Nothing changes," Corbyn repeats. "You hired a guy to attack me, and he did. Mission accomplished."

"Sir." The gentleman has been waiting patiently, but he's received a signal they need to control the situation.

He says, "You either need to continue out the door, or go back and take a seat."

"I'm leaving."

But, "Dad," is called. AnnaKay says, "Don't. I didn't mean to make it weird. I just wanted to know."

It is a moment where Corbyn could leave, or he could stay, and it would be fine. Unfortunately, Plinio opens his mouth:

"His intention was to strike you in the face. However, you reacted more quickly than he expected and squared to face him. After his first strike found your shoulder much more solid than expected, he became concerned. He decided to disengage, pushed off, and fled. He did not expect you to trip over the mooring and go into the water. He, of course, phoned us immediately and the appropriate authorities were notified you needed rescue."

This was listened to without interruption. This is an explanation that was repeated during the trial, and elements had been included in the agreement made between them – an agreement made for their child's sake. But it is a statement repeated at the exact wrong moment, and to a person that is no longer leaving – he is seething. He is a concern to the person called to intervene, who is no longer certain he is capable.

"That is not," Corbyn says – he slams a fist back against the door, and the finger raised and eyes turned to the man approaching, hold him back. Corbyn states, "That – isn't: That – is not – what happened."

"Corbyn?" Anika calls, and there is concern. He is in a place she's seen before. He is after a race where he couldn't find the extra gear. Where he couldn't push his body past the pain and limits of muscle function. He is where he's been after hours training, where his body's breaking down but he keeps pushing. He is pushing through the agony brought by injury and tasting its blood. His focus is on a single point, and as she'd found before, there isn't a way to break it. It can only be turned, and she moves to protect the others in the room, admitting, "It's my fault. We'd joke. I'd say, knock him off a cliff, but I wasn't serious. I didn't want him to kill you." She says, "I don't think he meant to," and she realizes she pulled the trigger, so quickly follows, "I'm sorry. I'm sorry, Corbyn. I never wanted you seriously hurt."

She's answered, "Seriously? Not – seriously hurt? What degree of hurt did you want?"

The doctor begins, "I think we all," but she's told, "Shut," and Corbyn stops himself from the vulgar response that was ready to flow intrinsically.

He steps back. He leans against the wall, and says, "All the excuses, all the lies, and it's changed nothing: You had a guy attack me. End of story."

"Richard," the doctor says, "Please position yourself in front of Plino and Anika."

"Don't bother." Corbyn moves to leave, yet again, and yet again, Anika stops him:

She says, "You're fine. I told you I'm sorry. It was never supposed to be – you're dead. Let's just move on and focus on what we were supposed to: You're daughter – AnnaKay. Can we agree on that?"

"Move on," Corbyn says. He is darker yet, as he shares, "I sleep with a light on, now. 'Cause I have nightmares that I'm drowning. I wake up and I can't breathe, and when it's dark, it feels like I'm in the water." He walks behind the doctor, back towards his seat, but he doesn't take it. He shares, "I run through water, and I hear that sound – it's the last thing I heard.

Before I went under. I hear that sound and I'm there again. I'm underwater – everything goes dark. I panic – I'm frozen, just like I was that night. I hear that sound and I'm hitting the water again. I feel like I'm having a heart attack; I'm frozen – I can't move. I'm standing there, and I can feel the freezing water. All I see is black, and I'm freezing. But let's just move on – right? Let's just forget that you're who did this – it never crossed my mind. Not once did I think that you would be behind it. And I sure didn't expect Wyl to keep that from me. Worse than the panic and the nightmares: I don't feel like I can ever trust anyone again. But go ahead – move on. I don't know what the point of all this is, but I think we should end it."

"We have jumped right in," the doctor says: "We are in the heart of what needs to be addressed. I had not expected the conversation to be so – open. And, straightforward."

"And, I'm just supposed to forgive her now. Is that what you're gonna tell me?"

"I have not asked for that," the doctor says: "People that you offered trust betrayed you. Anika: You asked for an act of violence to be committed against your ex-husband. You are the victim of that violence, Corbyn. You have suffered as a consequence of that violence. This is all deeply concerning, and we need to keep in mind that this has also affected your daughter. We have a little more than a year to make sure she goes into the world believing she can trust the people in her life. I want us to take a short break, but when we come back, we need to begin an honest conversation about how we have gotten here."

Corbyn says, "I just wanna go."

"I'm sorry." Annika pleads, "Okay? I'm sorry. You just make me so angry. But I never wanted him to kill you. We'll make it up to you: Whatever you want."

"I don't want – anything," Corbyn says, "From you. And I'm done with this."

"Corbyn," the doctor says, "I am not going to force you to stay, but I think it is extremely – it is extremely – important to your daughter, that you are a part of these discussions."

He looks over, and she's nodding. She no longer appears to be greatly distressed, though, still unsettled – but so is everyone. Regrettably, Corbyn nods that he will, and she smiles.

A stiff smile, but she whispers, "Thank you."

Shoes hit the water, and the sound brings a crease against the spine. Light fades, but there's also laughter. There's uninhibited joy that spills beside the ocean, and the shading that still drains life's color, can only paint it gray with alternating heartbeats.

They turn up the beach into the softer sand, and AnnaKay declares, "I love this."

It is exuberant. It is the satisfaction of using every last iota of effort. It is the escape from a complicated world with damaged people. It is legs that have been pushed past their capability, that feel like rubber bands incapable of functioning properly: It is the cold water against them at the end of the run.

She says, "That's my favorite. That's the best."

"Yeah." Corbyn agrees, as hands come to the waist as he paces off. He says, "That's the go-to. It's a pain to drive this far, but it's always worth it."

"Did you get the time?"

"Oh." Says Corbyn, "No." He quickly checks, and even with delay the time's still solid: "It was a good one. I forgot to check, though."

She laughs as she wanders back towards the ocean, and says, "Me too." She lets encroaching waves saturate her shoes, and continues in. She walks to where the waves crash above her knees, and it feels good – a natural icing for tired and aching legs. She turns, and calls, "Hey, dad," but a woman is loping off the old wagon trail across the river. She is jogging across the sand, and calls, "Corbyn."

She calls, "Hey – Corbyn."

A-K watches as she slows, as she approaches her father, and AnnaKay does the same. She hears the woman say, "You never called me."

Corbyn says, “Did I say I would?”

“Yeah. It was right after that guy attacked you. What happened with that?”

“Oh.” Corbyn watches his daughter approach, and says, “Long story.”

“Oh,” Jesty says, “Alright,” and she watches the young woman pull close. It registers – not really a question – but she says, “Is this your daughter?”

“Jesty – AnnaKay: My daughter. Had a great run. You’re getting started?”

“Ten steps out the door,” she says, but she questions, “Did they ever catch the guy?”

There’s a look exchanged between the other two that signifies the answers complicated, but that’s abbreviated, with another, “Long story.”

She says, “Well, give me a call. We can meet somewhere and you can tell me. Nice to meet you, AnnaKay.”

“Oh – yeah, yeah: Nice to meet you.”

Jesty gestures at her ear, and says, “Call me.” She waves and then moves to more solid ground to continue running.

“Who was that,” is answered, “We’ve crossed paths a couple times: Another runner.”

She asks, “You gonna call?”

He answers, “Probably not.”

She asks, “Why not?”

“Literally,” Corbyn says, “Second time I ever had a conversation. Ya ready to head back?”

She says, “Yeah. But, do you like her?”

“Do I like her,” is asked with the absurdity deserved, though, it’s understood the question’s asked through the lens of youth and innocence. Corbyn says, “That’s the second longest conversation we ever had. I don't know her."

AnnaKay says, "She seems nice," and suggests, "You should call her."

He ends that line of conversation with, "We'll see."

They begin the walk back and as they clear the bend, there are two figures standing on the large, embedded rock. They are easily identified, and likewise, quickly spy the two approaching.

Both leap to the sand and a peal sails down the beach: "A-K: Unca-C." They race down the beach and quickly greet them, "Hey, Unca-C," and Lia says to his daughter, "We're stealing you."

They are a whirlwind as they pull her away, and Shey leaves him with, "By, Unca-C. You'll have to find her."

They tug her off, and it's good to see her in such a better place than she was a year before: She goes willingly. She laughs easily – there are times she can be described as happy.

They greet another as they reach the breach, but the conversation is drowned out by the wind and crashing waves. Wyl continues down the beach, moving to intercept the last straggler.

He greets Corbyn, "How's it going?"

He's answered, "Good. You?"

"Yeah – good: I'm good. It's been a minute."

"Yeah. Ya know – busy."

"Yeah. Kinda feels like you're Corboidin' me. We good?"

"I'm not. Really – just busy: A-K's down every weekend, and – work. It's a lot of work."

"Goin' alright?'

"Yeah – good. It's good. It's a lot but a good fit. Keeps me busy. Any clue why I lost my daughter?"

"Yes, Corboidance, the girls figured they kidnapped her, you'd be forced to follow."

"I knew there was a Wylsplanation. What'm I being lured into?"

"It's a tradition we have: We call it breakfast. They know you'll have an excuse if they just ask you."

"Zing – Wylarrow. Only if there's plans. But I'm sensing a conspiracy."

"Unknown to me, Corborate manager. They just told us they're making breakfast. I had no idea you'd be down here."

"A not so random suggestion, I think."

"I might have said something."

"Said what?"

"Like, we never see Corbanished anymore."

"It is a change. I don't live in your shed – it's an adjustment we'll have to make."

"Seriously, Corbs: I know I screwed things up, but you told me – if we're not okay, I need to know."

"You're beating a dead horse. I am consciously past it, and subconsciously, ninety-nine point nine. I still have a small, red light that keeps flashing and I don't know that's ever going away. But that's there for everyone."

"I just," Wyl starts, but he's stopped. Corbyn tells him, "Don't. I've been busy – very – busy. Not avoiding. C'mon: We'd better get up there before the girls eat everything."

"No chance, Corbese: They went crazy."

"Not yours…"

"Shocking – I know: Oh," he says, somewhat shocked to see a head emerging from the waves. He nods, and says, "Your guy."

Corbyn turns to see Awrol emerging from the surf, the familiar spray of water shooting past him. He moves to meet him, and they greet one another like the old friends the other watching truly is.

Corbyn asks, "Cruising the coastline?"

Awrol says, "With every moment of freedom that I have. I was surprised to find you in this region."

There's a laugh – one only: One of the other two put off, and the third rarely finding humor. But Corbyn does. He shares, "Believe the kids are coordinating a date. You remember Wyl?"

"Unforgettable," Awrol says. He offers a hand, and says, "I pray life finds you well."

"Good," Wyl says. He says, "All good. You – good?"

He's answered, "I am present." Awrol turns to Corbyn and says, "As you were in proximity, I share with you in person: Proclamation of a new conquest will occur one week from today. We will gather with the informality that is protocol and I will certainly challenge. If you intend to avail yourself, arrangements should be made to discuss strategy. Also, I would like to practice at least once, if you are available, and regardless."

"Unless A-K doesn't want to," Corbyn says. "But I think she'll wanna be there. I'm free most of Monday-Tuesday."

Awrol says, "Seven – Monday. Confirm next weekend as you are able." He turns, and says to Wyl, "A non-expendable pleasure, as always. Give your delightful daughters my best."

"Yeah – yeah," Wyl says: "Good to see you. Another conquest – that's the adventure thing? The – where ya do the… Weird. Something."

"Something," Corbyn agrees.

Awrol says, "Impossibillis fix. It is the impetus to challenge – the crux and purpose of our endeavors."

"Yeah," Wyl says: "Okay." He remains uncertain what it is, what they do, and why they need a submarine, but he does remember, "That book had Latin. That's it – wasn't it. There was Latin."

Awrol says, "No."

"No?" He reflects back. Wyl tries to remember any of what they'd read, and recalls that most of it seemed like nonsense. However, some of it seemed, like, "Strategy – that's what it was. Or, observations. I remember, there were a lot of diagrams. Is that – for the challenges? Or, conquests?"

He's answered, "It is not for anything."

It is with that answer, that Corbyn understands the conversation should end, and he tries, "Good to see you. Plan on Saturday, we'll do Monday, and I'll get with Elkilia to cover strategy: She's got some ideas."

"Why was it there, anyway?" Wyl asks, because he's focused on what was written to offer understanding. He asks, "Is that part of the strategy? You leave clues around? That's your challenge – conquest? Something like that?"

But the man that's asked is dark from a starting point, and only darker as he says again, "It is not for anything."

"Then," Wyl asks, "Why leave it there?"

Corbyn says, "Hey," trying to gain his friend's attention, but Awrol answers:

"The blade and the notes are work of my wife. It is one of many shrines I have built to honor her memory."

"Shit, man." An entire world and compilation of devastation distill as the few words ever shared are sewn together. Corbyn says, "I am so sorry." He rests a hand in sympathy against the large man's shoulder, and says again, "Man, I'm so sorry – so sorry. We just stumbled on it. I tried to put it back like we found it. We didn't know."

"No reason," Awrol claims, "To be concerned. They are the artifice of moments."

"No, man – come on." Corbyn brings him in, and says, "That's sacred ground. I knew that. That's why we put it back."

It is at that moment that Wyl realizes what's being discussed, where he realizes shrines are being erected on sacred places of memory, and the person that memory's been shared with is only that.

He says, "Oh. I am – man. All I've got's – I can make it up to you: With the breakfast my daughter's made. We'd all love to have you join us."

The man is ready to retreat. He is unwilling to share company with almost anyone, but then, Corbyn says, "You promised magic. Got anything up your sleeve?"

Awrol says, "Indeed," but it's despondent. He says, "Regrettably, I have left my vehicle in a tow zone. Your cordial invitation is deeply appreciated, but I must defer to another time."

Wyl says, "They made raspberry Danishes that are amazing. I can run up and grab you one."

It's dismissed, with, "Unnecessary," Tim says to Corbyn, "I'll call you to hammer out Monday." To both – they are told, "Good bounty."

They watch as he begins down the beach, but not towards where he entered. He walks north, up the shore towards no-man's-land, and the cave with the buried treasure.

Wyl says, "I really botched that," but he's told, "Nah. He talks about her all the time – in fact, our team's named after her."

"Yeah? What's her name?"

"Apothocles."

"Apothocles?"

"Correct, Wylnouncing. I've got two complaints I want you to address."

Wyl agrees, "Okay. Whatever you need – anything."

"Firstly, Wylcher, my co-conspirator has been kidnapped by maleficent antagonists. I need your help to free her."

"Okay, buddy: You get weirder by the day. What else've ya got?"

"There is a hoard of raspberry pastries. We need to take as many as we are able as the spoils of victory."

"Sounds like you're walking right into their trap."

"The direct approach is usually the easiest path."

There is amusement as they follow the path up through the cliff, as Wyl says, "That's probably the most profound thing that's ever come out of your mouth."

"Try this: It's important to set a low bar."

"You took it lower, Corbvoyant." He opens the door, and offers, "After you."

"Oh – it smells so good." They enter and find the four ladies seated around a table filled with food. With visuals paired to the opening aroma, Corbyn's starving and moves to join them: "This looks incredible."

Corshae suggests, "I think somebody's missed our infrequent morning guest."

Corbyn says, "I heard the pastries are delicious."

Corsh teases back, "I heard you met someone."

"Oh yeah." Corbyn shares, "Tim's out there – Awrol. He says hi to everyone."

"Just walks out of the ocean," Wyl muses, and A-K asks, "Are we doing that today?"

"Not today," Corbyn answers. "Monday, he wants to practice, and El-Assissi's throwing down the gauntlet next Saturday."

"Can I skip school?"

Her father laughs, and tells her, "No," however, he offers, "If there's anything we need to cover, I'll drive up in the afternoon."

"Not Tim." Corshae clarifies, "A-K says there was a woman."

He says, "huh," dismissively. He assures them all, "Not even acquaintances." And especially, to his daughter, "We used to cross paths when we were running. She wondered where I'd been."

His dismissive answer leads his daughter to mimic the woman's action, and words, "Call me."

Wyl wonders, "Who the heck is this?"

"Jesty, Wylsumption. I've spent an entire three minutes of my life in conversation with her. She's just looking for the salacious details of my midnight swim. Delicious, by the way: These are really good."

Lia suggests, "Try the casserole. That was mine."

"Everything's delicious. Tim doesn't know what he's missing."

A-K asks, "Why's he here?"

Regrettably, Wyl shares, "I believe he's visiting a memorial for his wife."

"Oh," says Corshae. It was unexpected, and she has a moment of insight into those sharing his vocation. She offers, "That's so sad."

"She's dead," A-K questions. "I always thought she just stayed home. Or, she left him."

"I should have known," Corbyn reflects, "When he talks about her, it's always in the past – I should've realized."

Wyl admits, "I didn't know what he was talking about. I didn't catch it at first."

"You should have invited him," Corshae says, but of course, "We did."

"Unca-C," Shey asks: "When are you gonna see him next?"

"Probably Monday. Unless he's still around, but I don't think he's looking for company, so – Monday. Probably."

"Can you come by Sunday, Unca-C? We can make more Danishes you can give him."

They are small, and triangular. The filling in the middle is mostly exposed, with just the edges folded over. They are extremely rich, and there is a hint of alcohol – Grand Marnier; perhaps cognac – sprinkled with crushed macadamia nuts and finished with ribbons of white chocolate. They are less a Danish, and more of a desert, and they are unquestionably delicious.

Unfortunately, "I'm on call on Sundays: Tied to the dock. If there are any left, I can take him one."

"Unca-C," Lia lectures: "That's two days old and they'll be gross."

"Yeah." Her sister agrees, "We can make more tomorrow." She says, as a question to her parents, "We could drive them up."

"Yeah. Corbasta: I'd love to see the place – if that's alright."

"Not much to see," Corbyn says, but A-K offers, "It's getting better. I can come down if you don't wanna drive."

"Corbs," his longtime friend inquires: "Alright we swing by Sunday?"

"You can stop by any time, Wylmission. I've been informed – it's tiny, and dark. But as you know, I previously lived in a shed."

"Bathhouse, Corburger."

A-K offers, "I can return the favor – I'll make us dinner."

Lia suggests, "I'll help," and her sister agrees: "We can make it together. Can we make it together?"

It is moment that's a flashback to the past. A moment before worlds crumbled apart, where families spent time together – all, together. There is a memory of the moment an infant came into their lives, and for a few years, they had been together nearly every day.

Then they moved. The girls were always welcome, always cheerful, but with distance and intermittent interaction, those early memories had become capsules from the past. That had begun to change.

They were again seen more frequently, and they were even more fun than remembered. So, A-K says, and means, "Yeah: That would be fun."

25

The morning is exquisite. The sounds of the morning bay clang, and hum, and whistles blow under the slight veil of fog that hangs over the landscape, and heavier mist at higher elevations that hides the tops of hills. But it is soft, and quiet compared to what will follow, as the shore awakens, and visitors and weekenders flock to the western end of the country.

It is peaceful. Even conversations with those passed, those out on the boats are easy and relaxed. The world seems calm and untroubled, despite the great power of the waters that bring that sense. It would be the perfect morning to sit on the dock with a cup of coffee, except a bell rings to signify that someone's entered the store.

It's alright: The short reflection brings Corbyn in, and he greets them cheerfully: "How's everybody doin' today?"

What he didn't expect, and what ends that sense of peace and calm, is the surprised, "Corbyn?"

It takes a moment. It's the wrong setting, but then, it hits: The woman that entered the store with another and two children, is, "Jesty."

She asks, "What are you doing here," as if the same couldn't be asked of herself.

Corbyn says, "I work here."

"Here," she asks. She is shaking her head, her mouth's open – caught between laughter and abomination: There's true surprise, "I don't know what I saw you doing, but I didn't see you behind a counter."

"Counter," he says, "Monger, meet the boats – whatever. I cover it all."

She is equally surprised – perhaps an indicator she's impressed – she asks, "You own this?"

He laughs, "Heck no. Just work for the family."

"How long?"

"Oh," he says. It's a look back – a rewind back, more than a decade – he guesses, "Going on twelve? It's been a while." At that, she leans back and the surprise is gone. A smirk develops, and he questions, "What?"

"I'm guessing this isn't coincidence."

"Got me," Corbyn says: "I have no idea."

"No," she questions: "You didn't put someone up to this?"

"I did not." He says, "I don't even know what this is. I work here – that's it. You wanna find me, this is usually where I am." And he questions, "I should ask, what brings you in?"

"Your daughter," she says – he questions, "My daughter?"

She laughs, and she's relaxed again. She shares, "My brother and his family are visiting. We were on the beach a couple days ago when I ran into your daughter."

"Mine," he asks. "I don't think she's been around since the weekend."

He's assured, "Oh, she was. We talked a little. I told her – family's visiting. She suggested I should take them whale watching."

"Okay," says Corbyn, "Not a bad suggestion."

"She said, Friday morning was the best time, and she told me – I needed to stop in here. She also decided I should have your number. Should I believe you didn't know anything?"

He shakes his head, but he can't help but laugh. He tells her, "No. It's a long story, but my daughter and I were sort of estranged. She's become very involved in my life since we reconnected. I also think she probably had some help."

“Oh?”

Corbyn says, “It’s a long story;” she notes, “What isn’t with you?”

“Jesty?” The other woman calls, and says, “I’m gonna take the kids back up. It doesn’t look like they have much.”

“Okay. I’ll be just a few.”

Corbyn waits for the three to exit, before he says, “She’s wrong. We have everything you need – right here.”

“Yeah,” she asks.

“I assume you’re doing the two-hour cruise?”

Jesty says, “We were thinking one. Ya know – kids.”

“Tell them to take the two – you’ll thank me. And the kids are gonna love it – guaranteed. Just like I guarantee they’ll love the jerky.”

She looks, and offers, “Yih.”

“Heard it,” Corbyn says, “But it’s amazing. I recommend buying more than you think you’ll want, ‘cause the kids are tearing into that.”

“Okay,” she dubiously replies.

“I’ll buy back what you don’t eat, and I’ll pay you back for everything if the kids say they hate it. But they won’t.”

Jesty says, “I think they were looking for healthy snacks.”

“Packed with protein and sixty-percent less salt than beef-jerky. I also recommend the smoked fish. Everyone loves salmon but let me get you a sample of the trout – it is outstanding.”

“A real company guy,” Jesty jokes, but Corbyn tells her:

“It’s really good. Real good. You will not regret going with the jerky, fish and crackers, and we have some cheese sticks. They are the – perfect – snacks for an ocean tour."

It is meant as teasing, but fails to register when she says, "Sounds messy:"

"You're on a boat. On the ocean. Everything's messy. Just lean into it – I guarantee: No regrets."

She laughs at the enthusiasm, and agrees, "That is very good. I will take one, but I should probably also get some salmon. And, we'll try the jerky."

Corbyn volunteers, "Complimentary cooler. You'll want some waters."

"So," says Jesty – suspecting otherwise, "You had nothing to do with this – all your daughter?"

"Yes," he says. As he packs the cooler, he shares, "She's become very involved. She completely re-did the apartment, she's joined me with some of my hobbies, and she's synched our schedules. So, she knows where I'll be and when. I think she saw an opportunity."

"Maybe," Jesty suggests, "You told her you regretted you never called."

He stops, puts the lid on, and admits, "I was never gonna."

She asks, "Why," and he says, "Also messy."

"Let me guess," she says, "You're still married."

Quickly, he tells her, "No. No, no, no: That ship sailed and it can keep going. There's just been a – lot."

"A long story," she says, "Right," and he laughs, because it is.

But he says, "If I gave you a synopsis, you'd run outta here and never look back."

She says, "Give me a synopsis."

His head is shaking. Corbyn means to laugh it off, but he says, "Okay." There is a moment of recalibration where he looks at the slope to walk agreement down, but he says, "Okay," again, and the recalibration turns towards sharing, "The guy that dumped me in the river? Hired by my ex. Up until I found that out, I'd lived in a shed for the prior ten. But I found out the guy that let me stay there knew she was the one behind it, so I got pissed and moved into a tent on the side of the mountain. In the end, I lied to make sure she didn't go to prison. If you aren't ready to run, it gets worse."

"Kind of sad, actually." She asks, "What's worse?"

"This is where I live. I have to be on-call – at work – a hundred hours a week."

"Okay," she says, "I don't think that's worse. Is that seven days a week?"

"I have a seventy-two hour shift, and a separate twenty-four. A lot of that's down-time and I can do what I want, but I have to be available. Midnight's the end of my seventy-two."

Jesty says, "I'm still not running."

"Well," Corbyn suggests, "Here you go: If you decided – for some crazy reason – you wanted to stay up late and talk after I'm done here, you'd have to trust me enough to walk into the ocean and board a submarine."

"What?"

"That's the hobby I was talking about."

"A submarine, Corbyn," she asks.

"It's a fencing club – ya know: Long, thin swords. But we've created a game; it's part of that. We use it to collect information."

"So," she says, "I don't think anything you told me's true."

He says, "It's a long story, but all of it is."

She asks, "A submarine?"

"Yes," he says. And then, he pushes her out the door by saying, "My king built it."

She says, "Oh, boy. What do I owe you?"

He promises, "One hour's not enough. You just get started and you're comin' back. The kids aren't gettin' bored on the two."

"You understand," she says, "There's just a little," and she pinches fingers close together, to emphasize, "doubt about everything you said."

"And," he says, "When you join me at Billy's for a drink, it'll all make sense."

She asks, "What's Billy's?"

He says, "Long story," and she laughs, and for a moment, it's contagious.

She says, "We'll do the two, we'll try your jerky, and if that holds up – maybe – I'll call you. I'll see you, Corbyn."

"Enjoy. It's a lot of fun." He watches her leave, knowing he doesn't know that, but it's been said, and he knows the food is good. He watches her walk away, and mutters, "Dang kid," but he laughs, because exactly what she wanted just occurred.

However, there's also some concern that surreptitious oversight helped make that happen, so he texts, "Jesty stopped by." After several minutes helping another customer, there's still no reply, so he types, "I hope you didn't pull Tim into this. There need to be boundaries."

The bell rings as another trio enters, and Corbyn, says, "Welcome. Let me know if you have any questions."

They look confused, and one says, "They said we could get some snacks here."

Corbyn beams, and says, "Have I got the thing for you."

It's more of the same for the rest of the morning: A few random stragglers, but most are directed from the tours. There's a surge of three to twelve, and then a lull where it's lucky there's more than one.

It's after twelve when relief finally walks through the swinging doors. She says, "How we doin', Jimmy?"

He says, "The usual. Mostly tours."

She says, "I see you've been pushin' people towards the trout. You wanna grab me another tray?"

"You got it. You got help comin' in?"

"Not 'til three. No point having two of us watchin' the clock."

"Call me if ya need me. I'll get that tray in a bit – I'm gonna swing through the back."

She says, "No rush, Elvin."

He says, "See ya, Shirley."

The back is moving smoothly. The banter's a bit rougher than it had been, and an off-comment heard on entering brings the order, barked, "Clean it up. We got ladies here."

Of course, that brings the response, "Ain't no ladies in here."

Corbyn says, "You can fuck around and say – that. But that's as far as it goes. We all good?"

"Good boss."

"You got it."

The one woman that's present says, "I can handle them."

The noise that follows is a mix of wordless exclamations and vulgar interpretations.

It's shrugged off. Corbyn walks through, and the only person still remaining from his time in processing, reports, "It's good, boss. Everybody's havin' fun."

He says, "Keep it that way. You're my eyes and ears – lemme know."

The man says, "You got it, boss."

"Bowes," Corbyn calls: "Get a tray of the smoked trout for the front."

He says, "Yessir." The knife drops to the counter and he peels off gloves, and washes his hands. He quickly dries them and moves just as fast to follow orders.

The prior decade had been an unusual period in processing. It had been anchored by a pair that were there for the entirety, and others passing through had an example that kept them tethered. That was not the case, any longer, as the one that was entrusted to oversee the others had been there for under two.

He had proven himself to be less than trustworthy, but there was familiarity, and the few extra dollars he was paid kept him reasonably honest: He was on board with tamping down the worst transgressions – language, drugs; blowing off the work.

That made the day longer for everyone. On that, at least, there was oversight, and the worst of everything else occasionally got reported.

Corbyn leaves it behind and moves for the stairs. He walks through the empty receiving room, through the door, and past the empty office. He walks down the hall to another door, and enters an apartment that is nothing like it was when he first became the occupant.

The walls are no longer gray – one is bright green, one is orange, and the others are a combination of artistic expression. Of those alone the space is vibrant, but that was only the beginning of A-K's transformation.

The immediate space is occupied by the sofa of origin, but it's been pressed back against the closet wall, and it is joined by a small, round table and two chairs. The space beyond – where the window lets the light in, and, in front of the kitchen – it has been filled with a funky s-shaped couch with seats on either side of the colorful backing.

That is still, only the beginning.

Lights have been added and with the intent to give atmosphere. There are plants, and artwork has been hung on the walls. The small, quaint space that was moved into has become alive, and comfortable for small gatherings: Twelve still makes the space feel claustrophobic. But is a very vibrant space that no longer feels dirty, yet also antiseptic.

Corbyn is working through antiseptic numbers when there's a knock at the door.

It is after five and odd that expected company would knock, but he calls, "It's open," on the chance it's someone other.

He watches from the counter as the door is heard to open, and it's Elwhinnie that looks around the corner, and her eyes are wide. She doesn't say what she came to say, instead, "My goodness, Jimmy. You have completely transformed this place."

"My daughter," he tells her. "She had a vision – it exploded."

She says, "I love it. You think she'd take a look at our place?"

"You can ask," Corbyn offers: "She'll be here, soon."

It strikes him odd, she says, "I am so sorry – I was overwhelmed." She explains, "I came up to let you know she's here – with her mother. I wasn't sure how you felt about her coming back here."

Corbyn's quickly on his feet, panic tripping through scenarios explaining why they'd both be present. However, by the time he joins Elwhinnie, it's largely abated and thoughts have moved on to what Anika might be plotting.

He says, "I appreciate that – thank you. I do not want her back here."

"Everything I've heard," she says, "I thought you might feel that way." She leads him from the sealed apartments, down the hall and to the waiting space, where they're met with identical faces that wear disgust. She offers a smile but says nothing as she continues on.

A-K asks impatiently, "Can I go back?"

"Yeah." Corbyn says, "Of course. What's going on?"

The two are left alone, and Anika questions, "I can't go back?"

He tells her, "No."

Her eyes roll – she says, "You're acting like a child. I want to see where my daughter stays. I don't think that's unreasonable."

She's told, "No." Corbyn says, "It's got four walls and basic amenities. I'm sure you'd hate it."

"Whatever," she says – eyes roll again: "I just came as a courtesy." She waits. Expecting with the pause, he'll ask, but he doesn't. With more hostility, she says, "I'm staying at Corshae's. This weekend. I'll be there until Tuesday. So, don't be surprised to see me."

"You could call," he says, "Or text."

She says, "Whatever, asshole. Hope she gives you as much shit as she's giving me."

He jokes, "There's a good chance she'll stab me."

But there's no humor found: "Your stupid thing. What's even the point?"

He shrugs, and says, "It's what we do."

She is sour, and questions mockingly, "Do you win anything? Do they give you a little trophy."

The answer's, "No." Corbyn says, "I guess, bragging rights. But no one does – not seriously."

"So, what's the point," she asks again, and anger rises, as she complains: "My kid spends half her life fucking up the stupid costume she made. Why do you do this? It's a waste of fucking time."

He says again, "It's what we do: We like it."

She storms away, but turns as she finds him following, and asks, "Is there a problem?"

"I work here."

"And, your point?"

He points out, "I'm trying to get to processing. It's down the stairs."

She combines a third eye-roll and, "Whatever," before continuing down the stairs, and then towards the swinging doors. She's disregarded but then exits with an angry call as she punches through the door, "It smells like shit."

The man closest Corbyn gives him an eye and says, "Damn, I wanted to say something."

He's asked, "Why are we still working?"

"Coaching up the quality," he claims.

He's asked, "Is there a problem?"

"No, boss. I held a session to make sure we get consistent quality. You told me, take initiative."

Corbyn says, "It's after five, dude."

"Almost done, boss."

He lets it slide, and says loudly, to everyone, "Let's get it done."

He's mostly ignored, and he exits through the swinging doors to take the heat: "I didn't realize they were still here: I'm on top of it."

"That's why," Elwinnie says, "We wanted to keep you on the line. We knew this was gonna happen."

"I'll step in if I have to. You want me to take the counter?"

She says, "Go spend time with your daughter, Jimmy."

He says, "Thanks, Alice."

He finds his daughter is not in the foul mood advertised, only collapsed on the sofa and watching television.

He asks, "You hungry?"

She answers, "Nah," and asks, herself, "We goin' out tonight?"

"Midnight," he says: "If you change your mind, there's pizza, trout – help yourself."

She says, "We ate lunch, like, an hour ago. Maybe later."

She is where he's found she often is on Friday afternoons: Tired, not interested in conversation, and looking for space to just relax. He gives her that and returns to the counter to continue cataloguing inventory.

As the evening wears on, that begins to change, and excitement begins to grow as midnight approaches.

Corbyn exits his room, and attempts to draw his sword, but it hangs up on a chink of damage brought in practice. He asks, "How's yours?"

She says, "Better than yours," but as she says it, her eyes grow wide and there's an open smile as she marvels, "That looks like blood on your shoulder."

"Yeah," he says, and gloats, "They're startin' to look pretty good."

"Is he here yet?"

"Down the road," Corbyn tells her: "We can park at the campground."

She asks, "You ready?"

He says, "Let's see what we can rattle loose."

They exit onto the street where many eyes are watching – some passing, some hiding in the shadows. They leave the Benz in favor of the dated MR2, and as they pull away, a dark sedan begins to follow. As the dark sedan begins to pull away, a pickup pulls behind.

Elkilia notes, "They're behind us."

"Of course."

She says, "I can't tell who it is, though. Maybe a Honda?"

There's little room to maneuver – or lose them – so Corbyn doesn't try. He drives the curve he rode a thousand time, back up to the highway – any hope for a quick escape subverted by heavy, weekend traffic. However, that does provide the opportunity to take the slightest opening and at least get a small amount of separation.

A-K twists back and watches as the vehicle behind them juts into traffic. There is excitement as she realizes, "Oh my God: It's the Camry."

Corbyn smiles as he realizes, "El-Assissi."

His daughter teases, "Did you forget to pay him?"

"Can you tell if he's driving?"

He's three cars back and it's after midnight, so all she offer's, "It looks like – long hair. But maybe it's a hood. Was his car black?"

"Dark blue. He might be coming after us, so as soon as we stop, make a run for it."

She says, "Okay," and continues watching, twisting back to keep an eye on their bloodthirsty adversary.

They continue over the bridge and traffic slows – likely visitors looking past the jetties into the vast darkness of the ocean. As they descend, they continue to approach the recommended speed, until it's reported:

"He's passing in the turn lane."

It brings Corbyn to wonder, "What the heck?"

His daughter wonders, "What's he doing?"

Corbyn doesn't answer. He takes what remains of double-divided highway and punches it past two vehicles. He pulls back in as the pavement narrows and there is traffic in the distance, however, another turn lane is approaching.

It is shortly after that the speed limit finally raises, and not long after that they sharply turn. There is finally a brief stretch of road where they can accelerate at inadvisable speeds, and the car's driven quickly down to the parking lot.

The instant it stops, both doors fly open, and the occupants extract themselves and begin jogging for the beach. Despite their efforts, they have only made the bathrooms by the time the Toyota flies in after them.

Corbyn calls, "Let's go – let's go."

"I'm going," A-K says.

In their haste, they never see the truck that follows.

They move quickly for the ocean-packed sand and begin sprinting down the beach to a point demarked by a sudden break of the trees. It is a point where there are no lights, and no homes immediately on shore. It gives them the cover of isolation and darkness to begin their march into the ocean. It is a point where it is unlikely anyone will see them. That is, unless someone watched, and followed.

Someone follows that can nearly match their speed. She didn't notice the truck that entered right behind her, nor the five that move casually, farther down the beach. She only watches the two she saw walk out in bizarre uniforms. Two that drove erratically, who then did everything they could to run away from her after she found they'd parked. She watches as they walk directly at the ocean and wonders what they plan. She watches as first the daughter, and then Corbyn march quickly into the shivering water. She watches them wade in and continue. She watches as they push forward into ever deeper water, and then they are gone.

There is panic, and she runs to where she saw them enter. She is ill to think they actually went in, and her instinct is to call for help.

The phone is answered, "This is – uh – emergency. Emergency services. How can we assist you?"

She says, "I don't know. I just saw two people walk into the ocean. There's no sign of them – I don't know what to do."

The person on the other end inquires, "Were they dressed like Vikings?"

Jesti asks, "What?"

"Did they have on stupid uniforms?"

"They," she says – remembers, "They had – they had some kind of: Something. Maybe uniforms."

"Stay away from them," she's warned. "These are dangerous people. You should return to your vehicle and go home."

She pauses, and looks around, because, "How did you know I drove here?"

The woman on the other end, says, "You said so."

"No," Jesti says: "I didn't say that." She wonders, "What is going on?"

A man behind her says, "I have an offer."

She jumps as her heart begins to pound heavily in her chest, and takes steps away as she not only finds the man, but four others with him.

Jesti quickly raises her phone, and in a panic, says, "I'm just south of the park. Just south of Newport. I need someone here – right away."

The woman she'd been speaking with raises her own, and Jesti watches, as she says, "We're already here."

"Who are you?"

The man says, "We are Taborh: The Afrahm Band of Rascal Hunters. Consider yourself fortunate to have avoided direct contact with those Rascals. They are highly dangerous."

She says, "I'm sorry? I just watched them walk in the ocean."

The man shakes his head with disgust, and says, "An abomination, and probably illegal. At least, it should be."

"Okay," Jesti says: "You don't seem to care they walked into the ocean. Can you tell me what the fuck is going on here?"

The woman says, "Hon: They're fine. They had a submarine down there."

"That's for real?" Jesti watches as the man raises a single brow, and she asks, "Who are you people?"

The man says, "I am El-Assissi-Syrianni-Afrahm. I would like to enlist your services. I promise, you will be well-rewarded."

"What?" She asks, "For what?"

"Infiltrate the rascals," the man suggests. He says, "And plant a tag on their submersible."

"I'm sorry?" She quickly texts, "There is some man offering me some kind of reward to tag your sub. You want to tell me what the hell is going on?"

"Dad's busy," is the first response, followed shortly after, by, "Is he kind of a refrigerator? With dark hair and a beard?"

Jesti texts, "Who is he?"

She gets, "El-Assissi. Stay away from him."

She asks, "You guys are fine?"

She gets a question, "Did you follow us?"

She is typing, "Yes," when she receives the quick follow up, "This is Corbyn, now."

He then sends, "Is it El-Assissi?"

She asks, "Are you El-Assissi?"

The man says, "Take the deal: Twenty-five thousand. Tell him you want some answers before you'll agree to go out with him. Tell him you need to see the submersible."

She texts him, "This guy's offering me 25k to tag your sub. Tempted."

He types, "NOOOOO!! He is evil – give him my best. That's my lawyer."

"What?" It's said aloud, and she questions, "Are you Corbyn's lawyer?"

"No," he insists, "Ooothodaipsa are the enemies of all enemies: We will destroy them."

"Are you," she demands.

He still says, "Never," but then qualifies, "Not on the weekends. Not until Monday."

She types, "WTF"

Corbyn types back, "I told you to run."

Jesti turns to those gathered, and tells them, "Get lost, losers. I'm not taking anything from you." And then she texts, "Tell me when we're meeting."

It is a message that flashes on the phone as it rests on a bunk in a submersible that is twenty feet from the shore. It is first seen by a young woman who smiles as she watches her father help navigate, as they sail away, hoping they'll be able to pick up any conversation that will give them an edge. Though, like the rest of their efforts, it's mostly done simply because they can.

www.ingramcontent.com/pod-product-compliance
Lightning Source LLC
LaVergne TN
LVHW020659110826
845149LV00012B/2046
* 9 7 8 1 9 7 1 4 0 6 0 3 9 *